Fletch

MW01254261

Book I - Of Love

Book II – Of Death

Fletcher

Volume I
Book I: Of Love

Chapter I: Of Beauty And Music

A thing of beauty is a joy forever: its loveliness increases; it will never;

pass into nothingness

John Keats

I would have to say that all life tales begin before the first breath, for we have to learn about the situation of life the soul is born to before we can understand anything of the individual themselves. An example to contextualise you would perhaps be much like what grows in the womb of a Queen, that life has a chosen path before it gains consciousness or forms limbs, vastly different from that of the son of a coal miner. My father's family were a wealthy one, nearing one of the wealthiest in Northumberland. They were high in the profession of the transportation of coal, which was in high demand. Coal was 'the fuel of industry' as I was told numerous times and very important to the soap produce in our area. My father's family were wealthy yet my father and his father, my grandfather, did not speak to one another. Why I never learnt, I was only told he was a terrible man. Being estranged from him left my father struggling economically and falling down the ladder in our overly proud class formed Empire. In defeat, and yes I mean this without intending to mitigate his decision as quaint or romantic, in defeat he bought one of the best farmland in the North-East. And so I was born the son of a farmer, yet he distilled in me the values and education of a wealthier middle-class home. He aspired to reach a wealthy state of being for his family once more within the next generation, before obstacles came by.

I was born in 1824, but of my childhood there are memories here and there of only little value if I am honest with you, my reader. Life itself has always to me been an obligation to the fact I was given birth to, I had known of many miscarriages within families who lived near, my own mother had had several before my birth; and because of this, since I can remember, I thought of those who had died, those who could not make it to beyond birth, and felt obliged to live the life I was graced with; no matter how simple and tedious it was. I was not much beyond ordinary in this time. I had an education behind me which was rare in farming families, however other than that, I was the same as any other. I aged from my tender years until my seventeenth year with my dear sister Mary playing on father's fields. She was the only person in our family that actually saw me as a being with value, she was four years little to me and because of this fact she looked to me with high respect, one of the few ever to have done so.

Father was planning on leaving the land to Walter, my eldest brother, as well as Jonathon my other older brother. Father's plan was to take the North-East's farming land and dominate its exports to become a major power in the growing economy; all in the name of competing with his family's wealth. However over the years with less income than father hoped for, he found himself having to sell much land, until the farm became only of modest size and all workers were relieved of any duty, it was then that only his children worked for him. He and all assumed I would stay and work on the farm beyond it becoming Walter's, but I had no such plans. I cared not. I never told Mary I would not stay, however I am almost certain she always knew.

It was in 1841 when my life was altered from its course of monotony and a bleakly dull existence. I remember winter was vastly approaching, I believe it was October, the rain's surges were becoming heavier and the dark was setting in. My nights were spent with increasingly less comfort as the cold of the North came in through the weak windows. One of those nights I lay in bed strangely anxious, dreaming of a life where something new would happen once within a while. All souls should be filled with a joy of vague surprise most days, not the wearisome stationary routine that was my life at that moment in time.

I passed the night with a horrible absence of any substantial sleep, and rose before dawn to labour my duties. It was a dark and weary morning that greeted me, and the icy breeze from the North Sea was westward, ambushing us like a bout of harsh chill and blowing the foul smells of farming life forever into me.

After my routine morn with tending the animals I cleaned myself and received some sandwiches from Mary. Our mother had died giving birth to her, which in turn meant that she had learnt to feed and clean for us all more or less as soon as her soul entered this world. Bless her. Mary had just entered womanhood yet she had been the mother of us all for the past six years or so. She too was also educated by father's insistence, and would have been a prize wife for anyone in the county, yet until one of her brothers were married, she was desperately needed as the only woman on the farm. Mary my sister was my greatest and only real friend. Often if we had a spare hour or so we would play chess together and talk about all things from philosophy, politics to religion. She usually beat me at chess, and she did that day, but that mattered not to me, her time and conversation was the real pleasure.

As I was on the verge of defeat Walter pushed the door open forcedly, he was like a madman destroying all in front of him half the time. He thought himself the most superior of us for every reason under the sun. He was the eldest, but of a tall and well-fed family he was also the tallest. He had sharp facial features matching his character and his bold eyes were forever judging as they flickered around the room. Like mother, he had blonde hair whilst the rest of us were of dark hair. A trick of his to further his feeling of superiority was his daily tirades at me for not living up to father's expectations, that day was no different. I knew that it was his own needs that bothered him though, his reason why I had to get up and work was simple; the more I do, the less he does. And I was the youngest male which made me the easiest target. I used to raise my voice back in his imbecilic direction, yet father and Jonathon would always defend him, so I

began a policy of ignoring him; which worked perfectly until that day he began putting his hand in front of my face just to receive his much needed attention. What he said I honestly do not know, Mary brought him the sandwiches she had made for him, and though he surrendered to her gesture, sitting down and eating his food, I could see in the look he gave me that he wanted to finish asserting himself over me. After defeating his meaningless ramble with food, she fairly quickly aft defeated me in chess.
'Checkmate' she called, gleaming up at me.
'Ha!' Walter laughed a loud pointless laugh 'beaten by a girl, seems you are not as intelligent as you think little boy.' He spoke with food still in his mouth like a drunken pig, the manner-less fool. We both glanced over to him but paid little attention. He was no company for my tired and wearied mind. I looked to Mary with a smile and then walked out of the door for some much needed solitude by my lough.

I went to the stables and strapped my horses to my cart; it was by definition a wain, but more like a modest cart with four wheels and a bench than it was a wain. My stallions were perfect creatures and I loved them as if they were my own children, large brown beasts they were that I kept in the topmost condition.

I journeyed. Riding through England's wilderness as the trees dwarfed me, of conifer, willow and oak, in autumn shades. Rolling hillsides too, of luscious lime green fields with shades of faded yellow arable dotted about the area that were quite overwhelming when moments of appreciation were taken. And the glorious cattle scattered here and there, eating as if they were to hibernate for the coming winter. Though it was a chilly day, the sun was still working hard to make the day bright which gave it all the more beauty as it pierced through the clouds. The scent of salt from the sea joined me on my journey North.

Here is a pitiless truth my reader:
I cannot to this day think of any place on earth more beautiful than northern England.
If you have seen it and disagree with me, then you and I see different colours in this world.

But the lough, my favourite place, was the most spectacular in all the countryside of Northumberland. It was a fair distance away from where I lived yet it was worth the travel. A whole of two hours beyond the hills was the journey until I was at the most luxurious spot I could find.

On top of a modest hillside I looked down upon a delicate blue lough, was not a large lough like the lakes they have in Cumbria, this, more a sweeter and personally accessible variation. The woodlands to its side towered all so fearlessly as its reflection fell upon the water, giving it the appearance of twice its size. A breeze gently whistled passed me bringing fresh and brisk air into my lungs like it was blessed by God Himself.

The cart came to a complete stop and I reached for my quill, ink and diary, before absolutely taking in the depth, colour and wonder of where I was. I began to write:

All the beauty that is around me - yet I still sit here with a need for something more
Is all this beauty about me anything more than simple aesthetics?

As I wrote what seemed more like mind wandering than writing, I looked to the scenery; the insects that danced just above the lough, the leaves that had fallen from the trees floated on the water sweetly and covered large portions of it. And the smell of fresh air all around me was delightful, I would argue it as one of the best scents on this earth. I had all I could ever want of beauty there in that moment, and yet I still had a desire for something else, something more beautiful to enrich me.

What is beauty?

Is what I then wrote. What a hopeless query that came to me, there is no definitive or complete answer, of course, and because of that I tried to push the question away from thoughts, but it tickled at the back of my skull. Trying to both find another beauty and distract myself from the question, I strolled back to my cart and retrieved my violin.

The smell was nothing short of brilliant, I held my instrument loosely, stroked the sweet strings with the bow; just to get a feel of what I was about to engage in. I started slowly with a folk style melody, though the tempo gradually increased, and so did my swaying to the music I created until I was prancing in slight circles to a more virtuoso tune.

Music always stirred my excitement, I felt liberated from life for the prolonged temporality it gave me. How subtly morbid, letting go of life being liberating.

But the serene music I played was like opium to me, making every fibre within my insignificant body vibrate. My veins skipped with the rhythm, pulsating to no end with the music as my body became dictated by my artistic creation. I decreased the pace, back to andante in G minor. The violin began to cry with the slow dark sound and again I could feel the trembling of the instrument running through me. I grew to be completely swept away by the music, as if I had moved onto another realm where anything was possible and yet nothing was happening. I had achieved some form of bliss, which music is so capable of doing; I wish you were there to experience that moment with me. Yet the beauty was still not enough.

Amidst my playing I happened on glancing at the sky, realising not only was it much later than I had assumed, but also dark clouds were arriving, and with them, a guarantee of rain in just over an hour's time I judged; and so I headed back.

In the dry chill of my home Mary had pork stew and bread waiting for me and brought a towel for me to dry off. For the rest of that day I lay beside the wide open window so I could breathe in the vibrant moist air that developed as the rain fell so graciously.

I spent my next day thinking upon my question, 'what is beauty?' Not a simple thought when you think thoroughly about such you must agree. It ran through my cranium for the entirety of the morning, whilst I did my jobs, whilst I ate. I am to be honest with you my good reader, I grew tired of wondering. Beauty is beauty, beauty comes in many forms and even vile things that create horror in some, can be beautiful to others. Death is beautiful to some and so the thought of 'what is beauty?' is too devoid of content to be voluntarily engaged in. If I had three wishes from a pixie on that day all three wishes would have been to get the query removed from my mind; weary thoughts upon a weary head is an ill-state of being, one I did not care for.

That day started the same as the last until I left with my cart and stallions for the green of England. The hills and its curves were fine and smooth as the clouds from the distance rushed towards me. They were disturbingly grey, which created a parallel friction between the earth I stood upon, and the sky above me like two worlds colliding with understated grace. On the contrary however, for a day where dark grey clouds ruled the air so dominantly, it was in actuality a warm and reasonable day. For my life I could not help analysing every single particle within sight; the lough, the forest, the hillside, all was beautiful around me. My stallions themselves were touched by beauty. The greenest most luscious fields in all the Empire were on our own northern soil, how bloody magnificent I thought, the fact did make me smile a smile I could not contain. But its beauty was still not enough for my question to leave me be.

I had a contrasting relationship with the world. Sometimes I was deeply in love with life in a blissful infatuation that pleasured me through to the bone, and other days I was furious with how pointless every single thing in existence appeared, to the state of agony and an emotional field of powerlessness.

For my distaste of monotonous adventure I would often ride different routes through the country. That day was the same, I rode off to somewhere I had never been before towards the coast, where the air grew colder. Before long I found myself nearing a wealthy looking property. I thought maybe duke of county or a royal relative to own a lovely lucrative house that was perched in a hidden realm. At first glance I wished I was living in such a place, although as a house my current residence was of no issue. But upon second glance, I noticed something else.

Something instantly worth everything I had ever known; a face worth a thousand moments of woe or any other misery. A girl of similar age, I guessed, dressed in a practical yet perfectly flattering gown.

'Now that is beauty' I uttered to myself unaware. Finally I felt the query could leave me in peace, I had found the purest beauty. She stood before me just down the hillside, with long sand coloured hair and smooth skin, with a look of definitive splendour. Her high cheeks were rounded delicately to a youthful mould, and though her face was slight in comparison to her frail thin body, it gave her a more adorable appeal. She was breath-taking, fine and truly my reader. Something pierced straight through my form as she noticed me watching her watering the cheerful plants in her garden. Her delightful plump lips formed a smile as we looked at one another for several sweet moments. Though as sweet as they were, I felt an urge to look away, I feared her thinking me rude for staring for what felt an age; it was her however, who broke the reciprocal warmth by quickly averted her eyes down and continuing her business. Yet I witnessed she tried to look towards me in a hidden manner, which made me smile all the more at her. Her eyes were for me as mine were for her, confirming I was not perceived as acting with ill-manner.

One last curious look she darted in my direction before heading inside. I could feel she smiled as she walked away, but I could not help the thought of her getting her father to shoo me off like a dog. Assuming she had not, for I had caused little harm, I sat back in calm, visualising her gentle face. If only she had remained I thought, those eyes held some majestic truth behind them that I yearned to understand. Her twig-like figure odd but alluring still, and her sand hair flowed as if a waterfall from a mystical dream, streaming in its elegance down to the pool of her back as she moved away; there was something beyond this world about her brilliance. As I was imagining her and trying to recreate all the perfections I bore witness to, she came back into my vision. Attempting to give me a blank look of impatience, "leave!" or some other similar phrase emanating from her expression; but I could feel the true emotion of some connection bursting out into the world from her look as her handsome smile crept out of her. Her act was broken, and only magnificence remained as she tended back to the flowers. Her journey inside must have been simply to retrieve more water; I decided to go and speak to her.

At that point I was merely on top of the hill looking down to her from my cart but then I moved down to her. As I rode to her property my nerves tried to steal my calm state, however, I refused them assertively. She watched me with a charming look of intuition, endearing me to continue.

Out of the cart and towards her I walked, every step was a battle with my own composure. I could hear the birds chirping in the air, smell the freshwater on her hands as she placed down the bucket. She met me on the stone road. Face to face we stood; from the distance I was previously I could not see the chill her eyes distilled in me, the chill of a luscious ice blue. And that light colour of her eyes greatly clashed with that of her beach eyebrows in the most romantic way. Slowly I reached for her hand and in acceptance of my gesture, she held up its dripping form to me with a slight smile. My lips were pressed against her gently for a moment as she bent her knees in greeting.

'Morning my lady' I spoke, she smiled that beautiful smile again, making my body feel limp. 'Will you join me on a ride through the countryside?' I continued 'the countryside is very lovely, most beautiful and green land in the world might I add.'

'And how do you know that kind sir?'

'I am a man of the world.' I replied teasingly as she looked up at me.

'So will you join me?'

'Of course I will' she brightly spoke as if she had already told me her wish, 'excuse me a moment' her soft voice called with an innocent beam.

She rushed inside with her bucket for several moments before darted back out past me, blurting eager words and I followed. As she stepped up onto my cart, I found myself confused by her, she had the elegance of her household, yet the

12

frock she wore was of no grandeur.

Forth we went through the country but for the first time in my short life I did not take in the land around me, because the most beautiful thing I had ever seen was sitting by my side. I willed myself to act polite and so stare I did not, however so awestruck I was by the female.

'My lady, are you a duke of county offspring? Or upon that direction?' I asked trying to get an exchange of words flowing, as well as an answer to my confusion.

'No I am not.' She replied with an expression as if she had been asked numerous times previously.

'Well your home is grand in any case' I stated as my eyes flickered from her to the open air. She fiddled with her fingers as she gazed forward, yet our eyes met occasionally and those moments were nothing short of magical when they did occur. I perceived a spirit that was oddly bright to me, and I found it quite infectious and soothing as a silence washed over us. A peaceful silence. One where you know you are within good company, which is always a rare gift.

'Where are we heading?' She asked curiously as her glistening eyes looked up at me. I simply pointed forwards

'That way' we laughed together, and I took note of hers; high pitched and delicate it was but discrete in itself, like a soft giggle. 'I am not too sure' I continued 'is there anywhere you would like to go?'

'There is a lovely forest a mile from here.' She replied more as a question than a statement, but I took it as one, and moved in the direction she pointed.

By way of watching her, I saw in her aura, that she had a perfect combination of an intelligent being that was still rooted in humility. I could see it in the way she looked at the world; and at me. She had something else special about her too, but I could not grasp what it was; something I greatly craved to know in all its festering details.

'This is a nice surprise, I expected another uneventful day.' She spoke.

'Myself included'

'Tell me something kind sir'

'Well, let us see… Your eyes are so blue they are blinding, a kind of spring morning blue; it is as if you stole them from a fairer being'

'Perhaps I did using elf magic, and the forest I spoke of is where they all live, ready to steal your brown autumn eyes.' We both chuckled slightly, but with our talk of eyes we both naturally peered into one another's, entering a sort of motionless daze that seemed to last years. Our faces, almost expressionless, but smiling inside, she seemed to be searching my soul through its windows; but for what I did not know. The euphoric moment ended when she quickly looked away and fiddled with her sleeves again. I returned but to earth.

     I had seen a tall forest to one side of us and assumed it was the one she desired, I looked to her for confirmation of such and she nodded. It was quite spectacular, the first thing that hit me was the warm shade of brown from the vast tree trunks. They were thick and power stricken, bold and magnificent, the autumn leaves of reds and yellows covered the ground whilst some still clung to life from the branches above. The woodlands near my father's farm were dull compared to that find. I felt as if we had strayed from the known paths of the world and found ourselves in a hidden realm forgotten by time. And perhaps some malevolent elves would be waiting. As we entered, the smell in the air changed considerably, the smell of sea salt disappeared almost instantly and was replaced by a more broken branch and moss scent. I could taste it as I breathed in the dense air, quite pleasing. 'Do you come here often?' I inquired.

'No, I wish I could, I am not given leave of the grounds often, unfortunately. But I love this wood, it is wonderfully old and mysterious; and all the autumn colours are beautiful… Here is perfect.' I reacted by halting the stallions. I hopped down from the cart as the golden leaves below me crackled atop the mud. The sun's light still struggled to reach into the depths of the wood and because of this we were immersed in the warm shades; she was right about the autumn colours. I walked around to her and guided her down from the cart, taking her soft hand in mine once more, which was a delight in itself. My existence could not help but feel the world of hers.

I gathered a few sticks and proceeded with starting a fire, for it was not a mild day to begin with, plus the sun failed us in the wood. She sat herself down by my side, and held her legs up close to her breast whilst resting her head upon her knees. That cold pose I assumed was her need for warmth, though she was like a portrait of the content as she watched me trying to light the fire so patiently. The girl grinned at the first sight of an ember, and as the fire increased in size, I saw its intense colours glowing reds and oranges dancing wildly about her.

She quickly rose onto her feet and the moment quickly faded in my head. I, about to ask her the matter, watched her acquire fallen branches and accelerate the fire wildly. Though wildly it was, I was more merry to see than anxious.

Still standing once her deeds had been done, she caught sight to the figures under the cloth in the back of my cart. With care the cloth was removed, and my violin she raised preciously. If she were to have damaged it I think I would left her there, in the depths of the woodlands and gone back distastefully; thankfully though, she held it with attention.

'Could you' she asked gently, holding the instrument in my direction.

'Why yes my lady' I replied, taking it from her hands as she moved back towards the cart and held onto the Irish whistle I had rotting in there.

Before I began to play I tried to steady myself, for I could not keep the bow straight. "Nervousness is a sign of weakness; and no English man shows his weakness" I told myself, yet I started despite my composure. A sweat came down my forehead suddenly as the first note sounded in the open wood, but I kept myself contained. I began slowly, as always. Swaying back and forth near unaware as I raised the tempo moderately. After a mellow stare of pleasure that lasted a dozen moments, the girl began prancing around the fire to the music I generated; creating laughter in me that momentarily derailed the music, filling my soul with joy. The girl was a child at heart, and that was a quality I found most lovable in her; I first recognised that in her within that moment. As she began playing my whistle to the tune I created, I also began dancing around the fire; which due to her rash addition of branches and dry leaves, was rapidly growing taller than myself. Such euphoria I felt, my head snaked with wonder whilst dancing around the large blaze with her, yet dancing about her were the flames colourfully. And though she created quite the inferno, it was her smile and laughter that truly brightened the woodland.

In our prancing the music shifted to a more repetitive rhythmic feel; and such a delicacy chirped from the whistle as it floated in and out of the violin's harmony. My life, the meaning of existence itself, stood complete in that moment, on that day. And though I hardly knew the girl, she and our blissful dance amongst our fire was all I ever needed.

As the sun was setting to the West, the warmth and smoke raged all around us intensely, the heat became intoxicating, feeding me with a further desire to frolic and laugh jubilantly. Our dance seemed forever lasting, all time passed by us. The world, forgotten; my own self, forgotten. And all things drenched in glory.

When my breath became lost I retired from our eternal dance and placed my violin back delicately. I noticed there was an ample log near my cart under a tree and I sat upon it. The girl slowly joined me, her walk however, was still the prancing skip of a child. After a few moments of the fire and floating embers between us stealing our attention, I spoke
'If I were to ask you, what beauty is, what would say?'
'Beauty is something that touches your heart in the most sincere of ways' she stated in perfect response, before continuing 'whether the thing of beauty is abhorrent to another is irrelevant, I disagree with beauty in any universal sense.' I nodded in agreement and we shared a smile, not only was she my answer,

she also had her own.

I felt a longing for physical connection in some way and yet I did not know how. All day I had noticed she moved towards me with timidity and then slowly retreated in speech, it seemed she had that same longing; but like me, she knew not how. Yet we were comfortable in one another's company, the mood was that of two relaxed people, "that is enough for this day" I thought. And I hoped there would be many other days where we could achieve such contact.

'Are you a farmer-boy?' She called. Her words came so plainly I was unsure if she spoke with judgement or not. Though I was not ashamed and never would have been, I looked to her before my answer, and all I saw was serenity.

'I am. I am the third son of farmer Fletcher, just South-West of here.'

'It must be nice to spend most of your days outside, when it is not raining.'

'It is. I do not loathe farming. I just want more in life, it would seem such a poor waste of breath to farm the land forever' I said frankly as I pondered if I would or not. We gazed at the fire again, breathing in the silent tranquillity, and of course the heat.

'What does your future hold?' I eventually asked.

'My parents wish to marry me off to a man they consider a worthwhile suitor. Until then I will be little more than their ungrateful daughter.' She smiled cheerfully, but the eyes retained a melancholic note.

And of the trace of melancholy within me, it came from the thought of her getting married to some "worthwhile suitor"; which for simple minds means "not a farmer-boy". Understand my situation, with most marriages people simply married their neighbours or their dainty little cousins. Marriages were not about happiness, nor love, it was about practically. It was about learning to love the being you married whilst raising their children; and achieving to love was rarely the case. But we had no real neighbours, I was not deterministically linked in to any other family, and of cousins we were estranged from them all. Besides, father needed me on the farm for as long as possible. Since my early days I had wished some power above me had chosen some local village girl for me, it seemed it would have made the whole idea of finding a wife simpler; but with this not so, I could choose myself a wife, and perhaps this is premature in this tale, but in these moments I was dreaming of the beauty by my side being my future.

We talked further of our passion for music and instruments. She told me of her real parents owning many instruments when she was younger, of woodwind, percussion, strings, and she would love to play them all. Her mother was a cellist in the Chester area and they hoped she would follow suit. I confessed too that my mother had been musical, a violinist, and that these two instruments were once hers.

'Since living here in Northumberland, though' she explained with fading tone 'I have only had chance to play a piano, and even that is seldom.'

'Surely you have many instruments in that beautiful house of yours?'

'Only a piano, but it is for decoration more than playing. My parents do not like to hear it played. They see no utility in the art of playing it, only in the utility of presenting their affluence.'

'I can offer no piano here in this wood, or a cello, my lady, but of these two you can play as long as you wish.' She looked up to me with that warming beam once more, then putting the whistle to her lips, she played a soft, contemplative melody. All I could do in its ethereal tune was stare into the fire and listen to the flowing sound trickle its way up and down ever so tenderly.

She played that whistle for undoubtedly over an hour as late afternoon turned to evening. The darkness only made the failing fire glow the brighter as the disturbing clouds hid the moon and stars. She then stopped her playing to build up the flames once more. I simply left her to do as she wished and I watched her build it to a fine flame again. I could feel its sense of rhythm, as if the colours were designed in their manoeuvres as it danced. Its tones entwined with each other before separating, and swayed to and fro in the increasing winds as shadows flickered all about the forest with majestic innocence. However, my trance was broken by a fiercely sudden downpour as it seeped through the bare trees.

'The rain!' She called with elation, running into the open and dancing in circles, waving her arms gaily with gleeful expression. Her clothes became soaked instantly, I recall vividly the way her sandy hair turned black as it became wet, sticking to her face in clumps as the rain dripped down her cheeks. And mud splashed upon her legs as she moved on the damp ground. I would have joined her dancing, and delved into that stream of bliss that was her; but I could not help sit and admire her brilliance. She began singing also, and I witnessed in her a heart that was at its centre, freer than I could know. She had a love for life that cleansed my often miserable self and made me infinitely grateful to exist.

Her movements slowed to a halt, a stare of impatience came my way.

'Are you going to dance with me or shall I continue alone?'

How could I refuse her?

I stood up to join her and she greeted me with a beam, tainting me forever with her light. As I stepped into her and held out my hand, she embraced me with her own. We began dancing a waltz as she vocally imitated an orchestra, playfully alto. Oh how wonderful was she; my left hand rested on her soft waist and I gazed once more into those mesmerising lakes with yearning. I had been under vague shelter under the trees, and she was dripping wet, however she made sure I was of the same drenched standard before long, splashing and whipping her hair at me as the rain continued. The compelling joy from the clouds did numb to a gentle soothe after only a little while, yet she cared little. We danced by the roaring fire until the evening matured to night.

We only stopped when we she turned to the darkness, peering with an odd look and mumbling something under her breath.

'Is something the matter?' Spoke I with concern. She said nothing, and with her gaze still towards something I could not see she stepped several yards away to the edge of our opening. I heard her breathing become denser, and with an ambiguous agitation stained somewhat across her body, she continued to gaze into the dark.

'Are you quite alright my lady?' I called out. She looked to me, pausing for a second and displaying a bewildered expression.

'I thought I saw something.'

'What was it?' She did not reply, only looked back into the darkness 'come my lady, it is time I took you home.' She was not in fear, I thought, but peculiarly agitated nonetheless. She continued to look about as I walked her to the cart.

'Animals are scared of fire if an animal concerns you.'

'I thought I saw a man, but I must have been mistaken.' I placed my hand on her shoulder hoping to mellow the unrest in her, and lead her away.

As we left, the dimmed light of fire behind us gave a perfect sight to an already ancient looking forest, it produced a more sacred feel, as if I was dead and fleeing from the perfect light I should have been walking towards.

Our journey back contained little conversation. We were both settled with each other's company, watching the land as the shadow of night veiled all but above. I could see however, what she thought she saw did still unsettle her slightly.

When we reached her home, guilt itched at me for having taken her away for so long without her guardian's permission. I assumed we would be gone for an hour at most, how very wrong was I. Either which way the deed had been done.

'I shall apologise to your parents for your absence.' I spoke to her gently and yet with a tone of command.

'No need.' She replied with a smile for me, knowing this was the end of our time together. I walked round and raised my hand to assist her down from the cart, trying to be a gentleman. Her soft self was freezing from the rain, as was I.

'Good-night sir. Promise me that you will come for me again soon.'

'I promise. Good-night my lady, sweet dreams.' It was sad to see her walk away and enter the house, but I smiled to myself, thankful to God I had met her. I tried to straighten my face, I smiled plenty that day and my cheeks were tender from the strain, yet I could not release from the grinning. All for a good cause I concluded and gave into them.

Upon sitting back on the bench of the cart and heading to the farm, I heard a loud male voice resonating from her home. I heard not the meaning in its muffled form, but not only did it startle me in its apparent volume, it worried me. The noise was as abrupt to conclude as it had been to sound, I loathed it, yet I was powerless to him when it came to her. Reluctantly, I journeyed home.

'You are drenched' called Mary 'go change your clothes and sit by the fireplace, I shall make you some tea' she demanded lovingly as I walked through the door.

'Thank you greatly'

'You missed dinner'

'I am sorry, I...'

'Forgiven' she interrupted quickly, with a mischievous smirk as if she had been watching me all day.

Chapter II: An Encounter With A Dragon

Patience is a virtue, possess it if you can

Seldom in a woman and rarely in a man

Proverb

I lay in my tattered bed the next morn relaxed and calm, my mind, filled with her gorgeous smile. That bright smile as orange flickered all over her magnificent self, deep in the woods of my passion; that was her in my memory. Such thoughts lingered in me as I slowly came to an awakened existence. My bed lay in a dull chamber I shared with Mary, the room consisted of no chairs, no wardrobes, two beds only inside the grim white walls in all the barren simplicity I could conjure in your mind. It was no place of grandeur our home, and for that Jonathon and Walter also shared a chamber. Yet despite its timeworn nature it possessed the quaintness of an older time, and though it was increasingly failing accepted practicality, we were comfortable.

Mary was already up and about, busy with breakfast I assumed. I rested my head back gently, thinking of my day ahead. I had not done enough work on the farm the previous day I knew, I only hoped the others held the work in my absence. I also knew Walter would have an opinion on my absence, and that he would verbalise it once he caught sight of me, it was inevitable. So I knew it was imperative I did some hard labour for the day. Though I wanted only to see her again, her whose pure heart I hungered for, her whose name I foolishly did not enquire.

I sat up leaning against the wall, dreaming of her, wishing to be in the company of that sweet girl once more. But I had to collect my thoughts together in a strict denial, it was best to get along with my work before Walter or father came in.

'Morning' Jonathon called lively towards me.

'Morning.'

'And a lovely one it is. You missed the sunrise.'

'There will be another one.'

'You cannot be certain, do not take the sunrise for granted. I may kill you in your sleep to prove my point.' He burst into hysterical laughter. And I laughed too, but more at his own fondness of his own words, than the words themselves. He was a simple soul. The sort of man who enjoyed making jokes and laughing at most things in life. "Laughter is the best medicine in the doctor's books" he would often say to those that questioned his ways. At times his playful ways made him a nuisance, but he was a well-intentioned and honest gent, which was enough for me to render him a good person; despite his inability to adapt in serious moments. We had some well-humoured moments the two of us. He was my favourite brother and I cannot recall any serious quarrel with him, but in political fashion we were finding ourselves separating. He wanted to inherit the land with Walter, which meant he followed father and him in any decision they chose, thus indirectly and unintentionally distancing himself from me.

'Calm down Jonathon' I raised my hand to hush him teasingly. He responded by saying

'My point was, you are an idle fool'

'And you are merely a fool.'

'How disrespectful little brother, I am your elder, and you called me a fool, perhaps you need to be beaten into shape.' He spoke sternly but for the crescendo. His eyes lit up along with his smile, the silent laughter. He loved to play fight and pin me to the ground, that was his meaning. With Mary being female and Walter thought himself too great for joys, I was the only one who would allow Jonathon the pleasure, to some vague extent.

    He charged at me. Much like a bull, and I the Spanish matador in fine silk tried to dodge him and power him to the floor instead; but with my smaller physique I failed miserably. Hard down I went, he knocked me to the floor in a playful yet aggressive manner, knocking the wind out of my frame as I lay gasping and struggled to breathe. I was defeated as always. Instantly he jumped up laughing and heckling.

'Maybe next time little brother' he called triumphantly, before walking away. He was a caring person behind his façade of shallow humour, and a sign of such was he consistently knew when to halt his competitive will.

'He beat you again?' Mary came in smiling, helping me up to my feet and handing me some water to quench myself. I thanked her before she moved away, then I got to work.

First with feeding and tending to the cows, father aided me on that day which was a nicety. His limbs were not as agile as they once were, therefore him working with us was an uncommon respect.

'Where do you go my boy?' He enquired with a narrow complexion as we walked slowly side by side, nearing the sheep that grazed on the field we had just crossed onto.

'Just around to see the country father'

'There is nothing out in the world for you my boy. Beyond the fields there are only factories; and every field is the same. That is all, fields and factories. And we need nothing to do with them.' He spoke bent over in weary stance.

'To me the world is as interesting as it is dull father. And no two fields are the same, God would want us to enjoy His creation.'

'Remember the commandments? *"Thou shall honour thy father and mother"*, God would want you to remain here and work.'

His voice died in the late morning winds as a silence dawned over us; I looked towards the trees in the distance as they stood their ground to the fierceness. Father had a look of hopelessness about him as he looked up at me, trying to keep me uninterested in the world and remain with them. I witnessed in his fading eyes what he knew, and what he feared: he knew he could not stop me from my disappearances from the farm, nothing would, and he feared it would only become more frequent with my oncoming age, which would only be truth. In that moment I felt a crushing pity for him. My withered father. He was a great man in his own way, an educated Northumberland farmer; a blameless person. The hardship he had suffered in life had taken his youth quite viciously. Being estranged from his own family took away the concept known as hope from his mind; but the real event that enwrapped him in gloom was the death of his wife. He desperately yearned for her, it was as clear to us as the daylight, we all knew and we all pitied him for it. Jonathon said that he aged half a lifetime overnight when she died. Indeed something in him had died the day she did. And all that remained was a haggard and grey old man who bore the red and blue patches of grief on his face. He was a shadow of the man I vaguely recall from my early years. But he had four children to nurture alone, and bring them back to the comfortable wealth he once knew. He continued to live, and his offspring were the only reason. For that I admired his strength. As he hobbled away from me in defeat, there dwelt a turmoil in my head of apologising to him for my defiance; but I held back with a slight regret.

All throughout the day the girl of the night before stole my mind, I could not release her from my vision. And what vision that was. The bliss still tickled at me, everything from the girl herself in her handsome glory, to the autumn forest as the embers flickered a dance in the air to our melodies, was flawless. Oh how I longed to see her face again, even only a day without her smile and still I craved her being. I had made a promise to see her again, and I willed it to be that evening, I could not deny my fate anything less. I possessed the chance to visit her after dinner when work had calmed, and I used it fully.

I made my way as everyone sat down independently to relax. To the cart I went. If father would have spotted me leaving he would not have been pleased considering what he had earlier spoke of, nonetheless, I simply had to go. I was silent as I left but for a few tired noises from the horses, I had to be as obvious as a mere shadow, for the main window looked out towards my road. In the end I was unsighted and free for her.

The clouds supressed a red sky that seeped its way in sight as the sun set low in the West; overwhelmed I always was at the beauty of a dusk sky, for they are never lacking in wonder.

I sat relaxed and poised during my fair journey. A journey to the North Pole would have been worth another moment with the girl, thankfully though I did not have to go such a distance. I found myself at that same spot as the day before, on top of the modest hill by the nearby home, looking down enwrapped with the idea of the beauty I barely believed, yet existing with no plan on how I would see her. I had simply made the journey enjoying its solitude without thought, and expected her to be standing outside alone again, how very foolish of me. I sat in a confused reverie, I was not going to knock on the front door and ask for her company, what madness that would have been. My first fault would be I knew not the name to ask for, secondly that also was not proper for me to do so, not in the late evening, and not unless her guardians knew me themselves; and accepted my trade.

Despite my dilemma I took a moment calm, smelt the fresh air and inhaled it delightfully. I looked up towards the moon and it was shining down on the lands like a crystal jewel amongst cotton clouds. When taking in all the sensory stimulus that I could muster I felt a sort of sixth sense, a suspicion almost, as if I was being watched in curiosity. Slowly I turned towards the house, the hope of seeing her sprang up my form, but I remained composed. My eyes flickered around the building. No one outside. I do not advise such rude behaviour, gawking outside a lady's house in the dark, but I began peering into the house. In a room I believed to be the kitchen she stood, seemingly washing some item I could not see and gazing at me with an unreadable stare. My internal response was of astounding glee though what the girl most likely bore witness to in me was a mixture of joy and uncertainty as I froze still in my lantern light. For several seconds our eyes met, much the same way they did when we sat by each other's side the day before, despite the distance. Over the seconds her complexion began to break into a slight smile that she was trying desperately to hold back. That same playful game of the day before, and the revealing of her will as a smirk crept in. Then she walked away from the glistening window and out of sight. Though she hid her temptatious smile after only a few seconds the journey had already reaped its rewards. But a frustration loitered inside, for I knew not what she thought and where she went.

I waited for her to either come out the door to me or move back towards the window and within my vision. I stood down from the cart, scratching my head as I wandered several impatient paces away before returning to my seat. What could this all mean? I expected her return within a dozen moments but she did not. I waited with the agitated patience of God for the return of another Godly being; but even God becomes animated at that delay.

Five minutes or so had passed when she returned. It felt as if my heart had awoken again as it pumped a passionate warmth upon my glance. The curls around her face floated in grace and those pale blue lakes flickered at me for a moment that I adored. She waved only for an instant, almost as if she was flashing her palm before looking down and continuing her work hastily; with looks my way infrequently. I knew not the truth of why at that moment, I only knew that my fantasy of being with her again had died. Though my soul had been dented with disappointment, I understood, she was occupied. With warm eyes and a prolonged smile that she barely saw, I was about to turn away when I noticed in a window a few rooms right of her, a man was staring directly at me with a face of stern distaste. He startled me momentarily, so firm was he in his disgust for me. I gathered myself and nodded to him in acknowledgement, hoping for some sort of reprieve, but none was found. He was unmoved, and I took my leave.

The days after I was the one with priorities delaying our reunited company. Walter was awfully ill, pale as whale bone it reduced him to as well as a bedridden mess; and worst of all, we did not know what it was. He feared consumption and its ally death, however, it was not so serious.

Without Walter, father continued helping us maintain the standard, though after a couple of days he could not labour further, with cause of his elderly back. And so it became just the two of us, I and Jonathon, working the efforts of four people; though there should have been half a dozen at least. To begin with we dealt with the load of work well enough, but our days became harder as we grew to have little energy reserve. As we herded the animals he lumbered about yawning to no end, and I knew I was the same in his eyes, but we could not refuse our duties. Mary involved herself in our meagre jobs when she could, but she had her own feminine duties within the house to be doing.

Despite my over-worked state, however so much my mind was greatly fatigued, the girl was still all I could think about. I planned once Walter returned to work once more, that I would find my time to see her again; and keep my promise. I could not help myself dreaming of her somewhat more and more each day. She was the answer to my query. God must have collapsed in triumph when she was created. The exquisite smile she bore, the one that I could just not release, was her greatest feature I confess, but there was everything more. Her voice, oh so soft, yet it held power behind it; and those Artic seas that flickered about me with precision, delicately charming. Everything about her drew me in to think about her endlessly to the extent I questioned my own self, had she rendered me spellbound like some incantatious fiend? Or was she more like an impossible devil taunting me with her beauty?

Though it felt tenfold the time, two dozen dawns later Walter began to return to his stability. When he was able to leave his bed and walk around, as he would move past me I saw the only reason he did not pant and rave and yell was a lack of himself. I smiled to Mary as we saw the meaningless rage in his eyes without an outlet to defuse itself. In truth he was in a decent state well before he began working again, it became clear to all of us that it was nothing more than an autumn chill. But of course Walter would pretend the illness to be worse than reality, and receive great sympathy from everyone, but that was just the pathetic nature of the imbecile.

Eventually, after many days, I made my way to her property. Unfortunately it was after dusk once more, and so I was expecting not luck, nor even sight of her. It was simply my only chance to attempt to see her and the agony of the yearn had become too great to refuse. No clouds were above on that night and so the heat of the day had escaped me, yet the positive of that fact was the vibrancy of the stars, it was a cold but excellent night; one I could have wandered for eternity in.

I arrived at the same hill I had the previous two times, anticipating such a routine. I opened my lantern wider to light my small world on the hill and placed it by the side of me. Along with settling my impatient mind the light would make me more visible in the dark to the girl, if she happened to glance towards the way I sat. She was nowhere to be seen when I arrived. I waited with dancing eyes around the windows hoping to see her, but I saw nothing. Was she worth my effort? I began to question. It was a fair journey for simply hoping she was outside at night. And last occasion not only did her father make it clear he did not like me scowling around, I was also unsure as to how interested she was in coming out to see me. Maybe she did not want to converse with me, perhaps she had made me promise to return more in jest than earnest and smiled a grateful smile when I turned my back in leave.

I turned my eyes from gawking at the stately home for the beaut to the starlight above. Time came and went from me, and I concluded I had been lingering too long. The ill-mannered awareness once more. But as I was about to leave, I heard the door open. I looked back to the house in hope of seeing her, but it was not her, it was the stern-faced man.

He was stepping down the road and up the hill towards me with purposeful steps. I thought of strolling down to meet him half-way, but the fierceness in his manner told me not to. It felt an anxious lifetime for him to reach me. When he did, I hopped down to meet him. He was a cold-eyed man of around my own height, dressed in a large white shirt that blew keenly in the wind. Though I knew he was of a higher class, his threatening aura told me he was a brute of a man; and if we were to tussle, he would have been victorious with humbling ease.

He came pointing his finger at me, speaking in a thick and deep Geordie accent.

'If you know what is good for you, you will not come back again.'

'I come in good will to you both. Your daughter is pleasant company sir, and I would like to speak to her if you would allow it. She wishes to see me also, I think, will you not allow your daughters wish?'

'You smell of manure' he called mockingly with aggressive animation 'take a look at yourself. You and your farmers cart with hedge shears still inside, yet you come here as if you were Prince Charming in a golden carriage ready to take her away. You are not, you poor little thing; you are not fit even to wipe my arse! You will not see her again. You will not come here again.' As he spoke however, with his back to the house, I could see the girl in one of the upstairs windows watching us. She kissed her hand softly and blew it in my direction with a tender expression. I felt the world stop turning; and her action confirmed to me why I could not surrender to his will.

'I made a promise to your daughter, good sir, that I would come and visit her again, and I will not break that promise. With all due respect to you, her father, it is only she who could release me from my duty of that promise.' He looked at me with scorn for a short moment and as his mouth opened he resembled a foaming dog. I suddenly felt a rush of apprehension. He rushed the few yards between us sharply and pushed me in the chest, not solidly, but with power enough that I stumbled a few paces. When I turned to see him, he held my shears and forcefully swung them at my stomach. I crashed down to the ground in shock and terror. He intended to scare rather than harm me, and he succeeded. Pointing them at me with that same disrespect, he shouted

'If I cannot sever you from this promise, perhaps I can sever your head from your neck!' He roared with laughter and smiled maliciously to me, enjoying every moment of my disbelief and horror. Then he threw the shears in the back of the cart.

As I got up onto my feet, he turned away from me and walked back to his home, calling out arrogantly
'We will see how this promise of yours plays out.'

Chapter III: Dreams And Duty

Aimer, c'est d'admirer avec le cœur; pour admirer, c'est d'aimer avec

l'esprit

Théophile Gautier

'I made you some porridge sunshine' a soft voice spoke the next morning. My drowsy eyes opened to see Mary handing me a bowl with a hesitancy of disturbing my sleep.

'Thank you' I mumbled as I awoke into the early morning. With a smile, I took the bowl from her as she sat down upon her bed staring at me.

'Is something the matter?' I called of her.

'Something is different in you... and I cannot tell what.' She had the most curious look in her eyes, studying my demeanour, the look in my own eyes, and the words I then spoke.

'There is no change in me. What could have changed?'

'You are absent longer. Your duties are being neglected and your mind increasingly seems occupied in things elsewhere. I am intrigued as to why.'

'I am more absent simply because I can. Would you not if you could?'

'And where would I go brother?' She called jokingly, 'the road to church is the only venture I ever have; yet you disappear in the late evenings and return well into the night.'

'There is more interesting things out there than there is in here.' She did not speak or move in any way to indicate that she heard me, she merely looked into me, then got up smiling and left the room.

Enter the moment when the other feminine person I did know, the girl I danced with in the woodland entered my mind. Though her father left no ambiguity in his threat to me, there was no other way, I had to go and see her again. I wanted to look upon her again, but most of all I wanted to retrieve her name. Before any of that however, a day of work was my way.

After dinner I swiftly left, into the cart and into the evening for her; the sweet stranger I had only begun to know. I could not repress my smile in the hope of seeing her, yet at the same time my heart felt thin with the anxiety of her father doing exactly what he said he would.

In fair time I reached my routine spot upon the hill that looked down at the building the girl called home. Lady luck was with me on that day as I saw her upon arrival, inside the room I believed to be their kitchen. As a cool breeze came and went by me, those eyes fixed up at me, then came the gleeful and glorious smile that she possessed; which only endeared me further. But I was not certain of my next move, knocking on the door for her and having her father answer was not wise I thought. And so I did nothing, only stand down from the cart and share her gaze. Like the time previously, she darted out of my sight, moving where I could not see and I was left only to hope she would reappear. I looked to the upstairs room I had seen her in before, wondering if that was her chamber and praying to see her; to my surprise, she came out of the door and walked towards me with a smile. Her journey up the hill was magical yet almost unendurable, my breathing moved out of all control; like being asphyxiated by joy herself.

'I thought you never would come again, not after last time; yet here you stand, atop this hill again.' She spoke tenderly, and stopped a few paces away from me. The gentle dusk made her blue eyes gleam like divine sapphire gems.

'I made a promise to you did I not, my lady? One I always intended to keep it.'

'And I am glad you have.' She paused for a moment before continuing solemnly 'I would like to wholeheartedly apologise for the way my father treated you. He is wretched and you did not deserve his threats.' She had a stern look in her eyes which I took notice of, as if she expected him to see us any moment, and do worse this time.

'No need to apologise. I am still in one piece.' I looked to the house for several moments, and could not see him in the windows watching us. I looked to her again, reaching for her small paw and kissing it softly, speaking 'may I enquire, my lady, for your name?' 'My name is Rebecca' spoke the delicate voice with a slight blush of the cheeks 'Rebecca Hill by practice, Rebecca Evans by birth.' 'Rebecca. Rebecca, what a lovely name. Mr Robert Fletcher' I bowed my head in introduction 'would you care to join me on a ride through the county once again?' Upon my words her smile faded, saddening me slightly.

'I wish I could, but I cannot leave now' she looked up at me and gained half a yard. 'If you appear early to-morrow morn, just out of sight, I should be able to accept your proposal.'

'I shall see you on the morrow then my lady Rebecca, I will take my leave.' I could see as I spoke she wished me to stay, though, for both our sakes I had to go. "Lose the battle, win the war" is what I thought. I took one last long look at the beauty as her gorgeous smile lingered on her face. I absorbed all I could, every crinkle in her soft skin, those bright glistening eyes and the sweet aura of her.

She watched me disappear into the sky over the green hill. On that journey home my senses were ambushed by the darkening red sky through the clouds, the cool breeze; and the girl whose name I now knew.

Rebecca, Rebecca.

As you may know, a fair journey allows you the time to think about whatever is playing on your mind my reader, even if you wish it not to. I was not limiting her from my thoughts though, I willed to only think of her and her perfect name. Rebecca. With its coarse yet sweet feel, rough consonances strung together to describe feminine beauty in the most wonderful approach; giving her the essence of a rough jewel coupled with the common ending of female names by a vowel to maintain a harmless incentive. How very romantic. And we planned to see one another the next day. Truly wondrous was the prospect of sharing a morning in each other's presence and previous frustrations were forgotten quite instantly. I thought what we would do, and where better to take her than my beloved lough? A picnic for two, just me and my Rebecca.

I fell in and out of sleep that night, the eagerness for her left me restless and I could not find relaxation blessedly. Through the window I saw a sky that was on the cusp of closing night every time I awoke, as if it was a never-ending darkness before twilight, making me wait in an eternal night.

Mary also woke early that morning. We rested in calm before the day fully began.

'Who is this person you have met sunshine?' She spoke out of the silence.

'Mary, what makes you think I have met someone new?' I replied not worried that she had discovered so, but in wonder of how she had learnt such was so.

'You give me no credit. I know you better than anyone, I could see the change in you, it just took me another day to figure out its cause. Who is she?' Her face gleamed as she questioned. I hesitated at first, reluctant to say, not because I did not want her to know, for I did, but because I did not want the conversation. I felt revealing my passion for a woman was like announcing a weakness in me somehow. Is passion not a weakness within us, or is it the greatest empowerment of all?

'Rebecca is her name' I said, unsure of what else to mention. Upon the name alone the smile Mary wore engulfed her face, making me laugh, and she did too.

'Well what else would you like to know?' I added still amidst the laughter.

'That is enough for now' she spoke with serious eyes and a playful complexion. She smirked once more before leaving the room.

I rushed some food into a blanket, bread, cheese, fruit, as well as some food from the previous day. I did not want anyone to notice me until after I returned, and so with food all in the blanket, my violin still in my cart with varying other instruments, I decided not to wait any longer but go forth to her, the lovely Rebecca.

Thankfully on that day the sun was visible amongst only a few clouds, cold winds were present as they permanently were, though it was lesser than days hitherto; therefore I could not complain. The world was euphoric in its greenery and salty air, but I could not think to enjoy it. Reaching Rebecca was my end, and as I neared her home, staying out of sight, I saw her waiting for me on the edge of agitation, near the spot I had come to claim as my own. She stood elegantly, sporting a tasselled plain white dress, fur for warmth and practical brown shoes as the slow winds positioned her golden sand hair to one side and rested over her left shoulder. Those gentle eyes of hers lit up the world as she spotted me and brushed her hair behind her ear lightly; I was captivated by her splendour. She became more beautiful in her precious self than I had known before.

'Morning Rebecca' I called as I neared her. She simply smiled. I pulled the reins to my stop. I was to help her onto the cart like all gentlemen should, however she pulled herself up onto the bench and sat close by my side. There was no femininity in her manner there, and yet I adored her for not caring of such customs. Our eyes gazed into each other's for a moment as she turned to me; half an arms distance at most separated us. A passion roared, a melting warm yearn. I wished to kiss her plump lips and taste the girl who seemed so perfect to me. Even her scent was enticing, like the smell I expect of Heaven as I inhaled her. The moment ended when with her timidity she giggled under her breath with that unique feminine laugh I was so endeared by.

Conversation flowed between us like water down a stream. I tried hard to suppress my nerves to make the most of that time that I had been blessed with; and to conclude, I feel I did so to a fine standard. The suns journey across the sky was in full flow as we rode towards the mass of yellow, with its pollinating light showered upon us kindly.

'Where are we travelling to?' Asked her in her soft expression that I found to be a joy.

'To a lough East of here, it is a truly glorious place my lady.'
'Sounds wonderful Mr Fletcher.'

As we rocked to and fro on the stone road, the lough below came into sight. And beautiful was it as the scenery of tall trees reflected off the body of water, creating some symmetrical illusion of conifers with foliage at both ends. Beyond the foliage the sky could be seen on the water also, like the sky had invaded the body of water and claimed it as itself.

'Be this it?' She called becoming alert as to the marvel of the lough. I nodded. She observed the land, the water, absorbing all the delight that had become so familiar to me. 'It is splendid' she added with a smile directed at me. I reciprocated.

'I have not told you why we are here yet' I teasingly spoke, 'but you will know soon enough.' She too had a spirited look as her hair waved about her. There was something about Rebecca that I adored undeniably, our time together was of the most perfect harmony, like of a symphony that never lost its step. And I found her company soothing which was all too rare. Mary was relaxing company I admit, but being with her meant I was on the farm with Walter, and being near him simply meant no form of comfort was to be found on my part.

We came to a halt, my beloved stallions knew where to stop instinctively, for I had forced them to such a halt in the same place a thousand times previously. As the cart came to its standstill she lit up, I could see she wanted to sit by the water, and I would not deny her anything. I led her down towards the body as she walked closely by my side, entering my personal ether. I felt so frail, my heart was too vulnerable to her movements and speech; my weakness and strength. My passions weakness defined its unwavering strength for her.

We sat down ten paces from the water, the vegetation appearing all the more magnificent, with luminous grass, and a conifer tree that towered over us with a threatening sense of mystique.

'So...' her blue lakes sparkled with an overwhelming energy I could not decrypt 'why are we here?' I did not answer her immediately, only retrieved the cloth from the cart as she watched me patiently.

'Quite appropriate, I thought a picnic would be' I spoke as I unravelled the food and displayed it for her. She looked to the feast for a moment before looking back up at me with appreciation. We laid out the food upon the cloth together, presenting everything tidily.

'This is perfect Fletch'

'Please.' I signalled for her to eat as she pleased.

'Thank you sir.'

As she and I indulged in the meal I could not contain my thoughts of how fitting she seemed for me; it was as if the world was setting in motion for the both of us; a sort of fate unfolding that I could not wait to embrace. Yet I knew not the nature of love in any real sense. I had known no childhood romance, I had not been witness to love in my parents or grand-parents, and now I was old enough to marry, I had little idea how love or learning to do so formulated. How could I then show my affection for the girl? I did feel somewhat childish in this respect, but that is how I was in those days, and I believed she was too.

As we ate, I noticed her complexion fade and turn into a cold stare into the air.

'Is something the matter my lady?'

'Just tired.' A fake smile flashed upon me from her, but with an inaudible sigh her expression fell straight back to the blankness of before. She meant not for me to see that sigh, but I saw it, and I could see something troubled her more than mere tiredness.

'Are you sure it is only tiredness, does something prey on your mind?' A few moments passed before she said anything. A focus slowly ignited in her eyes. Then she spoke

'It is only, I have been having dreams the last couple of nights. A night ago, I dreamt of you... You were murdered by a man. A pale man of dark searing eyes, with long black hair and ruffled sideburns. He was of inhuman strength, and he crushed you to death with his bare hands!' There was a tremble in her voice as she recalled, and a hint of repulsion.

'You had come to see me during a horrible, and insufferably grim night, but my house was instead, a large shed. We were inside and so too my family. This man came through the door aggressively and threatened death upon me. My family fled at first sight of him, but you did not. He came towards me, but you stood in his path facing up to him. You would not allow it. The atmosphere was terrifying alone, the room, full of gloomy shadows that crept eerily towards us, eager to cause harm. The sky through the window was almost too dark, too black, like it had opened itself up to the final abyss. And he loomed over you, like a Giant from the ancient world, but you would not stand down. He roared at you to run in his rugged and foreign voice, but with courage you would not move. The anxiety of horror clamped me painfully, and I wept silently, prematurely mourning the fate of our existence.' I could feel the trauma in her words, like she felt the dream had some significance. I opened my mouth to utter words of comfort for her, but she continued further 'time seemed to drone on in an agonisingly slow tempo from there onwards. The giant pushed your head on both sides with his large palms until your skull began to crack. The sound was awful, like a creaking rocking chair on an old porch in the wind. You squealed a scream that disturbed me to a cold shudder; everything felt so heavy and slow in the dark enclosure. As his grip loosened on you, your lifeless body slowly fell into a heap on the wooden floor. Your limbs flailed as if every bone you had, he shattered with that one action; and as you descended, my very body was controlled by yours in the exact same contorted position. We fell as one. First to the knees as a tremor rumbled through us both with arms unresponsive, then with a crash onto our faces. I could feel the pain of your collapsed skull oh so unbearably as we entered convulsions of a demons possession. It was as if it was reality; or somehow prophecy.' She paused momentarily. 'But instantly I was on my feet, as I was before, facing the giant as you remained on the floor still jerking in agony. The man's eyes burned with an emotion I could not understand, it was not anger nor some contemplation, but whatever it was, it tore at my soul as he glared upon me. He then walked from the room to the outside. With slow harsh steps he did not intend, yet they thundered down like the storm itself. The door remained open as he left but he did not leave me altogether, he stood by the window, peering at me through the watercourses that trickled down. Fear gripped me to paralysis, I could not move, there was no escaping him.' A solemn tone ran through her frightened words. 'I do not remember anything aft. Last I saw he was watching me. It felt real, undeniably. He was evil, The Devil Outside Looking In; oh so evil. And I could feel the pain you felt when he crushed you, I could feel my body collapse to the floor as I heard yours, it was so real.' That is when she stopped.

Motionless yet visibly shaken, I knew I had to comfort her but I knew not the words. I placed my hand on her knee and in my own form of a comforting whisper I simply spoke to her 'It was only a dream.' She nodded to herself in agreement but I saw in her complexion that she thought more of it, her word "prophecy" still echoed in the air.

'Enough of my odd nightmares' she snapped 'I want to express how grateful I am that you did not yield to my father's taunts of violence. Words cannot express my joy that you came for me.'

'I said I would return, and I did.'

'But it is more than duty; I feel it, which is something I welcome.'

'And what of your duty as a daughter?'

'What exists between us is more than your duty of a promise. Do you not feel that too?'

'Of course I do. It is both of my duty of my promise, as well as my duty to you that I speak of. I am only concerned that your father will threaten and eventually harm me, and you, if we continue to meet with one another.'

'That is why we must be vigilant and diligent.' She had a gleam in her eye 'I think it best you do not come unannounced again, we should only meet pre-arranged, and you must wait for me out of sight from any of the windows.'

'Agreed. But will your father not know what is happening when you walk up the hill to where we have met before, and disappear for an afternoon?'

'I can leave through the door to the garden and walk round out of sight. As for my whereabouts, I shall try to find some story.'

Though her words were of everything I wanted nothing more, I was unsure of myself, and of her. She had negotiated her way around her father harming me, but I still greatly feared his violence upon her. My duty indeed was of both the promise I made her, and the girl herself, and I could not ignore this possibility of violence.

'Your father will beat you for our conspiracy. And you cannot escape him as I can.' She held a firm stare at me for a moment without saying a word, her brow creased as she searched my being for something in its caverns.

'Do not surrender me to his will. I swear to God I will beat you if you do.' A smile came after her words and I could not help but follow, whilst contemplating her ferocity and what it meant. Perhaps ultimately she was lonely, and lost within the conditions of her family like me.

'I am no brave Prince, I fear, I am not rich or particularly strong. But he is my dragon, and Rebecca I promise you, I will not surrender you to his fire.' She placed her small hand on my knee in appreciation, gently. I remained still, and felt the cold of her hand penetrate into my blood stream. I placed my hand on top of hers and our eyes met slowly brightening the world around us suddenly. I knew what the look we shared meant, we were bound to one another, by duty, and through whatever strife.

'I know of your father, but what of the rest of your family; your mother, siblings?' I asked trying to change the serious mood.

'My mother is simply my father's shadow and echo. Anything he says she simply follows. She is a poor, spineless creature. But I am adopted, they are not my real parents, so of siblings, I have two brothers, one also adopted, and the other of the same parents.'

'Where are your real parents?' I instinctively enquired, half guessing the answer after I spoke.

'They died.'

'I am sorry to hear'

'No do not be, that was some time ago now. Besides, I am lucky, I am alive and in good health when I could have died in an orphanage, like my brother Michael most likely did.'

'Then you do not know. He could be alive and well too; missing you as you miss him... Why was he not adopted with you?"

'My father would not take him, and because of that my hatred for him began before they even took me home. I begged of them both to take him with us, but they would not. Mrs Hill could not bear children herself, try as they did, and when Mr Hill was working for a time in Chester, where I grew up, they came to our small orphanage. They wanted only one boy and one girl, and for the boy to be the eldest. I was chosen because I was the youngest girl of the six there, but because Michael was three years younger than me they refused to take him with me. In the end they chose a boy named Oscar who is two years older than me.' A change came over her face as she paused for a moment. 'Fletch, we were both dying in there. Neither of us would have lasted another winter in that place; and so few of us ever managed to leave. For the sake of my life I was fortunate they came and took me when they did. And wanting a younger girl. However I did not want to leave, I was dragged out by my father because I knew I would be leaving my Michael to die alone. I know in my heart that he has not survived.' Her eyes grew weak as she spoke, looking casually to the Heavens. 'You should have seen him as I left, he was only seven and he knew he was going to die in there cold and alone.'

'Then he is with God, and knows no more pain.' She smiled for a brief moment but her eyes remained weak. 'Has Oscar been a brother to you?'

'No. He is not a bad person, we just never had a connection. He works all over the country for father these days, I have not seen him for a year or so now.'

'Come Mr Fletcher' she called as the day grew late 'I must retire before the sun.' It was unfortunate to hear but I knew the time was at hand, the sun was already setting. Setting in a scarlet that covered the land most spectacularly and shining warm colours about her face like our fire in the wood had done when we first met.

'Thank you for a perfect day Fletch' the soft voice spoke as we arrived at the destination, just out of view of the home. She smiled a delightful smile that made me grow frail, as if Cupid's arrow was causing my death accidently. 'When can you come again?'

'I shall return in a week, if that is agreeable with you?'

'Most certainly.'

'I shall meet you here then, at midday.' We went through our acts of courtesy.

'Sweet dreams.' She spoke as she retreated, I repeated those words to her and smiled as I watched her disappear. My Rebecca.

On my lone journey home I noted the silence of the world increasingly turned eerie. There were no words for it, and though no nightly terrors could overcome the glee she brought me, a sort of fear itched at my soul. The congealing darkness felt foreboding in an unexplainable way. Though I made it home without harm, I lay restless all night still feeling that phantom fear itching me.

I worked the next two days doubly much. I tried to focus upon my work around the farm, keeping father content with me for disappearing. But throughout all tasks I occupied myself with, she was inevitably in my thoughts.

Then came the Lord's Day, the day of a building that bore a sign outside that read "Jesus the Lord" in big bold letters, followed by a paragraph no one ever bothered to read. We went to a simple church of no magnificence, no tainted windows of beautiful biblical stories, no golden lectern bearing the head of a symbolic eagle for the sole reason of aesthetics. Our lectern was made of some dull wood. The priest spoke and then he stopped. I did not listen, it was only Mary and father who were concerned with the preaching and the prayers. The rest of us were Christians sure, and I had my connection with God as any other, but I did not concern myself with the insignificant details that others have died for.

The reason I mention of the church on that day, is to set you upon my mind frame that led to the want of my creation. Read on.

We left quietly, as always. Some reflecting, others had simply inhaled the gentle atmosphere churches can give. It was a nice day also, which settles the mind of anyone, and because of it, I decided to spend the remainder of the day by the beautiful land; a charming little place near home where I used to go as a child. However, father noticed me as I was preparing to leave.

'Where are you going my boy?' He demanded in a hush voice with a trace of anger.

'Out to see the country father, to rest in the green.'

'No, you stay inside on a Sunday like the example your brothers set.'

'But I want to go and enjoy the outside, it is peaceful, will you deny me that?' He looked at me with small eyes and breathed heavily. I did not want to argue with him, I never did. He was too frail to, and because of this, I thought myself a villain when I troubled the old man; but I was not going to give in to his useless rules. After several seconds of him wanting to speak, though he murmured to himself, in defeat he walked away.

My childhood spot was a simple and pleasant place. A stream could be sounded nearby, along with it came the fresh scent bodies of water give. The calm I felt laying in the lovely pale blue afternoon sky was euphoric. I fell in and out of sleep lightly, but when I was awake, the church's influence was about me. I thought of the idea of God being the creator of this world, the creator of the beauty in the sky above that engulfed my thought so tremendously. But when brought to its very minimum, the beauty of the sky was like that of a blue cloth. How did He create the sky when He previously existed in the empty void of She'ol? Would He have simply painted the horizon like a magical painter?

I delighted in such a grand thought, and had the sudden urge to create it myself; to paint the sky in all its grandeur like He did. I was a reasonable painter, though nothing special I confess, and was second to Walter in my family, who himself was surprisingly skilled at the craft. However, on that day I had no tools of craft with me, which meant I would have to wait for the next day to do my work. Thus I decided to make it the dawn sky by my lough that I would paint; the greatest landscape to paint that I could think of.

I continued to fall in and out of sleep until I left for home.

I got out of bed a whole two hours before dawn that morning and hastily prepared myself. I knew I had to finish quickly and be back to work for the family, but I was confident I would complete the painting in good time. Riding out, the pale winds greeted me. As I glanced upon the twilight horizon the birds sung delicate lullabies in the early morning, if only their songs could be transferred on the canvas in the same manner I thought.

My lough was tranquil in its atmosphere as ever, the birdsong was still echoing in its corners, enthusiastically willing me to paint; and how I loved the songs of my winged commissioners. The sparkle of ginger from the sun pierced the navy of the sky with great contrast and yet existed in a fiery harmony.

I placed the canvas upon a chair taken from home. I looked towards the sky for lingering traces of moon and stars, but none could be seen. I tried to catch sight of the birds I could hear so distinctly, hoping to work one into the painting, however, yet again, I caught no such sight. Time left me entirely as I painted, and few errors were detailed as I laboured the joy of a proud work. I shall try to describe to you my reader as best I can the end I fashioned:

My beautiful lough lay at the bottom and centre, shinning its silver as slight tints of the creeping orange sparkled delicately upon its rippling surface; water lilies still clinging to summer existed only in withered scarcity, but they existed beautifully nonetheless. The green hills were rising gradually to the East as the orange sphere poked its tip into sight from behind the distant land. To the West woodlands roamed gracefully with birds soaring carelessly above, I could almost hear their interweaving melodies in the canvas and smell the sweet perfume of morning dew. And to give the pleasant touch I craved, I added several dots of white as stars on the softly darkened azure horizon. It was similar in style to that of John Constable, though of a more realist nature.

I looked at the completed effort like God must have done when He created earth, greatly proud at the sight yet with a hint of perfectionists doubt. It was in itself a fair piece far beyond my own expectation, though it had those imperfections which my ability could not exceed. No piece of exhibition quality was it, yet I was most pleased with it.

I returned home to see the day's work had begun yet much more work was still to be done, my absence was hardly noticed.

During my days labour on the farm, thinking of the girl and of my creation, I never had doubt of my affection for her, but I did doubt whether or not it was right of me to cause issue between a young girl and her father. Surely it was not right of me to do so. But I thought of a gesture. To give my painting to her father in good-will, perhaps I could find myself in his favour. Its flaws came back to me, but is it not the thought that counts? I was not convinced he would feel anything for the gesture in truth, but once I thought to do so, there was no other path for me to take.

Chapter IV: Her Heart Sets North

Beyond this beautiful horizon lies a dream for you and I

Danny Cavanagh

Early the next morning I woke with firm determination to get my tasks completed as quickly as I could in order to hand the man my gift. And I did just that. By mid-afternoon I left, placing the painting in the back of my cart, and covering it carefully with white cloth in case it rained.

I arrived and approached as swiftly and quietly as I could, hoping to not be seen so when I knocked on the door, it would be him, not her, to come and I could hand it to him in person. I trembled as I neared their door, I was entirely unsure if the gesture would end well. I took a moment when the cart came to a halt by the door, breathing in a calmness. I could hear the sweet masters of the sky again, singing their songs as they did yester-day. Were they encouraging me further? Perhaps so. But it mattered not if they were, for I knew what my situation inevitably would be concluded with, me finally knocking on his menacing door. My heart pounded at the formality, I tried to swallow my anxiety, but it did not work. With a deep breath, my fist struck the door twice in nervous thuds. And then he came.

'Yes' it demanded. I should have expected just as much, but he startled me in his rude and direct nature.

'Mr Hill, I have a gift for you that I hope will mend the illness between us.' I spoke feigning a confidence as his eyes settled on me with a grim disgust, one that I had no respect for. I faked a smile for him and added 'come' as I waved him to walk with me to the cart. He remained still in the doorway. I retrieved the thing with care and presented it to him.

'I painted it yester-day of the dawn. For a new day, and a new beginning.' He took it from me with stiff coldness and an unmoved complexion; then he disappeared through the door to his left, leaving his front door wide open. How bizarre I thought, for someone to leave their front door open to a guest, neither bidding me good day nor inviting me in. As I thought on his ways, soft steps trickled out of the dark and into sight. Those icy blue lakes locked onto me momentarily; I so easily got lost in them. Like a seaman whose boat had sunk and all in sight was the overwhelming and rich tones of blue sky and blue water.

'I did not expect to see you to-day. What a wonderful surprise.' She wore a wide smile of enthusiasm, which was heavenly to see, changing the hostile atmosphere immediately.

'It is a wonder to see you too Rebecca' I replied as that beautiful playful smile turned mischievous quite suddenly. She looked behind herself to be certain we were alone, then hastily darted towards me with a kiss. Her warm lips caressed mine for barely a moment. Then it was finished. A sweet taste lingered on my lips and I sighed for more; but instead of looking to me, her eyes darted to her left, and the smell of burning came to me.

'Your gift returned, sir farmer' the male voice called mockingly. The Dragon pushed in front of her and handed me the flaming painting. Out of habit of taking something someone offers to you, I took it from him. I speechlessly looked at the fire spreading from the top and slowly engulfing the piece as thick black smoke started to form and bubble into the air. I was appalled at the sight, not for the paintings sake, nor the effort I put into it, but for the nature of the beast of a man. For a moment I looked to her, my expressionless gaze received hers; but the man whose shoulder she looked over glared at me with scorn. In anger I tossed the failing canvas on his lawn and turned my back to walk to my cart.

'Young farmer-boy, you have ten second to get off my land before I whip her to Kingdom come.' I turned back in surprise and disgust, he was in the action of taking off his belt and foaming from the mouth at me. Rebecca stepped back a yard with fear.

'I am leaving, do you not see me walking away?'

'I am coming with you' Rebecca called, quickly stepping past him and into my sphere.

'You bloody well most certainly will not.'

'You despicable man! Will you not allow me a friend? I loathe you and your cruelty. I have been a dove without wings ever since you brought me through that wretched door. You told me you threatened to sever Mr Fletcher's head from his neck, well you have already severed my wings; and my hope for that matter. You would do anything to see me miserable.'

'You petulant, ungrateful little thing. I brought your cold, dying body into a warm home. You will obey me!'

'I would have been happier if you left me to die like you did my brother than have been in this household.' He huffed in silent rage before puffing through his teeth.

'Go then, enjoy yourself my daughter. Just wait until you get back.'

'Come, let us go, I do not wish to spend a moment longer in his presence.' She grabbed hold of my hand and pulled me towards the cart. I could only obey. I whipped the horses to quick movement, and glancing back towards the house, he had already shut the door and disappeared. The fire on his lawn was still burning and smoking.

'Do you have any preference on a destination Rebecca?'

'Somewhere new' she said with a smile, forgetting everything of her father and existing only within the moment. But her energy soon fell and she rested her head upon my shoulder, closing her eyes and petite features gently. I felt her face warm and soft through my shirt.

'Are you tired Rebecca?'

'Far too much so yes, lately I have found no comfort in sleep.'

'Still having dreams?'

'Yes.'

'Of the man?'

'Yes I still see the same man, but I wish not to speak of this now.' I did not press her further.

I decided we would go upon higher grounds, to a location I had been when I was younger, one where unfathomable distances across the rolling hills could be seen. The sun was visible in the dimly white sky as the cold chill of the North-East was ever present. The crisp leaves clustered underfoot and danced in the winds with elegance. And the scent of those dead leaves lingered around my nose in beautiful fragrance. As we rode slowly, rocking to and fro in the sturdy cart over uneven lands, we were locked to each other by the indent of my shoulder and chest as she rested. I saw her peering into the world peacefully here and there through flickering lashes. It seemed her tiredness seeped through my shirt and into my form; or perhaps it was her tranquillity in the atmosphere. Either which way I closed my eyes, letting the cold air caress my eye lids as my head fell back slightly, to a more at ease state. My hand searched for hers, not in the timid fumbling I would have expected of myself, but of the conviction that should have been mine all along.

We made the destination in good time and I placed down the cloth from our picnic on the dense moss for us to sit.

'It is a glorious sight up here' she spoke, looking around with mild joy.

'Yes it is, incredible.' She looked to me and placed her sandy hair behind her ear, before turning firm in expression.

'I appreciate your attempt to win my father's favour.'

'He undoubtedly did not.' I laughed, but she did not move from her seriousness.

'I hope you know, it is nothing personal from him, his only rejection is your profession.'

'It is certainly personal to me.' I found myself in the same firm mind as her.

'I know it is.'

'Then what is it you are saying? Are you condemning or defending him?'

'His actions are inexcusable, and indefensible.'

'Are you condemning him then?' She hesitated with my words, and looked frightened for several speechless moments.

'Let us run-away together, now. And we shall never have to deal with him again.'

'Run-away?' I replied astounded at the mere thought of it 'and where would we go?'

'To Scotland, I have always wanted to see the Highlands.'

'How fantastical of you. Run-away to Scotland, now. What would we eat? How would we stay warm for the journey? Run-away you say? What madness that would be.'

'He will beat me senseless if I return to that house' she cried.

'We cannot just flee across the border without preparations and without money. Fear of a flogging is no reason to leave a country.' She looked to me as if I had gravely offended her; so much so that I was taken aback by it.

'That would be my unashamedly eclipsed second reason. You, Fletch, are the first reason.'

'Still, I cannot be responsible for you; yet. I am no breadwinner. I will not do such a thing until I can guarantee a comfortable life for you Rebecca.'

'I do not care for money, a life with you will be more comfortable than my current home regardless.' I had to turn away from her for a minute, her unexpected intensity had stunned me completely. I looked from the slowly setting sun in front of me, to my right hand side and eyed down the hill as it slowly wound its way to level farming fields that were lined with straight hedges and stray tress. And as my gaze moved from the land below to the wider world, I smiled to myself in the knowledge that I was unintentionally looking out northwards, towards Scotland.

'Give me a year, then, to prepare. I can save money for food, for warm clothes of our own. We can stay in an inn until I get some work on some willing farm. I imagine they look for labourers unlike my stubborn father.'

'I can get us warm clothes, my parents have more than they know what to do with, as for money I am not so certain I can get my hands on much. But what is it you are afraid of? Do you not want to start life afresh with me?'

'Of course I do, but what I am afraid of is us both dying cold in a ditch before we even reach the Highlands because we were imprudent and impulsive. And that is what this talk is, imprudent and impulsive.' With my words the ice blue turned to an oxidising flame, that was the one time ever that she looked at me with fire in her eyes.

'Take me home then. I want to be done with this flogging.' She stood up impatiently.

'Rebecca' I uttered though she partial ignored me. 'Miss Rebecca Evans' I called more demandingly which warmed her slightly 'I wish I could, I do. But I cannot. I wish I was rich so your father would be happy you met me. I wish we...'

'It is not about money, and it is not about him. Take me home now.' Her words came calm and subdued. For her, there was nothing more to say, and she was right. I took her home.

We said nothing on the journey. There was no animosity between us, only frustration. I pulled the reins by the debris of the painting. She smiled half a smile to me as her eyes flickered low about me, and then she hopped away. My heart sank to see the low look she gave me, I yearned to reach out to her and stop her leaving me, I wanted to say something meaningful, but I did nothing.

I had my horses turning when I heard the door open, I knew she was still too far away to have opened it herself so turned to see, inspecting attentively. It was The Dragon who came storming out, holding his whip viciously. And before either of us had the time to react he unleashed an unrestrained lash in her direction, cracking her on her arm as she shrank down to the floor, like a mouse who had lost all hope in the wake of a malicious feline. There was no attempt of words from him, I could see in his foaming mouth there was no lesson to be taught as he whipped her again.

'You deserve no less than this' the mother shouted from the doorway. 'Trysting with a farmer-boy, you ought to be ashamed of yourself.' Rebecca curled up and covered her face as his wrath came down again. I jumped from the cart and ran to the scene, hoping to take the belt from him, but that was hopeful at best. He saw me come down and turned his flogging to me. In an instant I too was on the floor and felt three or four rapid attacks on my back and legs.

'Get inside' he bellowed, and quickly Rebecca got to her feet and edged nervously towards the doorway. A few more lashes came at me closer to my head and I held my arms up to protect myself. Rebecca called frantically for him to stop. And he did for a moment.

'Look at you, you cannot defend yourself' he mockingly addressed me. 'I could not trust the safety of my daughter to such a lowly boy as yourself, cowering under my feet. You, get inside!' He screamed to her 'I do not want to see your face again today.' I slowly tried to get back to my feet, thinking any quick reaction would spark his fury again, but I was wrong, my movement was enough to ignite his rage. He began flogging me again with fumbling violence, and so quickly came the cracking all over me I knew not what to cover. The sharp pains were immense, I could not even consider rising to my feet and throwing blows his direction.

'How dare you step between a father and his disobedient daughter' he called, whipped me incessantly. I was paralysed in the succession of his belt.

'Fletch!' Rebecca howled as her mother clasped stiff arms around her. She tried furiously to break free but to no avail. I thought my torturous punishment would never end.

'For the love of God' she called out in desperate plea 'father, please stop. I love him!' He stopped instantly as if she had broken his will with those simple words that seemed to echo on the hillside. The mother laughed and pushed the girl away from her, and at her laughter The Dragon too chuckled in deep breaths. He scoured at me for the longest moment as if trying to pierce my soul with his eyes alone; then he turned away from me dismissively. Rebecca moved past him to my aid as he walked back into the house.

'In love with a farmer. Our love-struck Juliet is too childish for sense.' The mother muttered to him. With cradling arms for me, Rebecca held her fierce gaze at them until the door slammed shut. Then turning to me she helped me to sit up, and embraced me in a tight squeeze that made my bruises swell excruciatingly; she only wanted to give me affection.

'I detest that man, I am sorry for his actions. I am sorry you had to suffer injury for my faults.'

'Do not apologise on his account. I detest him too.'

'Fletch, it is true though, I do love you. My heart is yours, irretrievably so. I loved you from the moment I first saw you.' She held my face by both hands, unintentionally shaking me and searching my soul for its true reply.

'I love you too, irretrievably so' my exhausted and wounded self managed to word.

'Then do you not see why we must leave as soon as we can?' I let her words fade and the urgency in them die with the cold air.

'Give me but a year, my love, give me a year and we can leave.'

'He would rather kill you than see us together for another year. Has to-day not taught you that?' She held onto my hands tightly in her distress.

'I cannot, and will not, take you away from here until we are sufficiently prepared.'

'But I cannot endure this! I cannot endure his floggings, I cannot bear to see him do this to you again.'

'I tell you this now, he will not have the pleasure of doing this to me again.'

'And what of me? What do you propose for me? That I continue to see you and receive this punishment on a weekly basis for an entire year? That I cannot, and will not, endure!' She cried to me, and it broke my heart to hear her say such words.

'I can only propose, then, that we see each other more irregularly and plan our arrangements with more guile. A year will pass soon enough Rebecca.'

'No it will not, a year longer with these callous things?' she pointed to the house. 'No that is out of the question, and meeting more irregularly would be further torture, do not leave me to these heartless beasts, locked in this tower, do not walk away from this Fletch, I beg of you.'

'I will not abandon you to them, you need not worry of that.'

'I know I have, and I am, asking a lot of you, but you are the lighthouse to my stormy voyage, the dragon-slayer for my fairy-tale. I need you, I love you.'

'I feel the same, my love, however, regretfully, we have to suffer them temporarily. A year, please. Our escape will be all the sweeter when the time comes.'

'A year it is then.' She had an odd look of both defeat and victory.

'I promise you. Before next winter we will be far gone from here.'

'I will count the hours Mr Fletcher.' Her complexion morphed into something more tender, she moved closer into me, rubbing my palm with her hands and whispered to me 'I thank you for standing by me, for caring for me when no one else does.'

'Repay me then, with the patience we unfortunately need. But for now, I think it best I leave, the sun has almost set, and he is probably watching.'

'Promise me you will come for me tomorrow, at dawn. We can go somewhere' she eagerly implored of me. I saw a vision of him flogging her again when she entered the house, the idea of leaving her pained me; I could not refuse her.

'I promise you.' Her face illuminated into the sweetest expression, one that made me sad to know our day together, however painful, was coming to its end. We rose to our feet and I kissed her soft hand in leave.

'Remember, Miss Evans, not all dragons can be slain overnight.'

'Well this one could be, if stabbed in his sleep.' We laughed together, though I did ponder the chance of her having just announced her intention.

'Good night Rebecca.'

My journey back through the twilight and the darkness that followed was one I did not care for. My stallions became agitated by the sound of a painful, eerie and empty silence. I forced them on in spite of their discomfort and fear; and my own growing feeling that a danger loomed near. Though I told myself nothing was out there with me, that in the vast darkness no animal sizable enough to attack two horses and a human existed. But as I crept forward in the blackness and down a narrow, straight road that bore an adjacent woodland running alongside, I fancied I saw a man standing by the edge of the cover of trees just up ahead. He appeared dressed in an obscuring black. Of the man himself all I could see was his pale hands, and a beardless jaw from under what appeared a black hood that shadowed the rest of his face. Surprised I was, at the sight, primarily to see a man alone at that time of night in autumn without a horse or carriage to take him on his way; of alarm, I felt none initially, despite his ill appearance. However, once I caught view of him from the distance and moved closer, anticipating what a bizarre lonesome man may say at such times, he became lost from sight as if he morphed into the darkness around him, and no longer existed. Was it a mere shadow? Or did he wander out of sight? I looked about the spot I thought he stood, but no sight or sound could I detect. Confused and slightly disturbed, I decided to hurry home. But no sooner had I continued my journey on that dirt road did I see another human-like shadow in the distance, standing terrifyingly still like some misplaced gargoyle peering out from the shadows. The figure sent chills down the back of my neck and flushed over me the second time I saw it. I composed myself for a meeting as we moved to a measured trot, but again, he disappeared into nothingness as I drew near. Once again I decided to hurry home.

My lone source of light was a single lantern, and its flame only created shadows in the dark that flickered about me, forcing me to endlessly evaluate where every waving shade originated. And so a man garmented black in a nightly abyss was problematic to identify as material. Nevertheless, I would have sworn on the Bible that something was there, observing me; poised with a higher morose purpose than the watchful Devil's Scarecrow. I grimaced in trepidation of a possible confrontation, for I felt an

56

impending danger regardless of the being's existence. I contemplated if it could have been a ghost, but being certain talk of ghosts was nonsense and I was more likely going mad, I repressed my thoughts and tried to ignore the eerie phenomenon. I fancied I saw him several times that night, stood every time in the shadow of a tree on the borders of my sight, disappearing only to reappear further ahead; and every new time it happened the terror I felt multiplied. Ultimately I reached my sanctuary with only mental harm done.

No time passed between my waking and being back on the road again to see her. And how tired it left me, I could not keep my eyes from involuntarily closing. Gratefully, warm air greeted me, with only a slight chill of breeze from over the North Sea below a cloud-filled sky. I rolled about the hills until I came to the girl who stood waiting for me with an agitated impatience; adorning a casual white frock and a wide smile that won me every time I saw her.

'Fletch' she called with bright eyes and crimson cheeks.

'Miss Evans'

'We must go at once, I think they know I have left the house to see you.' She hopped onto the cart and perched herself close by me. I pressed my lips upon her soft cheek, then whipped my stallions into a steady pace.

'Where shall we go to-day my love?' Asked her.

'It seems there will be no real rain until late evening or even nightfall, so we should enjoy such a fine truth whilst we still can, but beyond that, anywhere your heart desires.'

'We could picnic on one of your fields if you fancy, I would much like to see your farm.' And so I took her to one of our distant back fields; one where we could be seen from only a couple windows and were far away enough from the family's presence that we would not be disturbed.

I set down the cloth behind a tree for some cover and she sat herself down calmly, I excused myself to get some food for our picnic from the house, praying that no one would bother me or tell me I should be working. But as I rushed myself in taking food from our kitchen I heard the door squeak open and my stomach dropped with anxiety and frustration.

'She is a charming one' spoke the voice. And relieved was I, to it being owned by Mary.

'Yes she is' I replied not knowing what else to say. She looked out the window towards a peaceful Rebecca who gazed out into the fields with intrigue. Mary had a complexion of curiosity, and a twinkle in her eye, before quickly turning to me and saying 'Would you like me to prepare you some cooked food?'

'I appreciate the offer, but we are quite fine with what I have here' I spoke as I held up the bag full of treats.

'How about some tea?'

'Perhaps later, thank you.'

"Be respectful of her, treat her like a lady." I invariable smiled when she, my baby sister, spoke in a mothering manner.

'I always do Mary.'

'Now go, tend to her' she muttered with a bright expression and placing her hand on my shoulder and urging me out the door.

Back to the field I went as Rebecca watched me approaching, sat with outstretched legs but holding a troubled expression.

'I apologise for my father last night, I wish there was more I could do. Are you badly bruised?' I lay myself down by her side, feeling my tiredness drifting me to the peace of sleep.

'I have never been happier than I am right now' I whispered 'do not be concerned of his aggression towards me.'

'How can I not be?' She put her hand on my chest in a bid to open my eyes whilst resting over me with her questioning. I ignored her question and asked my own.

'How are your bruises my love?'

'Painful. How are yours?' She looked deep into me.

'Mine are proof you have entered my world, Rebecca. And that is worth any bruise. Do not be concerned. Would you like some food?'

'Soon, Fletch. I have never been happier either; it is from this fact why I want only to leave everything behind with you.'

'I know, but I cannot allow you to fall sick because we travelled a long journey ill-prepared through winter. What would I do if you were to die?'

'My will to live with you would carry me through the coldest winter, I can assure you of that Mr Fletcher.' She pressed her thick soft lips upon mine for a long moment before retrieving herself and smiling to me.

'You seem very tired.'

'I am.'

'Then rest, my Prince. I am tired myself, I keep having strange dreams of that man, The Devil Outside Looking In.' She placed her head on my chest like a cushion and clutched into me warmly, wishing her disturbing dreams away that I believed were meaningless. Instead I concentrated only on the peace I felt with her as my hand found itself resting upon her shoulder, carelessly fiddling with her sandy hair. No man can explain why he is enticed by long hair in females, though we can all say it is a pleasure to behold. Perhaps the waving curls down the arch of their backs are nature's own baroque-styled decor. I closed my eyes and fell asleep for goodness knows how long.

'He is sweet when he sleeps.' A gentle voice spoke as my eyes flickered open gradually, seeing grass and the dusk of a plummeting sun. The voice was not the voice I expected though. It was Mary.

'I agree.' Quiet feminine chuckles followed those words as I pulled myself up; turning to see them both facing one another, eating and laughing in merriment.

'Quite enough sleep now sunshine?' Mary spoke teasingly with a chorus of feminine laughter again.

'Mary' I mustered in acknowledgement, the only word I could think to say.

'I came to bring you both some tea but your guest was the only one awake. So I thought she should have some wakeful company.'

'Your sister is delightful Fletch' their faces expressed an instant rapport 'I regret to say though, you will have to take me home fairly soon.'

'You will have to come again soon; and we can have another tea party.'

'Most definitely' they embraced each other and said their farewells as if they were long lost sisters. Mary then placed her hand on my shoulder again, looked to the both of us and then strolled back towards the house.

'It was a pleasure to meet her. She has a kind heart.'

'Yes she has' I replied sincerely, yet my gaze was stolen by a bemusing sight, I thought I saw a dark figure across the field by a tree.

'There is someone over there, by that tree.' I uttered, startled, and pointing towards the figure that watched us, the same figure I thought I saw the night before.

'Where? There is no one.'

'I swear I just saw a black figure stood by that lonely tree. It was the shape of a human shadow, facing us, watching us. Then he disappeared as if some trick of the shade.' I became wild with fever.

'Shadows can be deceiving, but humans cannot disappear. I could not see anybody.' I was certain he was there, the man of last night; my breathing paced beyond control and my veins pounded me from the inside.

'Calm, do not trouble yourself, there was, and is, no one there.' She placed her arm around me and continued 'it seems you are becoming a lunatic good sir.' She spoke tenderly, trying with humour to bring me from thought of the man. She comforted me until my breathing rhythm and sanity had returned intact. I had to give myself several moments of calm before taking her home.

The rain had not fallen in the evening as I thought it would, but it started to trickle into the world during that journey. The full dark was oncoming also, though the sun was no longer visible, I knew the darkness would have been fully realised by my sole journey; which I did not welcome. I trembled throughout the journey to her home.

'Do you feel quite well?' Rebecca asked of me in a worried tone as my gaze flickered through the falling world. I assured her I was well and decided to stop with my antics, for her sake; despite how hard it is to hide symptoms of fear. I recognised though, how guilty I was of unintentional neglect. First by falling asleep in her company, and then by my fretting over some man that logically could not exist. I closed my eyes for a moment to regain myself again; and opened them to see her smile underneath the surface. Without thought I moved in for her kiss, a short connection only, before retreating and seeing the lanterns light dance in those blue vessels of life. I willed for all that she was. Her velvet lips caressed mine once more as her hands ran through my hair.

'Good-night' she whispered, staring into me a mere breath away; then skipped off home.

I tried to conjure her presence, imagining her sat beside me, hoping it would build my composure before I got lost in my fear of the world of this Man Of The Lonely Tree. I sought not to search for him, I agonised not to, I told myself he was not real; however I knew my anxious scouring for him would be inevitable. And it was.

The darkness around me whilst alone turned wholly abysmal, it felt as if I was staring at an ink black wall that was no more than a foot away from me, glaring grotesquely and triumphantly back at me. And the rain steadily flourished, into a harshness that pounded on me, supressing all that I was.

The more I thought of him, the more I considered the possibility that he could have been some ghost or phantom-like creature; and once the seed was in my head I deliberated ceaselessly. If he was a ghost or of similar sorts, he most probably knew nothing of our property lines, whereas a living man would have known to some degree. He appeared and reappeared on the roads which was frightening enough, but it was on our property that distilled the most dread in me, yet if he was a ghost what fault could I give him for standing in a field of ours? Even if I did feel miserable intent brewing in the shadows he was in. However, there was still the thought that he knew who I was and what he wanted from me. What then could he be, a demon? Though I thought of all possibilities of him and the consequences of each, I did not see him again that night.

The next morning, with a mind removed from the feverish emotion and settled in its ordinary state, I thought nothing of him. I accepted my sight fell upon a man yes, but only one of terrifying fantasy in an active mind playing fiendish tricks on itself. And I was safe and well.

Father had me working arduously the next day by handing me the most laborious tasks, due to my unexplained and unannounced absences. Seldom did he question me of my whereabouts, he knew his defeat. He was not punishing me with labour, that I knew clearly, he was only using labour as a tool to keep me on the farmlands; and for that I could not begrudge him. Walter on the other hand, was perfectly himself and had his opinion on my "disrespectful actions".

With that in mind the day came and went by me without my knowing, as if Satan tore the colour from the midday sky with an impish impatience, and with the inevitable night came an overbearing anxiety that putrefied my stability. "He is not real" I told myself repeatedly, "I am more fanciful than I do myself good for". I sat in my room trying to write something, anything, but the sound of the quill scraping along the paper infuriated me; I had to look to the tree, to see if he was there. I do not know if I was compelled by the wish of proving he was the hallucination of a mad fool or to have my inescapable fears realised, but I stepped into the kitchen with my eyes barely open, dreading every step. I looked out from the window into the moonlit darkness, and to my disgusted horror by the lonely tree stood the same virile figure. My blood turned cold in an instance as my countenance crumbled with shock. He existed. My God he existed; and he faced the home from his distant, desolate spot.

'Mary, come here at once!' I shouted urgently.

'What is it that you so demandingly call?'

'Do you see that man, standing by our tree?' As I spoke to her I instinctively momentarily turned to her. And when I turned to see him again, he had gone.

'No, are you sure there is a man out there?'

'There was a man, he must have gone.'

'No one comes out here, especially at night, we are perfectly safe from unfamiliar visitors.' Mary spoke simple words and I had no other option but to accept them. But what could I do, wait for him to come to the grounds? Watch over the tree until he returned? 'I think you should get some rest. Stop looking, there is no one there. Go... I will bring you some supper.'

The next night I strained to fend myself from looking over to the tree to where the man would surely stand; but miserably, I failed. I looked to the tree at the very edge of the field. And with bleak hope, there he stood. But that time when I called Johnathon and father, The Man Of The Lonely Tree stepped the few yards behind the tree and was no longer in sight, so that when those two came to my calls, they saw nothing. They gave me the same assurances Mary had done, and I had to accept them. Yet I remained in the kitchen and watched the tree for a full hour after they left, only to see nothing; he appeared to have gone.

Was I under threat? He had been facing our home yet I could not tell if he saw me particularly. He stood as if spellbound in some dream. I thought of him as some lost soul but that simply could not be the case, he followed me as I rode in the darkness. He had very definite consciousness; and to what will I was yet to know, though I knew in some way he was charmed to me. For the sake of my rationality, my sanity, I had to confront him. There was no alternative to test if he was reality or wild delusion. And if he did so exist, hopefully I would be able scare him away with a weapon.

Hiding an axe behind my back, I walked towards the tree he so cared dearly for. To be clear, I intended not to use the weapon. Its use was for my own self-assurance more than violence, and his shock if necessary; though if he was aggressive, I had no qualms with striking a blow. I trudged through the dirt and grass as quietly as a horse on cobbles. The night felt much more foreboding out in that field than it did in the warmth, but I had to face the phantom, there was no alternative. When I reached the tree I could not see anything untoward, the side in which he obscured himself revealed nothing. I looked around confused, and slightly triumphant, before stepping beyond where I had last seen him. What frightened me the most was there was no warning, he made no sound in the dirt, he just simply appeared to me like a material revelation from Hell a yard away from the tree on its opposite side. I gasped and shuddered for an instant before instinctively holding up the axe. He bore no weapons himself, though he was taller than I assumed.

'You are trespassing sir, who are you and what do you want with me?' I called out to him, trying to be as imposing as I could.

'Nothing... yet' he replied with a deep and gruff continental accent. I was as astonished by his accent as I was horrified by his words; why a continental would be out wandering on our lands at night was something I could not even imagine.

'Who are you?' I firmly repeated 'and what will you want with me?' He did not answer.

With casual yet powerful steps he moved behind the tree and was no longer of this world. He was gone. I frantically ran round it, chasing him, but he was gone. Only fields were within direct view, he could not have escaped my sight so quickly. I was dumbfounded by his escape, and filled with a grimacing fear of what was to come from his words. Then came the thought that he was of the same description as The Devil Outside Looking In, and that the man could have been terrorising both me and Rebecca, and in very different ways.

Was The Man Of The Lonely Tree a ghost or some demon I ask of you?

Next chapter my reader, if you care at all for our well-being.

Chapter V: Weeping Beauty

Ever has it been that love knows not its own depth until the hour of separation

Khalil Gibran

It is nice to have your eyes upon my page once more, you must be sincerely concerned for the well-being of both myself and Rebecca; but then, perhaps you simply have nothing better to do. Any which way my reader, I am glad you are here with me again to share my life. Allow me to continue by describing the state of northern England.

The daylight hours were stagnating poorly as frequent onslaughts of torrential rainfall occurred. Winter had, for the most part, come with all its bitter influence, though regrettably, its glory was yet to arrive. The stale light of day was plagued by the gloomy clouds that drifted with grief for the summer and all sense of day became humbly overthrown by the most desolate nights I had ever known. This state of affairs coupled with my father's policy of overworking me left me both indoors and with the family more than I anticipated. Conversation with Walter resumed, but as destined, they were fleeting and fruitless. Yet effort was the merit that was important.

No more delay my reader.
'How is Rebecca on this lovely cloud-ridden morning?' I called with affection for the girl as she approached me. I had gone to her home in hope of seeing her and expected no luck, but to my delight she was in sight through her kitchen window and received my waves to come meet me.
'She is in need of one of your outings Mr Fletcher.'

'Then hop along.' A smile blinked across her small face yet the eyes gave away a dullness as if something was preying on her mind, I added 'is something the matter my love?" She jumped up onto the cart with my help and held her hand around my arm tenderly.

'Nothing new, I despise my prison and my nights are filled with horrors.' I did not want our conversation to so suddenly turn to the man I had spoken to, but it had, and I had to explore the villain in her dreams; how could a man I spoke to take flight in her dreams?

'You have only seen him in your dreams, true? Describe him to me again, The Devil Outside Looking In.'

'Only in my dreams, of course, but he feels real. He looks in through my window and waits with an appallingly serene stare. He wears all black garments and a black cloak. I can see he is clean shaven and sometimes I see his pale gaunt eyes staring into me.'

'Sounds unpleasant to say the least, I hope your dreams give away soon. Remember, they are only dreams.'

'I know, it is only, I have not had a fair night's sleep in far too long.'

'Then relax with me. Is there anywhere nearby you would like to go?'

'There is a small stream nearby, I know somewhere peaceful for us. We could walk from here.'

I tied my horses to a nearby tree, telling them I would not be long, and followed her lead as she skipped eagerly onwards. I could hear the gentle humming of flowing water from the road though I could not yet see it. The broken trees began to arch over us as we paced through the crooked woodland area with an aroused excitement. And just into the closed atmosphere of the twisted trees I caught sight of the stream. It ran shallow and swift, flowing over jagged rocks that were perfectly overwhelmed by the moss clinging to them. The fresh scent of the cold water radiated vibrantly into the enclosure. Deeper into the increasingly condensed woods we moved, stepping along the stream. Despite the beauty of all around me, all my senses focused on the being that floated with every yard as the icy winds blew her hair elegantly over her left shoulder. The body of water gently widened alongside us as the current gained momentum; here and there my girl would stop for a moment and looked back at me with a questioning if I would be able to keep to her. Then with the grace of a unicorn, she skipped across three stones that lay in the clear water, reaching the other side effortlessly as splashes kissed the bottom of her frock. She turned to me but remained wordless, standing with a slight smile upon her face with an expectation of me to skip across to her. The rocks in the stream took her weightless form perfectly fine, but I doubted their ability to hold me; though I could not refuse the look she gave me, and so I took the leap of faith.

'Come…' she spoke with her hand extended for me as I reached the other side tastelessly. She linked her arms under mine and together we continued our venture.

Not long was it that we reached a destination she found quite suitable. A large oak tree slumbered with a cradle-like base that she could not resist sitting in. She let go of my hand when she saw it, completely forgetting my existence momentarily to be cradled by the giant oak tree. Her arms lay casually resting on the thick roots as the tree trunk curved a perfect back rest for her. She seemed as comfortable as if she was in the arms of a birth-giver, and as beautiful as if it were an ancient Celtic throne built just for her.

As I beheld her in her cradle, I felt a burning desire to outlay my heart to her. We had spoken of everything but what unexpectedly skipped in my mind. My eyes fell to the dead leaves all around me that were compressed into the damp soil, the wind drove past me like a wall of numbing cold, slowly I worded my thoughts.

'Rebecca, you are the most wonderful person I have ever known. I want you to know that. I sincerely hope you have a mind to be my wife once we are in Scotland and I can afford a ring for you.' A quick shudder ran through me as I felt more vulnerable than I have ever felt; the cold felt suddenly harsher, the damp soil suddenly bog-like. And all I could do was wait for her in her throne to call her verdict.

Her hands moved gently onto mine, and slowly she came into me, resting her forehead on mine. I could feel the emotions running through her as her breathing became so faint I could not detected it; and those two sparkling icy lakes gazed into my muddy ponds for an eternity with a devious glint.

'Runaway with me now' she delicately whispered. I felt compelled by her spell to obey; but to do so for me was still impossible. 'You know we cannot.'

'Fletch, is this not perfect euphoria?' Rhetorically she asked, reclining in her cradle before continuing 'I feel a pervasive darkness closing in, I do not understand but I feel it. And my father still beats me, want to see what I hide from you?' Beginning to undo her lace

'Please do not. It kills me to know. I too feel a pervasive darkness. But winter and illness will not yield us to pass, I know it in my heart. Rebecca, give me but six months. Only six months, and then we can start our new life; you and I, a beautiful existence.' She had a puzzled look about her, dismissive yet embracive; and dejected all within the same expression.

'It would be perfect, my dear, yet I cannot endure his floggings. I have spoken of it before and I shall say it once again, I cannot endure him.' It broke my heart to see a solitary tear slip down her cheek as she spoke. She trembled, though tried hard to keep her composure. I thought of words, but they were futile, what could be said my reader? All I thought I could do was console her with my empathetic embrace. And calm her in time.

She let me take her throne, and as it encompassed me, I held her, and we lay admiring the wood and brook, talking of our future in a little cottage by a quaint village in Scotland that would look out over one of the beautiful lochs. We spoke until the light began to fail and the inevitable formation of darkness came along with her home beckoning for her safe return.

It was that time of the year where there were many moonless nights, and in them, my lantern held no command over the invasive black. My stallions began making ruffles of uneasiness and a restless agitation as a threatening silence surrounded us in the all too still air. The decayed wood by our road that was so picturesque during the day soon became the mother of menacing and almost hostile shadows. I tried stubbornly to ignore any thought of The Man Of The Lonely Tree but could not. A whisper came to me in the air and I looked to Rebecca.

'Did you say something?'

'No' she nonchalantly replied. I shuddered in thought of what could have been. If it was not her then surely it was him; it certainly was not some noise from the horses and it felt too close to my ears. I began looking for somebody stood by the road, however the darkness masked all into an abyss-like chaos, my lantern only served to prove its vastness by revealing so little, no matter how I tried. Again a whisper breathed in the air. So unclear it was, but I was not mistaken, there was unquestionably something sounding silently in the failing night; and so close it seemed.

'Did you hear it that time Rebecca?' I called.

'Calm yourself, you are becoming hysterical. I heard nothing, what do you think I should have heard?'

'I heard a whispering in the wind. I fear someone is out here with us on the road. Tell me you heard it.'

'There is scarcely a gust to misjudge. There is no one else here Fletch. We would know if there was; and if he was a danger to us as you seem to imply, he cannot outrun two horses.'

'I sincerely hope so.' I spoke in jest to her sobering words, but there was only seriousness in their meaning, I had already witnessed him travel absurdly far in short time in his appearances and reappearances.

I tried my damnedest to be composed for her, to not let her see my eyes flickering for him, nor my form dancing with trepidation but my agitation only swelled further. I had the sensation that someone was running alongside us, teasing me with unreal words from an eyeless and malignant expression; once the feeling came to me, it riddled me endlessly. Through the depths of my anxiety, and appearing without warning, came an infinite urge to scream out in release. Yet I could not do so, for the sake of her. Instead I sat still and said nothing, trying to subdue my ever grimacing face.

Despite how distressing my journey seemed, my solitary one was substantially worse. As I headed away from her land and she stepped down on the cobbles I knew whatever this tormenting malevolent fiend was doing to me, would be tenfold. I heard scowling whispers hissing coarsely in the ether, floating about me with attack and persistence. I tried to decipher words but could not gather a clear syllable, which only added to the terror that consumed me. I looked out in every direction for the source, for the man I suspected, but only saw road and field and tree in desolate and unending principles. I even noticed my horses peering into the night themselves as their trot diminished to little more than a crawl. It was then, when I whipped my horses back to a moderate pace that the hairs on the back of my neck stood up as if struck by lightning and every muscle in my body tensed to a stiff shudder. The whistling noise instantly came closer upon me as if the voice had murmured directly in my ear, and with bitter horror, I jumped to face the seat by my side where the voice was sounded. No one could I see.

To quieten the plodding of the horses step, I pulled the reins to our stop. Silence. I, motionless and dwelling on the edge of cowardice listened intently for anything, and speculated the truth regarding The Man Of The Lonely Tree; the haunting nightly spectre that was and was not there. Having disappeared behind a tree, the full potential reality he could wish for would be a sinister ghost I concluded. And a ghost could scare me to my core, plague me with voices and riddles and appear as a material being, but ghosts being immaterial could not harm. Or so I hoped.

I paused for a moment, taking in the air and soaking up the darkness, regaining my inner strength before coming down from the cart. Cautiously, I stepped down onto the dirt and began searching for the ghost. I looked to my stallions who seemed calmer, plus their glances were only casual and in no direction specifically, they feared nothing in immediacy; yet I myself, was too afraid even to tie them to a tree. To do so would have been to lose my guard for a matter of moments which I could not allow myself to do; however if I did not, and he frightening them to a start, they could have fled without me and leave me in a predicament I fancied I would not live through. I decided to risk it, I was not for idle focus for a moment longer than necessary from him and why he would panic them when I was wandering elsewhere seemed illogical. With my insignificant light in hand I crept delicately and silently enough that not even a fox would hear. Despite myself and the unmoving air that gave the atmosphere of a soundless tomb, I searched under the dark, twisting and ominous trees just off the road.

With my lantern held high above me, I feigned bravery and ventured into the unknown; feeling like I had stepped a yard too far in Baal's garden.

'Come out you ghost, you phantom' called I, 'I have no fear of you, you cannot harm me. You are nothing but a shadow.'

I received no reply. The black around me was as empty as limbo, and I knew he was the cause of its menacing tone. No wildlife had settled there that night and I was witness of it. At first I convulsed at the thought of him watching me, following me, hiding in the never-ending shadows when I had called out to him; but then I perceived it for the timidity that it was. He would not face me. A sort of triumph came over me, and with that triumph I had less fear in walking through the gloominess to find him.

I searched and passed through the woodlands for him and saw nothing untoward or troubling. And after a thorough search I came out the other side, seeing sheep out on the other side of a sloping field. Seeing them took me from the horror that had built in me and was yet to disperse. They brought me back to my own life, to the simplicity of farming and the lack of external troubles farming brings. But they were all as far away from the wood as their barriers allowed, and they had a strange nervousness about them. Noticing that, it was then that I heard his voice again, yet it was full and distinct, it was no trick in the winds but his actual voice about ten feet behind me.

'I welcome you' he spoke, with his deep and harsh vocal cords. I turned to face him and could only just see his foreboding shadow figure in the lantern light.

'What do you want with me?' I demanded feigning my bravery once more.

'I do not want, I claim. And it is the girl that I claim.'

'There is no girl to claim.'

'I admire your bravery young sir, and for that, and my generosity, I shall allow you to live. But step in my way, and I will not. Good-night.' He turned his back and lumbered his large steps away.

'Consider me in the way, she is not for claiming' I shouted as he strode out of sight. I sighed in relief to see him disappear. In seeing him again, he appeared material, and had I had my axe with me I would have charged him when he turned his back, but it had been left at home.

I moved through the dark where he had stood and to my stallions, greatly fearing him, but hoping he had moved on elsewhere for the night. The silence of the world was no longer deafening. I thought I had won my battle of courage, and so I continued the short journey home.

I reached home safely without further issue. As I came through the door Mary must have seen the distress in me. 'What is the matter?' I looked to her for a moment, wary but glad to be in the safety of her sympathy and seeing a pleasant being once more.

'Nothing. I am just cold and tired.'

'How would you like some food to calm you?'

'Thank you.' I sat down free from the fear that my life was in close peril though my pulsing angst still singed at me. With a sigh, I stared up towards the dull ceiling, trying hopelessly to collect myself. I could not return my mind from the man, the experience of him made me sick. There was no eating, no relaxation. And he seemed too physical to be a phantom or fantasy. The ill-intent of his words then became my focus, his dismal resolution of claiming

Rebecca. It was only when I had reached my own home and safety, that I dared to think of anyone else's, what if he went there to claim her before dawn? And planned to kill her? I rose in panic, rushing towards the door.

'Stop lad' Jonathon's voice came, behind me as I faced the door. I froze in my stance momentarily with anxiety of what lay both in front and behind me. My mind whirled with far too many intense thoughts to recall altogether, but I debated the use of staying, and saw none; it was simply imperative that she was kept safe from the entity. I continued to walk out the door. Jonathon rushed his steps and held onto my shoulder.

'Sunshine, please sit' Mary's voice spoke out with a frail tone 'I am setting the table for you both.'

'I have to go, I shall be back soon' I uttered with authority, and no thought of returning soon. But as I faced them both, I could see the genuine concern for me. Jonathon in particular, Mary knew she could get me to sit with her words, she knew I would listen, yet Jonathon had not the tools for such situations. And neither did I, the tension was unbearable. I needed to leave, but Mary came closer to me and held my hand as Jonathon led me back inside. In acceptance they had for the time succeeded, I closed my eyes and let them take me to the table, I had no plan. Significantly, I was thankful it was these two inhabitants and not the other two; and for that simple reason, I sat down as they asked.

For a moment I sat still, trying to breathe in the warm air emanating from the fireplace. But when the image of him harming Rebecca came back into me, I suffered extremely and held my head with both hands, trapping inside myself the intolerable anxiety.

'Brother, what is wrong?' Jonathon asked sitting himself carefully opposite me, as if I were to spontaneously bite him at any moment. I heard his question perfectly well, yet my mind only searched for a way to escape and somehow protect Rebecca. I needed to know she was safe.

'There is no man by the tree' he tentatively added. I darted my look to him.

'I know.' Trying to not show him that that man was my anguish. 'Then why are you acting this way? Find your sanity.' He tried to smile as if joking with me, but I wilfully ignored. I could not laugh when she was in grave danger.

'Food' Mary whistled trying to lighten the mood and bringing some in for us both 'eat up.' Her hand rested upon my shoulder, she paused for a moment and looked to Jonathon, then disappeared.

We sat and ate in silence, every now and then he seemed to stop and look at me as if examining my state of mind, then continued eating. In that room, without another word spoken and sitting with Jonathon, I felt soothed. His presence caused me to think of my actions, and the more I thought, the more I leaned towards the rationality that the man would not have come to me if his wish was to abruptly harm her, he would have gone straight to her, warning me first would have only wasted his time. That then meant he was still planning the foundation of his actions, the Devil would still be Outside Looking In. That thought settled my mind sufficiently, like someone had lifted a ton weight from my chest and I could breathe again. And even if he did wish to harm her that night, The Dragon would protect her for the night; her having a violent guardian suddenly became useful.

'Are you quite alright?' Jonathon questioned, looking unsure of me.

'Yes thank you.' We retired to our chambers when he felt I was settled enough that he could leave me alone, and I thanked him.

Despite the fact I was not tired I willed only to sleep, it was much earlier than I usually slept, though frankly, I had had enough of the torture of a shadows doom. I lay in my bed discerning the horror that had fallen over my simple life and the danger he was to Rebecca. What he meant by claiming her, what intention lay at the centre of his claim, I did not know, but I knew I could not allow him a moment with her. We spoke of leaving for Scotland and the best I would do for her was next summer, however, it had become apparent to me that her wish for as soon as possible was the best solution to the threat of the man. He would never find her in a small town across the border.

Mary wandered in warily, not wanting to disturb me from sleep, but when she noticed I was not gone yet, she relaxed herself. On her bed with a slothful crash she lay down.

I woke in a ruffled state, eyes burdened with the pain of a rough sleep and the first real thought that entered my mind was of apprehension for the safety of Rebecca. I had to visit her, to know if she was safe and tell her I had changed my mind, I wanted to leave as soon as we could. All day I tried to get away and see her, but I could not find myself a moment to fly to her, frustration at the obstruction of my obligation itched under my skin, but father and Walter lectured and whipped me for my agitated manner and refused to let me neglect my responsibility to the work on the farm. Regrettably, it was moments before nightfall when such an escape was possible.

For the third night on the trot not star nor moon could be seen as the clouds ravaged above. I rode across the sinister land as if being chased by the Devil himself, the winds grew stronger and whistled past me with a fierceness that on another day would have forced me to turn back, however, nothing under God would have kept me from reaching her. I brought my axe in case he showed any will to harm her or me and took two lanterns to light my path. They revealed the first line of trees on either side well enough, plus the direct path in front of me so he could not get close enough to harm me without me first sighting him. The inner turmoil of my stallions returned, they at times became hard to control, but I felt some comfort with them, I was not alone in the grim, atrocious and bleak atmosphere.

In those wildest of winds, a whisper came to me again, piercing the veil of my composure. I twisted myself round frantically but there was no one to be seen by the road, or by the trees. And again it came in its violent breath as if it was sat by my side; yet all I saw was a deep diabolical darkness. I pushed my hands into the seat beside me, trying to feel a supernatural ghostly form, nothing. My hands did not go colder, there was no sign of him. And her home was in sight. I grabbed a hold of the axe.

'Who are you? Come out from the night's shadows and reveal yourself' I shouted into the night with no reply. The voice had moved on.

As my gaze came over the house, to my astonishment I saw her lying in the middle of her garden lawn dressed in a frayed white nightgown. Languid she was, and in a peculiar and limp position. Another brief look into the dark I took. Accepting he was not going to show himself and hoping he was not present, I ran down to her, carrying one of my lanterns.

When I came to her side I noticed her eyes were not open and the cold windy night had turned her awfully pale.

'Rebecca?' I called trying to catch her attention.

'Yes' mumbled her voice with little movement, her eyes remained closed shut and I fancied her somehow spellbound by the demonic being.

'Why are you outside? It is dangerous to be out here in the dark alone.'

'Are you an apparition?' She spoke without a trace of human emotion; the beautiful feminine tone had morphed into something unsettling.

'Can you look up at me?' I tried to free her from whatever reverie she was under. 'Please open your eyes. You will fall ill if you stay out here too much longer.' I put my hand under her head and raised it slightly. Her eyes gradually trickled open, coldly looking past me as if I was not there. Then with an unsighted flash of humanity through her, I recognised the blue lakes for their serene nature. She woke from the deep sleep spell.

'Fletch. Where are we? What is happening?' She spoke surprised, forming the smile of a simpleton and seeing that she was outside her home.

'I needed to see you, to see you were safe.' I looked about the area once more for a vision of The Devil Outside Looking In but all I saw was morbidity stretching beyond sight. The only light to be seen was the deserted lantern behind my stallions upon the hill, and they did not rest easy; it could have been the harsh winds they did not like, but I feared it was the presence of him nearby. I feared him hearing my words, it would have grave consequences for both of our lives if he did, but I had no choice but to speak them.

I moved closer to her and whispered in her ear 'we spoke, my love, of leaving for Scotland. Let tomorrow be that day. I want nothing more than to be with you.'

'Is this real? Or have I woken from my darkest nightmare into my greatest dream?'

'This is real Rebecca. Tomorrow we go.' Her face lit up and I could see a colour returning to her. She gently touched my cheek with her soft lips and we held each other tightly. I never wanted to let go, I feared the end of her life if I ever did. I had debated confessing to her that the Devil in her dreams was somehow real, it was something she deserved to know, but I could not communicate to her the grave news of his will. If I could get her to Scotland and beyond his reach then she need not know I thought. And of starting our new life together, the girl rose wearily to her feet and turned our contact progressively to a dance with a happiness I simply could not find. I knew her life was in severe danger, she knew only of the new beginning we were to have. The girl twirled herself under my arm with a soft smile, and I went along with the movements, though still deep in contemplation of revealing the truth of the man. However practical it seemed to do so, I could not destroy her cheerful mood, not in those moments; I reassured myself that he could not possibly find us once over the border. Her father would be her protection for one more night, then he too could never harm her again.

I do wonder what you would have done in my situation, how anyone would save their darling in such a predicament. And I hope you feel empathy for my dilemma my reader, for there were three villains, not two; the nightly man who haunted us both, The

Dragon, and the very real threat of illness during harsh northern winters.

My lack of excitement must have been apparent in my expression. Though I tried, I could not hide my burden, and Rebecca could see something was not as it should be.

'What is the matter Fletch?'

'What happened just now in your nightmare?' I could not help but ask.

'The Devil was Outside Looking In, I came outside myself so he could not see me.'

'So The Devil is Outside Looking In, and The Dragon is inside soon to come out.'

'Sometimes I awake without knowledge of what it was I dreamt, though I always feel a dread for what seems inevitable.' Our dancing moved to a halt, her touch filled me with awe as her words consumed me with despair. She was not being spellbound but attacked in her dreams. I was completely lost for words and growing weak, the whole ordeal was crushing me.

'What is wrong?' She spoke 'you look troubled and in need of some good sleep. Fletch go home and get some rest. You are right my father will be out here soon, and that will not be good for any of us. Go home and pack provision, I shall see you on the morrow for our new start.' A thrilled smile became her as she comforted me. She was right, I needed rest, especially with such a big day ahead of us.

'Rebecca' I spoke as I clutched my hands around her figure 'keep yourself safe tonight, keep close to your father, he will protect you for one more night, then it will be my sole duty... I shall return just after dawn.' She came into me, concealing herself under my wings as the sweet scent of her fine hair floated about me. The warmth of my body sent a shudder through her cold self and I squeezed her a little tighter. Overcome by ecstasy we were, ecstasy for the moment, for the future, our grip turned into a breath-filled kiss. Slowly I drew back, gazing into her bright eyes for a moment, the deepest lakes I had ever known. I could see in those depths a beautiful future of married life, of children, of music and lochs and anything our hearts desired. I wanted nothing more. Her plump wet lips greeted mine again with an euphoric rush. I felt light suddenly, as if we were drifting up into the night's sky to soar above the rustic trees, an immaculate sensation. I pressed my lips into her with soft delicacy at first, but a puckered rigor singed through us, desire overtook me. Her cheek brushed my nose lightly, every sensation aroused as my hands cupped her hips impeccably. Then we released, delicately, peering further into each other's souls and tasting the air we both exhaled. I loved her.

It was then that I left her, leaving with a splash of guilt that I had to and praying her father would protect her if the need arose. I rode away mentally exhausted, too tired to be as alarmed as I perhaps should have been. There were sounds to be heard in the distance, whispers willowing in the travelling chill but I dared and willed not make them out. I returned home in no harm.

Straight to my bed I moved and made my plans for leaving. I thought at great length of taking fathers only carriage, but I could not do it, the farm would stand still if I did, and I could not cause that. My cart was unfortunately the only option, which would have been an issue if it heavily rained; but we could shelter in the cart with leather or fur covering us and the moment illness became apparent in her I would take her directly to the nearest doctor.

Mary walked in with a smile for me, and sat herself down quietly on her bed. A wrenching pain slowly burned inside my chest, knowing it was the last night on earth I would share that chamber with her; and worse still, I did not know if I would ever see her again.

'Mary' I spoke in the cold air, with an agony of confessing my plan 'I am sorry this is all so sudden, but I and Rebecca are leaving to-morrow, to Scotland.' I could hardly look her way as the sadness built up in us both.

'Oh sunshine, I knew this day was coming, that you two would leave together, however I did not anticipate so soon.' I saw the despair in her waning eyes, though she sat up facing me and spoke only with an eager flow 'she is the one, is she not?'

'Yes. She is.'

'She is lovely, and beautiful, I wish you the happiness you deserve. Though I too wish you would both stay a while longer, that I could get to know her better myself.' Her bright demeanour and wide smile was precious to me, revealing her truly loving nature.

'I want a letter when you are both married.'

'You shall get one Mary.' She came to me with delight, putting her arms wildly around me.

'I love you my brother, have a great life and marriage.' Her show of joy for me began to dwindle as I could hear her attempting and failing to fight back her tears.

'I love you also my sister. I hope you have the same fate. Do not cry, I will give you my address when I know it, we can write to one another. And hopefully meet again one day.'

'I sincerely hope so. I cannot accept our last day together came and went without my knowing it.'

'Do not worry of that Mary, we shall meet again.'

'When are you leaving?'

'Just before dawn.'

'Wake me before you leave.' She spoke softly and helplessly, still fighting off her tears.

'I will.'

We blew out the candles and attempted to sleep. She slumbered instantly and with ease but I struggled to find my peace. I lay in a reverie, thinking of the life I had spent comfortably on the farm with my family. Nothing would ever be the same again. In departing so abruptly and without warning I knew only Mary and Jonathon would ever forgive me, therefore they were the only two I could realistically hope to see again. Walter and father would hate me, and further still, I would not see them before I left in the morning, thus I had already seen them for the last time. How pathetically dishonourable of me not to even say farewell to my own father; instead I planned on taking some of his money as I left. He had suffered plenty, both of my doing and not, and I planned to give him the greatest of all disappointments. Of all the wretched and shameful events of my life the one thing I regret the most is leaving the man who raised me alone, the way I did.

But for all the woe of departure there was the life ahead; and how splendid it would be, to start a new life with my love on the morrow. It was a joy of course but then I remembered the true reason why we were to leave, the demon of my senses.

As I found little sleep that night, in defeat and fear of sleeping through the dawn, I made the preparations necessary early, and therefore in good time. Clothes, what I could bring of my own and water resistant materials. Food, the remaining scraps left around. Candles, two lanterns and plenty of firewood to alight our journey, along with the instruments I had left in the cart for some merriment. The horses were well fed for the day, The Man Of The Lonely Tree seemed to only show during the night and we would long be gone by nightfall. He would come by The Lonely Tree and find we had vanished, by then we would be too far away for him to trace.

'Mary, I take my leave now.' I awoke her from what seemed a pleasant dream.

'No' the word fell out of her mouth without thought, before she opened her eyes and called it out again with distress. She found herself on her feet and squeezed me with a firm enough hold that I could barely breathe; still, she could not help herself. She wept softly, I could feel the tears on my clothing, only reaffirming the sibling affection we felt for each other.

'You will always be my favourite brother.' I could scarcely recognise the words through her trembling as she buried her face in my chest.

'And you will always be my favourite. My baby sister, my mother, my best friend. I will miss you.' I uttered under my emotion. This was the goodbye to the sibling that I had shared everything with since her birth, and she had shared every experience she had ever had with me; there was no filling the void our departure would create in both of us. I longed to take her with us, there was about enough room in the small cart, and Rebecca and Mary had enjoyed one another's company. But Mary's life was there on the farm, and fully ahead of her. She would marry there and raise a new family. Besides, our family would have been lost without her, wholly and completely; and I could not be the cause of that. Father and Walter would barely notice my departure in any compassionate sense, but the loss of Mary would be devastating to them.

'I do not want you to leave. Why so soon?' She spoke releasing me, her cry became an audible sob.

'I have to sweetheart, it is now or never for us.'

'It is now or later. Traveling to Scotland at the start of a bitter winter is certainly not advisable.'

'Please do not Mary. We have to go. We will be quite fine.'

'You look after her, you hear me?'

'I will Mary.'

'And write to me when you are settled.'

'I will, hold me to that.' Her countenance fell into abject defeat and her weeping became stronger. She held her hands to her face and I held her once more, the last time. Though I showed less of my emotion than she did, I am quite sure I felt the loss more than she did, she would still have two siblings left, I would not.

We stood apart when the air between us became more positive, and my chest was damp with her cold tears. I looked to her, trying desperately to mentally imprint the girl in my memory. Her hair was still rough from her sleep, curling every which way gracelessly. She held her small frame in simple posture as she trembled in her dark gown, elegantly wiping the channels of tears that ran down her swollen red cheeks with a handkerchief and snivelling to stop the weeping from overwhelming her. Every time I think of her now, I see that grief-stricken image.

I endured the misery, gently placing my hand on her tender shoulder.

'Farewell.'

'Good luck. I will be waiting for your letter.'

     I moved from the chamber grateful she did not follow me to the cart, I would have crumbled if we had another ordeal of a parting. As I rode and the house was on the edge of sight I looked back one last time to the home I had known since birth and felt surprisingly little. It was Mary only that I yearned to still be acquainted with; the home itself meant little to me, it was only the arena for my memories. My reader, it is the company you keep, or leave behind, that really matters.

     The journey to Rebecca's home was in low spirit, I felt not the delightful joy and optimism of starting a new life, only the misery of my loss.

'Mr Fletcher, the beginning starts here.' Rebecca welcomed me in the high spirit I hoped for, bearing a joyous and beautiful expression.

'It does. Come along.' She hopped up and we went on our way.

'You do not seem so pleased'

'I do not know if I shall ever see Mary again.' Her mood died with my sorrowing words. And seeing that, I wish I had not spoken them, I wanted her happiness for us both, not my melancholy. She played with my hand sensitively as I rested my head upon her shoulder, wallowing in the sadness of losing my only friend and lone sister.

'Rest easy Fletch' she spoke as took the reins from me.

     We rode watching the sky blossom above us, starting from a pale red, to a pale blue, to a beautifully vibrant sapphire.

Chapter VI: The Border And The Desolate Highlands

Hell is empty and all the devils are here

William Shakespeare

'Mary is a special person' my love stated in a gentle manner. 'She is. She is the most generous and kind person I will ever know.' Rebecca looked to me with a tender smile and I reciprocated. She knew throughout the day that Mary was still on my mind, but she tried to press my mind to the future; one that she looked at with great glee. She herself had also taken money from her father, and a much more useful quantity than I could get, as well as a tent for us to camp in, thankfully. The plan was that we would find a charming quiet inn to settle in by a nice location as we would look for local on-going labour; assuming we had escaped the evil entity.

Throughout the daylight hours she made minor suggestive movements that held a certain rhythm, I knew perfectly well that my Rebecca wanted to stop travelling and dance in our freedom, but I pretended to be oblivious. My reasoning for purposefully depriving her of such joy was that I wanted to take her as far as I possibly could in a day's journey from him. Neglecting her of her dance would be the necessary evil. The horses, however, suffered the most from my will to travel so far. Stopping regularly to rest the poor horses was for me a risk not worth taking; by the time the sun set and we prepared our camp I was certain we had travelled far enough that the ghost man would not find us, even if he knew the direction we moved. The horses made a very relieved sound when I pulled the reins, and credit where it is most due, they had been on their feet most of the day.

The darkness that night was not nearly as powerful and overbearing as that of the previous nights, the winds were mild;

plus I could taste the cold moisture and dead leaves in the air, what I would call the taste of winter. The moon was also in sight again, shining bright and brilliant as it moved in and out of the concealing clouds. She and I lay with the same awestruck contentment by the sweet light of a campfire admiring its full white richness. But as we gazed up at the moonlight, she still wished to dance and asked in her own special way 'Mr Fletcher, are you ever going to ask me to dance?' which made me chuckle at her direct nature.

'Of course. Miss Evans, would you do me the honour?' I stood up and glanced out into the pleasant silver night, there was no hissing in the winds, no shadowy figure lurking in our woodland by the road; just the divinity of Luna's light that put me perfectly at ease. I offered her my hand and she accepted with a smile that was half sweet, and half mischievous.

'Mr Fletcher, I thought you would never ask.' An excitement pulsed through her form and I could hear a trace of that laughter I so loved from her, singing its own magical melody. There, under the moonlight by our campfire, where all we could see was fields and some congregations of trees, we danced a delicate and tender waltz until the night grew late.

'A toast...' she called halting our motions, holding her hand in the air with an imaginary glass. 'To our new beginning, Fletch' her sweet complexion sparkled.

'May it be prosperous and wonderful my dear' replied I, tapping our glasses together.

We retired to our camp and buried ourselves under as much warm clothes and furs as we could, whilst also leaving the fire to burn through the night. I was warmer than I was cold that night, which was a pleasant surprise, and I was delighted with the distance we had made. I was certain that already we were too far to trace or be followed.

A couple of days and nights passed much the same. We would wake an hour or so after dawn as the beauty above us crept through the thorny trees and into our tent. I would lie by her side and watch the light slowly make its way into those blue lakes until the day was truly upon us and there was no more delay. We would then have breakfast and press on with our journey North. When the night came we would set camp and I would keep an ear and an eye out for any indication of our fiend. But there was none. We slept with relative ease, and I took note of the fact she was not having any nightmares. I fancied him still there by The Lonely Tree, and that thought amused me. He would keep looking into mine and Rebecca's homes to find neither of us. He would not know the direction we had gone, and even if he had chosen the correct road, by craft of tracking or mere guess, we were days away by horse ride. I was comfortable in the knowledge there were countless reasons why he would not find us, and because of this, he became in my memory more like a distant but vivid dream than a bleak truth. We were free in increasingly distant lands, never to be troubled again. Rebecca had sensed something was not as it should have been with me the first two days, that I knew, and so I tried to focus only on her and our future together, as she did.

A few days into our journey, when we stopped for two hours in the afternoon to let the horses rest and we built ourselves a fire. Just like when I first met her, she wished to play my whistle whilst dancing in elegant drifts around the fire. I reached for my violin as she did so, attempting to play to the rhythm of her beat and bowing with the same ferocity as her steps ventured like the folk rhythms of the Irish. Fervour pulsated as we pranced together; and with a wily grin to match the pied-piper she led the music to andante. I followed the tender drone. Our pagan dances in Christian Britain, how mischievous we were in our love, our 'perfect euphoria'. I wondered through the melodies how it had been that I had become the luckiest man on earth; perhaps God does love to see an impeccable romance.

We found ourselves back on the road soon enough and my horses continued their good pace, which left me more grateful than they, or Rebecca, could have known. But nightfall crept back over the chilly world, and the winds grew more treacherous as if they did not want us out there. With those winds, suppressing thoughts of The Man Of The Lonely Tree became futile. I fancied I could feel him in the distance behind. My poor stallions had paced well throughout the whole day and had lost most of their strength, but because of my feelings of him, I kept them going far into the night. They were nourished sufficiently, but for all my meagre efforts at such, there is no substitute for sleep, and I had to accept defeat. They had to stop eventually, and we camped for the night.

Her high moods when leaving had remained through our journey, and she became a calm aura that I relied on amidst my growing madness. To the girl, stopping meant only rest. We set up camp as always just inside a woodland not too far from our road; so no passer-by would disturb us. When she sat wrapped in the furs with an innocent face, I thought it best to collect some firewood from the woodlands, rather than use our limited supply needlessly. I left her safely there, as I roamed nearby for wood.

The wood was only of small capacity, little more than a couple dozen trees, however enough to leave dry wood on its rustic surface. The world around me was obscured by an empty blackness both from within the wood and from the sky, but from my lantern to hers, I could identify her shadow inside the tent, and I continued to collect firewood whilst remaining aware of her safety. The enclosure seemed usefully dry compared to the rest of the world, I could smell its crispiness floating in the air. I extended my arm out to grab a suitable stick, barely able to see it despite my lantern. Once I held its form however, I noticed the underside was disappointingly damp and insects crept along as if they had somewhere in particular to be. It was that that made me realise those beings were the only sight or sound I could experience outside the four of us; me, Rebecca and my two horses. And how familiar that seemed. I tried to ignore the omen but a queer sensation came to me, my body began to feel incredibly heavy as if standing upright was an effort beyond myself. I stepped a few yards and tried to regain my posture but its impossibility was apparent, I fancied my weary spirit was losing its connection to my material self, and my body was sinking to the ground as a result. I closed my eyes for a moment as my mind turned cloudy with an incompetence; something devastating, and uncontrollable was happening to me. From the silence and stillness of the air, a strange wind drew forth freely. It seemed at first only a refreshing feeling as the cold air brushed into me, reminding me my body was still mine, but when my mind had come back to me somewhat, it did not sound quite so natural. It then came back stronger, directly into me as if the sluagh sídhe had travelled in the westward winds to personally condemn me, and in those winds I heard their hollow murmurs. I shuddered and moaned with a bitter dread as I collapsed to the floor. The horror had found me. My consciousness recoiled into its own abyss of insanity for several still seconds, I was terrified of peering into the dark at what I might see.

'Where are you?' I commanded out, holding up my lantern to the trees when I regained some courage. 'Stop with the trickery you Devil!' I scorned out into the world with bitter rage for him. My only reply was that the great black of night seemed to enhance its foul gloom in but an instant, as if the sky had somehow collapsed on itself and its shards etched at me supressingly. My mind fell only to my love and her protection. I turned to face her direction and my straining eyes saw with clarity no movement in the lantern light from inside the tent. With a deep agony shooting through my form, a panic filled me. I tried however, to remain as composed as I could manage, for I felt certain the demonic thing was watching me and hiding nearby in the darkness. Running and screaming for her would only play into his torturous game.

I hoped to remain diligent and move to find her, instead, my eyes caught the appalling sight I feared the most. The dimness deceived me not, it was him. He waited unmoving, hunched over and languid like a beastly imp lurking out in the centre of an open field that I faintly could see through the trees. He wore the same black attire he did on my lands, concealing himself as completely as he could like the most sinister shadow amongst shadows. My heart sank with apprehension as I bore momentary witness to my peril, unforeseen and far from home.

'Fletch, where are you?' I heard through the trees behind me in a feminine and concerned tone. Instinctively I moved towards her, walking as fast as I could whilst trying not to appear desperate or frightened to the unmoving phantom. She moved leisurely into the woods towards me without any form of light and with a step that contrasted wholly with the danger she was in; like a beautiful night maiden wandering in treacherous obscurity as the preying Diabolus loitered nearby.

Her cheerfulness melted when she saw the grave urgency in me. I grabbed her arm with more aggression than I intended. 'We have to leave now. Quick.' I demanded under my breath. 'Why, what is wrong?'
'Just get everything ready. Now.'
'I thought we could have supper and some conversation'

I led her to the cart with a force I regret. I regretted it at the time, but that was better than telling her the truth of him. She objected to leaving sternly but I pulled down our camp with much haste and resolve. I barely heard her words, I had seen the horror of a lifetime, we were leaving. I looked about the place frantically as I prepared to leave. He was not in sight. Temporarily.

I offered my arm out to help her onto the cart and she looked at me with a puzzled glance which lasted for several long seconds. Reluctantly she accepted. Even as I untied and whipped the dismayed horses to a rapid start, she still looked upon me with a reserved questioning. For a time I ignored her, wondering where he was and how with two horses travelling for days this man's wandering legs had not fallen behind our pace.
'What is the matter?' She spoke calmly, in the same sincere tone as before. I could not answer her, I thought of how I would respond, but in the end, I said nothing; only looked behind myself into the impenetrable dark, expecting him to be chasing us like a ghostly canine barking his vengeance upon me. I whipped my horses into a faster pace once more and placed my axe on my lap; which alarmed Rebecca all the more. I wished I had carried a weapon for her too, some hedge shears or some other ploughing

blade, anything she could strike him with; yet as I packed provisions for the two of us, I had only thought of getting away as soon as we could, I was certain he would not find us.

She placed her hand on my shoulder, commanding my mind as only she could do, and spoke. Yet though her mouth moved with some worried meaning, I did not receive the sound of her voice; instead a deep and coarse noise came in the air all too near me. It was his, uttering something I could not define.

'Can you not hear that?' I begged of her hysterically.

'Hear what? The cries of horses dying of exhaustion?'

'You cannot hear it? Hear it!' I ordered of her, grabbing her wildly as if she could wake up and hear the voice I heard. Helplessly I looked to her, and only saw a terribly frightened expression. My sanity was crumbling in front of her. I was not strong enough to cope with the impending doom. I felt frail and exposed, like I was falling off a cliff onto jagged rocks below, and in but a few short moments my irrefutably feeble form would shatter.

'Fletch, sweetheart, calm yourself. There is nothing to hear.' She held me like a mother would, trying to protect me from my terrors and shushing my mad ramble. But I heard his voice again in that same sinister undertone of a whisper. It was an endeavour to grasp any clarity, but once I knew his voice, it was unmistakable. I swayed and groaned in my struggle to endure my torment, and I called in the name of the Holy Spirit that he would be struck down into the chasms of Hell!

'What is going on? Why so frantic?' She tried to gently exert some influence over my state, but the mothering proved hopeless. There was nothing of coherence to my thoughts; and the only further word I seemed to call out was "no". It spewed out of me austerely but became a roaring scream from the depths of my gut, and I screamed until my throat gave in to coughing violently. The girl continued to caress me, kissing me and smothering me with love in an attempt to return me to a vague notion of myself, yet my mind's stability had fallen completely.

After my distress and coughing harshly I had no energy left in me, and I fell victim to unconsciousness against my own will.

The poor girl I loved sat and watched her protector from dragons and demons go mad, pitifully, and fade away without an explanation.

I awoke in our tent facing up, seeing the daylight penetrate the gloomy green. I did not want to see the world yet, nor smell the smoke of a dying fire that came into me. What I wanted was to fade into some distant magical dream where pleasant fairies would tell me to rest awhile, that everything would conspire into pleasantries in due time. But I only saw the inside of a miserable tent.

'Are you going to tell me what happened to you yester-day?' She asked in a monotonous and slightly impatient manner, seeing that my eyes had been open for a minute and not yet turned to face her. When I did look to her, she had a keen scrutiny in her eyes. She sat opposite me hugging her knees, holding her stern expression. I took some time before answering her question, and heard the wind outside. The wind, those ill and vicious winds that too often contained his voice. Any trace of optimism I had awoken with was shattered; I realised, the real answer to her question was unavoidable.

'I apologise my love, my Rebecca, I sincerely apologise.'

'Tell me what happened. Tell me why you were acting nonsensical. I was afraid you were going to cause yourself harm, or even me, clutching your axe like that and acting so wildly.'

'I would never hurt you.' The very thought turned my stomach.

'I know.' She faintly smiled. Though faint it was, only she could perform such a tiny yet significant thing, the cheerlessness of our conversation had been lifted to something more endurable. 'But still, you could have hurt yourself. Do I have to change our course to the nearest asylum?' Her smile lingered on one side. The scrutiny of her eye had faded.

'I will explain to you Rebecca. But not now, later, you have my word. Let us get back on the road first.' My words were well received by her and I kissed her pink red cheek as a gesture of agreeing our deal.

Something I had guessed and saw as truth when I returned to the world, was that we were still by the same woodland of the previous night. As soon as I had lost consciousness she must have stopped the cart to the relief of our horses and set camp for the both of us, and the fire; all the while he was nearby, surely watching her, but not yet exacting his will. I was anxious to get moving again, he had come this far for her but to what true purpose? Whatever it was, I fancied he was only prolonging our fate in his vengeance, because, to him, I was only a stubborn obstacle to be removed. I knew I had to be more vigilant than ever and I could not risk letting her out of my sight unless it was absolutely necessary.

As we rode on, I gathered my thoughts and began to wonder how I would speak to Rebecca of him, of his reality and his intent. I also thought of my madness the night before, his whispering in my head and the dreams he had previously brought to her. This man was a master of minds, I knew he was also cause to her state when I found her on her lawn, either directly or indirectly. Her not knowing of him meant that I could pretend he did not exist when we had our merry conversations, however, I recognised then that keeping him a secret put her in more peril than knowing, it had become a hindrance to our safety.

'I owe you a picnic' my arm found its way around her small frame as I kissed her sand hair.

'You do.'

'And so it shall be, if God allows it' I spoke looking to the forbidding clouds that began to cover the vibrancy of the day with threatening rain; subsequently, we would have to stop to shelter.

'My guess is it will not rain until nigh on dusk.'

We sat opposite one another, and had our picnic for the sake of conversing, nourishing, and resting ourselves, as well as for the sake of our horses.

'I gave you my word, my love, that I would explain myself from yester-night. Here it is...' Her relaxed body twitched to life as if by Frankenstein's lightning when I spoke unexpectedly out of the calmness. I paused for a moment, uncertain of how to articulate

92

the events and still unsure where to begin. Moments turned to a painful eternity from the last word to the next. Eventually, knowing Rebecca would speak herself if I did not continue my confession, I stumbled out my words.

'There has been someone following me as of late. A man. I have seen him by several roads. And when I was with you on my father's fields. At first I fancied him an apparition, or the result of a fanciful and diminishing mind, but he has spoken to me from a distance of but a few feet, he is a being of material flesh. Yet I have heard him whispering to my mind when no one was there.'

'Oh' she pronounced in recognition of my words whilst taking in the farfetched details. 'You heard his voice in your head last night then? I thought you were hearing voices from your peculiar damning of someone. But I was sat next to you, I heard nothing. It was the most silent night.'

'That is exactly it Rebecca. It was too silent, eerily so. Where were the ever-watchful hooting owls? Even the fluttering bats were too scared to make an appearance. The very world cowers away from him, fears him, and so should we.' She looked at me as if I was whimsical and descending into lunacy, but I continued on 'you could not hear him when I could because he has some command over our minds. I know this because he has revealed himself to no one else but you, in your dreams, The Devil Outside Looking In.'

'They were just the dreams of a weary mind.'

'The way you described him was vague, I agree, but every detail is the same as the man I have seen. You said yourself it felt like prophecy'

'No, it cannot be' she said dismissively 'it did, but they were just dreams that passed by. I have not had those nightmares for a while now.'

'He has travelled this far with us, walking, following our tracks only in the dark and across around fifty miles as I take it; plus another fifteen today. My lady, he is real, and he is here.' Still she did not believe me, but the fear had begun to boil in her to an agitated impatience that she wished our talk to be done with and out of her mind.

'So what now? What does he want?' However much I wished not to speak of his reality to her, it was the answer to her last question I loathed to reveal most of all. I looked to her as she knelt in front of me, peering into the centre of my soul with the command of her pale blue eyes and striking a chord of weakness in me. I had to turn away, I could not bear to bring her despair. 'When he spoke to me the second time, he said he "claims you". And that if I stepped in the way he would not allow me to live.' It was only in guilt for disregarding her well-being that I hopelessly looked to her; her, who was the real victim, the one who I should have been supporting devotedly, not cowering in selfish misery. In her, I witnessed an expression swell slowly as a look that resembled sadness came over her, though the pure emotion she would have felt is quite beyond me.

I longed to hold her, or some other form of affection, anything to comfort her from the thoughts that numbed her. Yet I remained motionless. And of her, no motion came either, like the cadavers of Romeo and Juliet, devoted partners wishing to love each other limitlessly, yet they could not move. I had to fill the silence.

'I...'

'No one can take me away from you, I hope you know that! We are together now Mr Fletcher. You cannot leave me, never; and I cannot leave you. We agreed to be together, there is no parting now Fletch. Not even the Devil himself could separate us.' She spoke with that stern will of hers, a fresh glimpse of what I admired most of all in her. And such a comfort her adamant words were, they gave me the strength to fight when it was beginning to seep out of me.

'He will have to kill me before he could lay a finger on you.' I replied to her, though knowing that was precisely what he intended.

The thick raw emotion between us remained as we continued North. I studied her throughout the journey, how solemnity and quiet invaded her. There were times when I thought she still did not believe he was real, then other times she seemed as deeply concerned as I was. I was fortunate in some way that he had tormented her previously in her dreams, if he had not, I doubted she would have fallen to belief.

'You said he only appears at night, and tracks us, then let us obscure the track at a crossroad. We can try to lead him down another route.'

'Wonderful idea.'

When we reached a crossroad we turned right and rode for ten minutes until the next crossroad, so that our tracks were firmly committed to that route, then we turned around and kicked the dirt in such a way that unmarked our turn. With my axe I carefully, and ever so precisely, finished both sets of wheel tracks so that the one he followed would go off into a field in the opposite direction, and the tracks we were now making came from another different field. That made our tracks go into obscurity while the tracks we then began to make would appear unsuspicious. We smiled to each other once we were done and continued throughout the day in lighter moods.

Though I did not speak such words directly, Rebecca knew to be perceptive when night fell. She had the idea of camping in a field away from the road so that from all sides he would lose any cover for surprise, which we did, and we both stayed out during the darkness, scouting for him until she could no more and retired. I was restless and so stayed out watching for a few more hours, but he was nowhere to be seen. Neither whisper nor dream came to us and I fell asleep out there by our fire in the freezing cold.

I found when I woke up that it had softly rained in the early hours of the morning, which left me wet and flushed with the cold. Rebecca came out fretting that I was going to fall ill. Besides the cold and the rain, I was under-slept, and my neck hurt from the way I had rested; however all that was a small price to go through the night unscathed.

We agreed that our workings with our tracks had either lost him completely, or given us a day further on him, and we agreed to do it again every night thereafter. We had breakfast. I dried myself and changed, then we took to the road again and I conscripted my stallions to ride another gruelling day that had circumstances been otherwise, I would not have dared put them through. Poor things.

Of our location, we increasingly saw signs directing Glasgow to the West of us and Edinburgh to the East. I felt encouraged by those signs, not because we chose to be in the city areas but because other tracks on the roads were becoming more common, making it harder to focus on just one for any length. With the Highlands being our chosen destination I knew other tracks to help us would be scarce when we reached there; it was paramount that we lost him in the Lowlands. I felt confident with our new technique that we could move faster than he could track and chase us, and when we were to reach the Highlands he would be two dozen miles behind and accept defeat.

We were relaxed and mildly cheerful that day. The threat of him seemed faded for the time being, and within the comfort of daylight we could hear the birdsong hanging handsome in the air for only the second time since we left home, that was a priceless omen.

Nevertheless, all that calm and heightened tranquillity fell along with the sun. Deep in the insecurity of unknown lands, the darkness came on us condensed and disturbing. The omen of sound too left as night fell and the only thing to be heard was the rustle of trees in the swelling winds. The altogether noiselessness of the atmosphere felt oppressing, I needed all my will to stop from heaving in its sickening nature. I feared we had come full circle and he had found us again.

We did intend to camp out in a field away from the road again, it had worked the previous night, however not long into dusk it became apparent that our horses were in desperate need of stopping for the night, there was no going further. Where we found ourselves that night lay at the foot of a ridge that loomed tall and had a woodland encroaching up it. We camped just by the woodlands away from the road and built a much needed fire. As the night moved, the shadows that the fire cast from the trees became progressively insufferable.

We sat out together engaging in tedious conversation, though we both knew our real reason for sitting out was in watch of him; even my horses seemed to search the parameters for the danger they knew. I could see Rebecca's hand tremble with distress, she distrusted the dark as I did. She did not need to state the fact she fully believed he was real, it was plain as day for me to see; she feared him as much as I did. I held her shaking hand tightly, emotionally protecting her from her horror and dreading to ever let go, as if he would come from out the shadows up the hill to clasp her from me the moment I did.

We remained out there for quite some time that night, neither of us dared to sleep. I was convinced he was relatively close to us. It was undeniable that his presence had come back into the world around us, whether on the road behind striding towards us, calculating our path with his loathing and violent assurances; or dwelling in the shadow of a tree, watching us from the invasive black with hawk eyes, waiting to pounce with any opportunity, I did not know. If my stallions had not have been overworked during the day I would have had them take us further; sat out in the dark and expecting him at any moment was unpleasant to say the least.

Under my arms I felt her pulse quicken sharply as if taken by some swift and unbearable fever. But before I had chance to react in any way, she threw herself away from me with a sudden roar, screaming the most violent and high pitched sound I had ever heard. Impulsively I covered my ears from the pain she induced. It was not a typical feminine scream which can be ear bursting enough, it was something frightening and all too diabolical. I thought it was her reaction to seeing him in the darkness, and that our final ending was upon us. I tried to calm her in her frenzy and see where she looked to, but if she had seen him, I could not. With intent I wish not to speculate, she found her feet and began running towards the woodlands without her natural graceful step. Like a Banshee screaming a reply to Lucifer's call, she ran for his domain. I bellowed out to her feebly, too stunned to really react at first, but soon found myself running into the dark after her.

The girl had made her way through the bog-like mud and into the murky black wood as I lost sight of her momentarily. Above me, the winter branches looked like claws willing me into my finality; despite my wild apprehension, I had to follow beyond the threshold.

'Rebecca? Rebecca? This is not wise' I shouted from my gut hoping to somehow break her from the spell, and noting amidst the high towers the air had turn unnaturally coarse. I had a fear, and expectation, that I would not see her again, that she would have "disappeared" and only the man would be standing in sight. My eyes darted every which way trying to spot her but there were only trees to be seen, and I perceived no movement.

I praised God when to my relief I caught sight of her. She had fallen to the ground some ten paces ahead of me and continued crawling her way forwards silently.

'Where are you going Rebecca?' I called gaining the necessary yards. I cared little for an answer to the question, for all my thoughts were on the menacing spectre I anticipated was watching us. I glanced again into the dense obscurity and saw several long, gloomy and twisted shapes. My blood turned cold with each one fearing it was him; they proved unmoving. I hoped they were trees. Looking behind us, only a dim glowing fire was sign that our camp and road were really there. I felt we were lost in a black sea, and the leviathans were all around, lapping angrily in the deep and sniffing out our fear. I held her hands tightly and tried to examine her soul, but her eyes looked up at me in a chilling manner. They were red-rimmed and cold as if the life behind them had dissipated, I do not know if it was a tear of sadness or the cold had dried her eyes and forced a biological reaction, but a droplet trickled down her flushed cheek as she trembled softly, somehow emotionlessly.

The desolation tried to close in on us yet I wilfully ignored it as I crouched down to her, and beheld her, her who I would

98

have done anything for. I embraced her frozen body hoping she would feel my warmth, but she did not move. I began to despair gravely.

Breaking through the clouds the moon trickled slowly into sight. I saw it behind her through the trees shining like a bright silver jewel. Even in the deepest darkness it shines as hopeful as ever.

'There is no parting now, remember Rebecca? Not even the Devil himself could separate us.' I worded into the most remote recess of her spirit, trying to touch a nerve that dwelled so deep in her that even he could not reach. My heart ached to end her torment. Her mouth moved open marginally, though I could not tell if she meant to speak. No sound came. My words did, however, have some vague effect upon her. Her limbs softened their stiff anxiety, I could feel it in her as I caressed her hands gently and attempted to let my calm settle in her.

The low lingering moon caught my attention once more, moving into clearer sky, and it distilled in me a sort of ease; with its tender light I could see the landscape enough to navigate us both as the bleak shades passed.

'Come now my love, we are safe, Luna guides us.' My speech brought a tentative smile to her. Slowly I lifted her from the ground and patted the mud off from her stained dress. Diminished had our fear by the time we walked back, the serene melody of Luna serenaded me triumphantly, it gave me a divine peace that I could provide Rebecca with.

She went straight into the tent and fell asleep within moments. I on the other hand sat guard with my axe and watched the moon travel across the increasingly clear night's sky; worrying only little, and sleeping at first sunlight.

I came to a wakeful state wretchedly, only waking because the sun through the tent allowed me no further rest, not due to a sufficient amount. Rebecca, on the other hand, somehow still lay deep in sleep. I got out of the tent and saw a world that was perfectly malnourished by winter; it seemed to mourn for itself. I relit the fire and sat in miserable reflection. No birdsong dwelt over the trees like the morning before. And the dreadful silence lasted all day. My eyes flickered to the gods drearily, but I only saw clouds that abused our skies and created a feeling of impending doom within me. I do not know if it was concluded by how awful I felt, or how bleak the morning was, but I thought he would try to take her that night. I did not speak my blind suspicion to her, it was too final for speculation, however I could see behind her brave face the tremor of dread that dwelt underneath the surface.

We continued North as ferociously as possible, flying with speed I feared would take my beasts. They would not die within a few days but their premature deaths were on the horizon due to my need for distance; and that was heart-breaking my reader, I had had them most of my life.

We did our deeds of concealing our tracks during our mid-day break. We spoke little of our peril and instead turned our minds to the increasing raw wilderness of the land. It was a beauty to behold of course, however I knew it would only bring further desolation when the night came.
'What do you believe it is?' Her words as we rode on, spoken with a voice that was almost too afraid to ask as a fragile stare came upon me. I looked away with a sigh and remained silent for several moments. She watched me with intensity and persistence. It was a question I had speculated much, before pushing it to a distant and neglected corner of my mind, wishing its possible answers would not haunt me, but the conversation by her insistence was to take place. I had to answer.
'I am certain he is of flesh and blood. I know that, though he feels grotesquely demonic... What do you think?' She blushed miserably for a moment before speaking with her own certainty 'I think it is the Grim Reaper coming for me.'

What do you say to such a thought? My love believed the Angel of Death had claimed her life. Worse still, she spoke as if it was inescapable; no matter what we did he would have her death shortly. My whole world passed before my failing eyes; the whole life I had lived, and meeting her, the beautiful future that seemed all ahead of us. I cannot put into a poetic melancholic phrase my emotion, I simply felt I had died myself as she spoke; as if all reason to live had been violated from me. I looked to her for some sort of relief, yet with a commanding presence she still held that morose complexion. I needed the happiness and joy of her that I had come to expect, I needed it to infect me as it had when we first took to the road. I moved to her, filled with my desperation, and touched her lips with mine. With the delicate touch, I could feel the gloom and distress of everything we knew fade into the ether. And I wanted it to fade forever, perhaps I should never have stopped.

It proved a great temporary relief, as if a bridge was built between our growing isolations from everything. We were together still, and more devoted to one another than ever. But there was more to him than I knew, he could have taken her when I fell unconscious in my madness, yet he did not, and I could not make sense of his motive. The only thing I could make sense of however, was that since I had been carrying my axe with me, he had not wanted a close encounter; which further proved to me that he was of flesh, and could be harmed if struck by a blade. That gave me only little hope for the fight ahead though, because regretfully, I seemed only to know how to play into the miserable role he wanted of me. With a heavy sense of helplessness, I knew the decision of how it would end was entirely his. Taking another road on our journey would change nothing for us, same was true of distance, he seemed capable of molesting us regardless, and for that reason we decided to take longer and more regular breaks so that we could continue riding during the darkest hours of night. Sitting helplessly for him to come created a greater ill than riding through the night, for when we did ride through the night, I felt active in trying to defend her; even if in only a meagre way. He did not come.

We rode through the next day hardly saying a word yet we held each other without end, through an anxiety of loss, more so than passion. We took our regular and long breaks taking note of the sun's movement until the invading darkness took control of the skies. And as it did, we turned from two embracing beings to two detached beings side by side, clutching hands and working solely from the instinct of survival. We searched the terrain intently, never so much as blinking lest the demon appeared. The blackness of the night in its own searing way was deafening. I felt attacked by the blatant tyranny of the night itself, as if it willed our demise.

'I need a weapon' she trembled quietly in my ear. Though as quiet as she attempted, her words still seemed to echo into the empty night. Without further warning she hopped down from the moving cart and walked as calmly as she could towards the woods on our right. I still cannot decide if flirting with her own existence so simply was her greatest act of courage, or of sheer stupidity. I pulled the reins, to the relief of my horses, and jumped down too; holding a lantern in one hand and wielding my axe in the other, terrified he was breathing his quiet prowl in the shadow of a nearby tree.

I ran to her side as her steps reached the outskirts of his woodlands. She took the lantern from me and searched the ground, finding a large fallen branch and preceded to strip the fingers off it; all without thought of what may have been in the dark a few feet away. When she had fashioned it to her liking she held it high in the air as a slight grin traced across her face with violent intent. I doubted how effective her weapon would have been against him, however I could see the change in her, from someone who felt powerless to someone hungry for the fight to begin, and I would not taint that with doubt. But as she lifted the lantern from the ground and its faint light drew shifting shadows, I saw a flicker in the black inky mist that did not move with the rest. It was a vague upright figure, no more than twenty yards from us. I stumbled backwards with a mortified gasp.

'What is it?' She screamed, holding back her flurry of panic, looking to where my eyes could not leave and seeing nothing of what I had seen. It had disappeared right before my sight, becoming one with the shadows about him and no longer existing there.

A rage crawled its way up my spine and I boiled with scorn. He was mocking me. Having seen nothing she tried to calm me, but I jumped back to my feet and held my axe up high like she had. With a battle cry, I screamed an unmatched abhorrence 'show yourself you wretched fiend. Grim Reaper or whoever you are. I am going to kill you. I vow it!'

Nothing. My violent voice echoed into the awful depths repetitively and died down in unbearable humility. The only beings I seemed to distil fear in were the two of us. I searched frantically for where he had moved to, but there was no sight of him. From behind us the winds strengthened vigorously, suddenly. She clutched into me and I held her tightly, we both knew it was not wholly the doing of Mother Nature, but in part the will of an altogether malicious being. Its cold bitterness thrashed at us for several moments, stealing what little morale we had left. And the slumbering trees that towered above us swayed fiercely, creaking in their own weight and creeping over us execrably. I looked directly up at the phenomenon, initially only fearing the possibility of them collapsing on us. But I saw it, a formless figure darting across the trees directly above us, as if it had wings, and gliding soundlessly into obscurity. Rebecca cried at the sight of the menace. I tried to keep my eyes on him but once again he seemed to morph into the shades and somewhat, or completely, disappear.

Her cry of dismay echoed too keenly in the night, too grimly, as she clutched to my arm with a grip of claws. As her sound began to fade, the faintest laughter trickled in the air from the man. What startled and shocked me the most however, was that it did not come from above where he should have been, it came from an unknown distance in front of us. She looked to me with the same knowledge, as well as searching me for some form of bravery. She found none. Another, louder cracking sound came from one of the trees near us, shrieking a slow noise in agony as if it was soon to collapse to the ground. I did not look to see if he was in the tree causing it or not, instead I hastily ran towards the cart dragging the girl along with me until she found her stride.

We ran franticly for the cart to find my stallions too were gravely anxious, and were already stepping to an escape themselves. I saw nothing chase us or them, though I certainly felt it. I whistled for the horses to stop for us, which they complied with momentarily, and with much apprehension, though it proved long enough that we both could get on. They soon ran as fast as they could by their own will. I fancied had the horses left us behind we would not have lasted the night out there with him, with only a lantern, an axe and a pitiable stick to defend ourselves. But we knew we were still not safe from him, we held out our weapons, waiting for him to come out of the murkiness with the speed two galloping horses could not master.

However, there was no sign of him again that night. We eventually camped and lit a fire after my reassurance that I would keep her safe as she slept; which she did. I remained awake all night, sat on the edge of intolerable apprehension and cold, dreading he would come once more to "claim" her.

The feeling of night did not disperse as the light of day began. Mild rainfall at dawn coupled with a sunless morning left frost to formulate. I could see her breath in the lethargic winds. Clouds threatened further rain all day, however, it did not release itself before the twilight. Our day itself was like no other, so lowly, so bitter. I felt the world roaring in silent anguish. At times I felt it manifest in my own chest in a terrible scream that matured with its own tremble; yet it could not surface or dissipate.

The previous night troubled me immensely, I witnessed his capability of dwelling in two places in an impossibly short time and I did not know what to make of the fact. I reminded myself that the main concern was Rebecca's safety, that was my duty, and it was intact. Until otherwise, I was winning the battle.

Any other time in my life I would have been delighted to know we had finally reached into the realm of the famed Highlands, where the greenery is of a wild vigour only comparable to a dream seen through the eyes of an emerald jewel. But I could not be taken by its splendour, for its antiquate wilderness filled me more with danger than enchantment. The mountains loomed like rocky volcanoes from an abandoned land as thin ash clouds drowned their peaks. And each of the numerous valleys were more immense than the last; reminding me of my own insignificance. I became almost afraid to travel along the unending roads within the cavernous depths. Even the lochs that lay scattered in every direction of the mountains gave me no comfort, they were of an ill and gloomy grey. The comforts of my lough back home, of home itself, seemed like an uncanny dream.

Out of the valleys our road moved through dense woodlands. Oak and beech and willow that stretched out into a great expanse. Within two hours of being in there however, with the road moving further uphill than I expected I began dreading the thought that we would not reach the other side before nightfall. The wilderness would turn perilous and I sensed I had caused our own downfall in taking that path. Conversely, I had experienced him in open lands, and that was no better. Perhaps his flying in the density of woodlands would prove a quicker release than seeing him come from a mile away.

We found our way into a small meadow of an opening with a river drifting by and stopped briefly for some respite. But even in that space, the close and eerie tension in the atmosphere did not resolve. It was apparent nowhere would give us the ease we strived for, and Rebecca seemed more dispirited there than she did in the wood; we moved on before long. On the other side of the meadow the foliage only became denser, and with a harshness that all Scottish folk-tales seemed to elude, as if merely mentioning the horrors that lurked in the district was blasphemy. We saw not the end of the remote forest as darkness approached in brazen agony. My tiredness had been overtaking me throughout the day, but I was too anxious to sleep, and as I remained so, my weariness increased. As the light fell in the distance, tremors ran through my sensibility and my nerves ached an unsettled fear; I knew I could not sleep until night had passed.

As we moved in the enclosure, every stiff footstep of the sluggish and unaltered plod echoed solemnly in the barren and defeating night; revealing in every second how inconsequential our efforts were in the peril that suffocated us.

'There is no end to this wretched woodland Fletch. I feel him near, I feel him watching us' the girl muttered in her most helpless expression.

'I would die defending you, if need required, Rebecca. Neither the Devil nor Christ could part us, remember? He will move on or die.' My words helped her as much as they could, but the crippling despair we both felt was consuming us. When someone so full of love and life thinks they are about to die violently, little of comfort can be said.

Nothing more did we speak, we dared not. And in our wretched silence we listened for an encroaching demon. Much like the sun during the day, the moon and stars were hidden behind the misty masses of rain, leaving the night so utterly black, so contemptible that I felt bombarded with its overbearing desolation. And in that ambiguous dark the tree stumps by the road appeared to me as vile gnomes, silently laughing at my apprehension and frightened quake. Both lanterns were lit, yet they only created flickering shadows in the depths of the trees, assisting my mind to create creatures that mocked me incessantly.

I was not sure if it was one of those created creatures, a real creature or my villain, but I thought I saw black shapes dart across the road in the distance frequently. I anticipated that the haunting hands of the unknown were upon us for our final end whenever I perceived them. But Rebecca never seemed to notice them, and I let myself believe they were just my own conjurations.

I held my weapon ready in hand, prepared for a battle to the most bitter of ends. She held hers too, but I noticed that she often held extended looks my way; longingly, as if saying "farewell" with her bright lakes that glimmered an icy December on a hopeless night. Yet I could not reciprocate her stares, my eyes only existed for the thing that threatened her.

Two harsh and stern footsteps sounded amidst those of my horses. A frozen chill singed my spine and lingered in my neck, and the top of my head so concentrated with a convulsion, felt like Satan had his despicable hand clamping on my skull, shaking and squeezing its hind for his own appalling pleasure. The steps sounded around fifty yards behind us, but before I had chance to turn myself round and see, the walking steps turned into a pounding gallop full of cruel intent. I turned as quick as my horrified body would allow, and from the vicious sound of the feet on the road, the violent thing should have been but a pace away from me when I turned. Yet nothing was there, save the hostile silence, and the bitter depths of winter. I felt no relief in not witnessing him though, I still felt he was in fact within that yard of me, merely unperceived, sat by my side glaring with hostile fury and a devilish grin. I grimaced in abhorrence, and gazed at the girl to see if she had experienced all I had. The speechless, desperate stare she gave me confirmed it. And the silence afterwards tormented us as much as the gallop did itself, as if there was an explosion of absolutely nothing, and its shards of debris penetrated our skin vehemently. I felt I would die of fear before long.

I found my courage and tried to sight him, but to no avail; the darkness was far too dense. But out into that density, the winds found a new source of potency and a subtle mass of sound hissed with it. A dreadful voice it was, one that was too close for comfort and yet existed faint and unclear as it interweaved in the rustling North winds. Rebecca heard it too and dived into me. I sheltered her under my wing whilst moving my axe in front of myself, trying somehow to ward off the air that seemed to close in on us. She had no further thought for him however, I felt her soft hand caress my cheek and guided me into the serene mystery of her stare. It became evident in that moment that I would never see her again, somehow we both knew it was the end, and that she would be his by the end of the night. And I did not even know what that meant.

So elegant. So pretty. She was simply every female superlative our savage language has. I yearned to smile to her, to tell her we would survive; yet my glance only deteriorated into powerlessness. The loss of losing her had already begun to eat away at me, my heart fell from grace, and shattered, before I even lost her.

Thoughts of losing her not only curdled my blood, but curdled my hatred for him as well. I pulled the reins in blind anger and jumped down from the cart. She came down too, clutching my clothing and standing desperately behind me.
'Where are you?!' I screamed with blistering rage into the bleak night; my words echoing into nothing.

Something moved slightly to my left. I turned to face the flicker I had witnessed and Rebecca shuffled herself behind me. A poised silhouette it was, behind the shade of the trees. His very stench was evil, his very aura felt lifeless. In a placid manner he stepped with heavy feet out onto the bank by our road, miserably dwarfing me. Yet I stood facing him, as tall and strong as I could, and wielding my axe ready to strike him.

As I mentally prepared myself for the fight I feared would leave Rebecca mourning my humble demise, abruptly, I found myself on the ground. I knew not what had happened except for the excruciating pain in the back of my head, Satan's false grip on its form again. Warm blood gathered under my face on the frozen road; I was quite critically bleeding. Something had struck me from behind, but the man had not moved.

The world swayed slow as I lay there, as if my mind could not perceive my sight as clearly as custom. Turning numb with agony, I rolled to my side and the red liquid of life covered my face. It clung to my form and wished to return to its meaning.

As I struggled to retain consciousness, I saw Rebecca held off the ground by the large man, both hands crushing her throat brutally. Of him, I could only see the black clothing and pale hands. My fading eyes moved to the girl, my love, who looked to my motionless and debilitated self with that same mysteriously serene stare. I think she tried to say something to me, but nothing could she muster through her airless frame. My will screamed in desperation to get up and fight for her, to release her from his vile grip. I desired so enough that I could feel myself rising from the ground and striking him with my axe repeatedly; but I could not see it.

I could not, and did not move.

'You have her now sir' I heard. But to my shock, it was a southern accent and a female voice. I then perceived two more of those black figures, wandering calming on either side of me as their cloaks swayed with their steps. They moved past my body towards him and Rebecca.

'Come now, you have her, can we go back to the capital now?' She spoke again. The Man Of The Lonely Tree only nodded, still clasping Rebecca's throat. Yet as her tranquil complexion began to fail, it was only me she noticed. And that was my last memory of that night.

End of Book I

Fletcher

Volume I
Book II: Of Death

Chapter I: The Grave Abyss

Nous devons mourir à une vie avant que nous puissions entrer dans

un autre

Anatole France

     I had no conceivable idea how long it was before I felt awareness of myself again. I would say it seemed a lifetime at least when consciousness came back to me in a somewhat vague sense; certainly longer than my life had been thus far. Longer than the process of one God dying and another taking in its place. Though simply put, and with all distorting speculation aside, I knew not the scale of time, only acknowledgement of endless darkness and ever-present agony presented time as unfathomable. And of emotion, it practically did not exist anymore to me, and thought too. Without the solid ground of thought, I could only accept simple sensations that came to me when I retained life for a mere moment.

     For what seemed weeks upon weeks, my 'mind' appeared to flitter freely in the realms around my body aimlessly. I felt light like I could fly. Floating in the forms of the ancients, one might say, before drifting back softly to myself and lingering in my rightful place again. These moments in my rightful place were the moments when I began to feel faintly real again. And with that twinkle of life clinging to me in scarcity, spawning from the deepest corners of the world and hopelessly stumbling upon the weak lifeless recesses within my skull, were the thoughts:

"Rebecca" "Where is Rebecca?"

The phrase came to me like an echo of some nebulous emotion from a past life, all meaning left me as briefly as it came, dispersing back into those hidden corners of the world. Silence. I tried to grasp the idea behind the phrase with what little sensibility remained in me, but I could not recall a face to the name of Rebecca. I sensed a sphere of a personality to the name, though I could not decipher any of it. There was in me as simple as this, merely a name.

In defeat that I would not recall who the person behind the name was, I tried to stop all mental strains completely, for thought was only a delicate burden, a tedious pain. I tried to move but it was beyond me entirely; though there was a throbbing agony within my torso and limbs, I could scarcely feel my own form. Did I feel the ache of a warrior in his ghost limbs? That would certainly explain why I could not move I thought, perhaps I had lost my limbs. But it would not explain why my mind could not think coherently, I could not be certain of anything. And I lost consciousness.

When either I awoke once more, or simply regained enough strength to sloppily control my mind, all the same thoughts ran through me. I tried to remember who this Rebecca was, but it was hopeless. Enough fragments lingered in my mind not to fall into a desperate panic, but I was not fully certain who I was myself. What even was my own name? I was exhausted of nearly all livelihood, simple as that, homeless from any stable mind, naming a woman whom I did not know.

More time passed, another lifetime perhaps, another God reluctantly crawled onto the throne of Heaven. Eventually, in one of my periods of wake, I knew I would have to try to move, to learn the shape of my existence again. And so, lying there, with such weak life-force within me, I tried to move my fingers, enforcing with all the might within my being to move the things at the end of my arms. Nothing. Still nothing. No sensation running down the arm, no proof they were still attached to me save for the silent agony that was the shape my body once was. The frustration came upon me like scolding a wound, I tried to shake my fists in fury, but could not. There had been no sign that I still truly existed. However I had not the capacity to dwell on such negative thoughts. I tried to move until my wake collapsed. And this happened several times as far as I can tell.

At the time I did not believe in souls as ethereal entities intermingling with our bodies during life, and at the moment of death drifting into the world as immortal beings, no I did not believe any of that; but I felt in those moments, as if my soul had left my body. I could not feel my physical self, I felt absent with exception to ill-defined remnants of pain, and though I tried to move my body anyway, I simply could not. Eventually, after several waves of consciousness and on the cusp of passing back into sleep, having willed myself to move all the waking while and unsure of night or day, I felt a faint tingling sensation in the tip of my finger; awaking my sense of touch, as if without a source, feeling slowly itched back into my knowledge. The shivering feeling soon became clearer and moved down my finger increasingly, spreading to others. And suddenly I wished they had remained at a physical loss, for thorny knife-like pains twisted into my little revealed form with the great torture of all dwelling agonies. The pain worked its way progressively into my hand, then up my arms, revealing to me that I did exist. Indeed I could feel for the most part my arms and fingers, but of my chest I felt something peculiar, I was certain it was there, I knew, but I had no sensation of it. And I knew at least the main bulk of my head was still there, for I could think; but still, other than my arms, I could not feel the shape of my body entirely. My legs could have been severed and I would have been none the wiser, and such thoughts panic one into anxious fevers. I tried to scream, tried to shake an unmoving form. Then tried screaming again, but neither could I do. I remained a dormant ruin. Often falling from consciousness when my panicking wore me to sleep.

Somewhere down the line of my panicking and feeling more of my form, when beginning to understand the top of my chest was still mine, I realised, there was an overwhelming weight on top of me, crushing me constantly. I groaned terribly, overcome with pain and unable to relieve myself of it. I wondered if it was the cause of the pain I felt in my limbs the whole time? No, it was an internal affliction, and the new discovery was unquestionably external. And how excruciating and final it was, like being trampled by a herd of raging bulls without a foreseeable end. Again I tried to scream and writhe but nothing could be done to end the abusive oppression beyond lose consciousness.

Every time I awoke I suffered the agony both outside and within, being crushed to death and having to accept it was my fate. And I did just that. I pushed the pain into as much passivity as I could, numbing it slightly, moving my thoughts elsewhere. I thought it imperative to understand the state of my being, if I could see where I was I could try to make sense of everything with a foundation. I needed to open my eyes. I struggled. It took quite a while of arduous effort to recall how those muscles were used. But as I willed to open them, the sensation of my own face slowly returned, droning into painful existence like a never-ending cry of a nail on a chalkboard. I felt like the layers of my skin had been carved off, but it could not deter me, I needed sight.

When I finally was able to move my eyelids, it seemed all the force in the world was needed, for the weight of the thing above me fought my restless attempts persistently. With a low tremor of energy, my eyes came back to life. I could feel my lashes fold under the weight and brush against the bottom of my eyelids, gradually opening, burning with the most wretched agony. And where air should have caressed my eyes with a moist and fresh sensation, a tremendous sting scratched me; some unforeseen stale mass filled the space. My mind was too wearied to comprehend anything of what was happening, all I knew, is that something strange and unexpected occurred; and curiously so, I saw only utter blackness regardless of whether my eyes were open or not. To shield myself from the itching sensation of the unknown bizarre thing in my eyes, my natural instinct was to instantly close them. Again this was not without painful difficulty.

Of what had happened I could not ponder, my mind was too crippled, and my senses almost entirely failed me. I was reduced to nothingness, only pain. I needed to send myself to the most basic of functions. That was all I could see as necessary; and as I thought of it, I could not think of a moment when I had done so earlier... breathe.

I attempted the basic function, suppressing the pain that swelled in my recalled lungs, yet no air could I retrieve into the deep barrels of myself; only those stale clumps of mass could I inhale, which came in a harsh mouthful. My instant reaction was to, in motion, twitch upright and cough the thing out of my mouth, but the weight that crushed me in place refused me of my reflex. Instead my head challenged the crushing form with power I could not bear. More ache in dulled torture. The cough I had attempted to remove the things that rested in the back of my throat was partly successful, some of the things shot out of my mouth. But without air, I panicked of suffocation and impending death. I tried once again and like the last attempt, I could only inhale thick clusters of mustiness. The reaction to spit it out once more, and again, I was downright suppressed.

Terrified I was, I could not breathe, all I could do was lie defeated to the fact, motionless and in a dreary reverie. My mind commenced its wandering in and out of the vague shape of my body again, my own soul trying valiantly to escape. But still, every single cell in my body endured a tiresome numbing pain. I was burning to death, yet my end never came. And at times, I fancied myself bleeding, yet I could not see anything to verify. Was I dying? Was I already dead and feeling only the agony I died with still pulsing through me? I did not know. I only knew that I had never endured something so overwhelmingly coarse before, so excruciating that I could not conjure a scream of agony or fear; whereas with lesser pains, that is all you can do to mask the harsh reality from yourself. In the end, I concluded if one cannot breathe for such a length of time, they must be dead.

I attempted to clear my mind and forget the searing intensity inside myself, to forget the shape of my existence entirely and fade away, out of consciousness. And I believe I did for a while.

Once I awoke, I struggled with the state my life was in again, going through the pathetic reactions I had previously tried and failed with. But after the same feverish actions, I rested and tried to become rational about my state. To trace my steps back and see how I had come to that disabled and hopeless existence. Nevertheless, in those moments thought itself was a great effort, it seemed as if all the links and associations within my brain were lost, and every single one I had to put back to their rightful place, practically re-learning everything I had ever known.

How did I come to be here? There was nothing in my mind, I searched back further and further for any form of memory, but still not even my own name came to me. I still knew who I was, like a shadow without context, but I could not recall the name given to me. Frustration became me, the only thing I could remember was the name Rebecca, and only so, no image, no personality or sensation of emotions she distilled in me. Just a frozen name.

Overtime through several wakeful periods, deliberating both my name and who the name Rebecca belonged to, I eventually stumbled upon a solitary and distant memory. A girl, dancing merrily. Nimble she was in her movements as a flame roared behind her; and though I knew she was a beautiful being, I could not fully see the features of her face, nor any of her surroundings past the fire. Such details were still concealed somewhere in the rubble of my mind. And oh how I willed and pained for further recollection of her. I assumed the girl was Rebecca at the time but with absolutely no certainty; and being my only remaining memory I assumed the scene was of some special significance. Which of course it was.

I wondered how I had come from a place of seeing that prancing being, to a fate where Hell had been bestowed upon my body, what turn of ill-fate had led me here? Had I been crushed? It certainly felt that reality, as if a rock had fallen from a great mountain onto me, and I had lived; somewhat so.

117

I contemplated if I was actually alive. It seemed as if an alive thing could not endure the hurt I felt for so long a time. I listened for a pulse within me, at first I thought I felt nothing. What seemed minutes moved by and I could not hear nor feel the deep thud of life inside myself. But there was no panic, no fear, for no pulse alluded to a possible and welcome end. With that thought, it then came, astonishing me, out of the darkness like a ghost on the moors, the pump of something snaking slowly inside me. Then gone again. Too delirious to emotionally react to the fact, I only listened and observed. The pulse was dim, and each time the bloody throbbing wounds of mine gently numbed for a moment; a half bliss. However, morbidly so, after the rhythm-less beat, it took minutes for it to reappear and invariably it seemed it would come to its final stop; but that was not to be. And what little memory I had of her, little more than a word and a shadowy image kept me from truly wanting that final end.

There was no time, no memory, no situation or life in that endless void of Hell. Deep in the bitter, lonely emptiness the notion of having died passed me once more and for a short while, thinking the vague noises of my pulse could have been something beyond me, I believed it to be true; I could not even breathe let alone move. Yet I was conscious. I was able to think, that must have stood for something of life running through me I thought. I considered all without any real conviction. Neither life nor death seemed possible. For with death, I was not in Heaven, that much was clear. Same for the true concept of Hell. My body tensed itself suddenly, as if I was being pulled in all directions; the pain, relentless, oh so relentless and never ceasing. So much so, I believe I fell unconscious once more.

I awoke to the smell of soil, bringing me dreams of the farm. My family. All the relevant faces vaguely came to me, Mary, Jonathon, Walter and father. Even my tender youth briefly faded into my thoughts before leaving me, the only face in that was Mary's; I concluded the bleak truth that I had no companions outside of kin; life's grim reflections.

118

Slowly I opened my mouth marginally to breathe, gulping down, wanting to feel the moist fresh air, but that was not what I tasted. That clammy mass again, collapsing into the depths of my mouth, violating me and filling my throat with thick density. And again, the same hopeless reactions of coughing and trying to spit it all from myself, only to fail miserably whilst being refused movement. I simply had to let it all lie inside me. I tried to breathe again, but only the dingy mass existed outside. Of the stuff inside my mouth, I tasted...mud. Mud? And the scent of the thing lingering about my nostrils was the distinct scent of soil, how bizarre I reflected. That was as far as I thought of it, for mingled in with the scent came to me the smell of the farm. Another memory, The Man Of The Lonely Tree standing with his foreboding frame erect in the darkness, staring with unseen eyes in my direction, oh the horror! And the hatred for him bubbling in me. Though I knew why I felt fear, I knew not why I despised him so greatly.

Gradually however, stemming from that image of him, flashes of flirting memories passed by me. The girl who danced by the flames previously sat by my side on a cart, we were in some far off land and she was holding a measly stick in the air, searching for the source of her terror. For a long time I could not link the connection of these fragments to that of the dark figure by the tree, yet when a dreadful memory came to me of indistinct words in the night and fearing for the life of the girl, this Rebecca, my memory as a whole started shaping the pieces of my life again. She was not just a being who would dance in forests and sit by my side in carts, she was the woman I loved, the girl of my dreams and feverish haunted sleep. My one.

With the time of mountain formation, or the so very slow march of the autumn snails my reality pieced itself together. Firstly, I could not move a muscle in my horizontal body and as I tried to open my eyes, a coarse burning mass filled them, blinding my sight with only darkness. Then when I regained more of my bodily sensations, I felt the great weight of something crushing me. And finally, I tasted and smelt soil. Grim Reaper or ghost; The

Man Of The Lonely Tree, The Devil Outside Looking In, whatever he was. Could it be? Surely not. Had he buried me alive?

I questioned my own conclusion. Buried alive? With bloody rage and a bitter anger only a dying man can have, I forced a scream from my gut, taking all the strength that lingered within myself. Of course the scream meant more mud was able to fall its way to the back of my throat, drying my already dry mouth completely; and in turn, leading me to coughing uncontrollably with the impulsive reaction to sit upright. The state of affairs was unbearable, the pain within me alone was harsh enough, but then being dragged ferociously in circles with frenzy and soil was maddeningly torturous. And here still, as far as I was aware I had not drawn a breath since I found myself in the pit. No such thing could be done, every attempt led to the crude thing strangling me. I panicked several times when I thought of the fact I had not taken in any air, yet it was pointless worry, without air, I did not feel necessarily breathless, only numb, and more importantly, I was still conscious.

The weight of all had conquered me. I felt certain I had died. I considered that perhaps I was not even buried alive, just simply buried, and my spirit was trapped in the body as it decomposed; that would have explained why I felt pain in every ounce of my flesh. My body decomposing. I shuddered at the awful thought. I tried again to move and scream but I struggled with both; and the deathly circle of rage and mud came again.

If I had been buried in a coffin like most, then at least I would have had the choice to attempt to scratch my way out, or bang on the inside with the slim chance someone would hear me. The chance to breathe. Yet I had none of these things. Just the throbbing ache of a weak body that I have described to you a thousand times. Tear your limbs apart with some grim torturous device then crush yourself under Ben Nevis, then you may comprehend my plight.

But I ramble. In truth my reader, it is a pain in itself to recall the dull, endless misery of that time, and the confusion of everything unexplained crippled me as much as the earth above me. My dear Rebecca seemed a remote notion to me when I was down there, like that of a peculiar emotion only experienced in childhood and you cannot tell if it was an ancient dream in your life or a dusty antique memory; one that's lasting value to you, you are yet to discover.

Some great time had passed since I regained my initial consciousness in the claustrophobic dark. Eventually I recalled most of my time with Rebecca, our lough and picnics and dances and music; though for all these great memories, all I knew was the grief and despair of her loss. The moment that preyed with most vivid emotion on my fragile mind was the stare we shared on the cart the night we last saw each other. She knew it was the end, deep in those tranquil seas, she knew; it knotted my heart in sorrow when I thought of it. Every time the image came to my thoughts I willed to hold her, to comfort the conflict inside her, but nothing could be done to relieve my dear of the horror. I failed her. Oh I failed her, and I wept for our fate; like Hērō when she discovered the corpse of Leander washed upon the shore. There was no hope, no salvation, no more life to be had. And much like the tragic character, if I had the power within me to end it all, I would have done so.

Perhaps, under the soil of the earth, God could not see me, for He certainly did not smile upon me nor did He answer the prayers I tried to utter.

As I wept bitter tears, my blubbering mouth found itself open many times, filling completely with the tormenting soil that I could not rid myself of. The Devil at his most wicked. The tears that came from my eyes only remained there without gravity to lead its way, liquefying the soil, sticking to the corners of my eyes so infuriatingly. I was so hopeless, so insufferably helpless. The pain, the misery, the fact I could not tell if I was actually alive all flooded out of me, drenching my itching dry head, mixing with the dried blood and solid soil. And the pathetic nature of tears, they help nothing, they do not reverse time, nor could they bring her back to me. They only added another emotion to my already despairing being, the new emotion was a realisation of my own pitiable self, an internal revulsion. For I despised myself when I wept, I despised the moment utterly, tearful seizures are the quickest way to remind one that they are infinitely weak.

But as I say this, I am describing the only time I can recall when I have wept. I did so until my body could take no more, my will to wake buckled from within.

I came to, slowly. I do not know whether it was my extremely deep sleep or exhaustive release of all my negative energy, but I awoke somewhat peaceful. My mind was rational and calm, and instead of weeping over the lost Rebecca, hating the man that had done such and accepting I was going to breathlessly cease to be. I decided it was time I tried to move out of the enclosure.

Firstly, I needed to feel myself as a man again, to clear myself of the discomfort of being only a violated muddy corpse. I began swallowing the compost within my mouth to empty its influence. It took several painful gulps to force it down as it frayed my throat from the inside, like the filth was made only of sharp stones against my tender self. A noise of agony came from my depths but could not fully be released for obvious reasons. Once I had the majority of the soil down me to an extent where I could feel more comfortable, I tried to get a sense of the position of my body. Here it was when I realised I had not been buried fully horizontally, my head was considerably lower in the soil than that of my feet and having a constant rush of blood to the head must surely not have helped my dizzy spells. Once I came to realise this fact, it became a painful frustration that I could not correct.

The racing madness within set me on the great track of doubt that I could not be free of that hole, for all I began to think about was the end of time. That seemed the only destination for my failing body. I fancied volcanic lava would cover the dark Scottish earth before I could climb my way to the surface. The Deity would not help me, I was utterly alone. Being abandoned by no one is infinitely more lonesome than being so by someone. I pitied myself for it, pitied myself more than anything I have ever pitied before. But pity is an hollow emotion, and very rarely does it cause action. The root of the word is lined more to its heritage of combating what appears to be instinctive shame than it does from its bastard line of sympathy.

I had failed my love so terribly. I fell with ease in the eyes of my foe, I did not fight to my last waking moment, reaching for a weapon until my last breath. I did not even die for the cause of my female like the knights of chivalry once did so honourably. But as the disgrace covered my skull with a prolonged sour regret, a sense of life sprinkled through my hands. Tickling the tips of my fingers at first, slowly working its way up until my hands began to shovel the soil about them. More in circles than anything else, however I managed with great effort to funnel the soil that was above them, below; cupping my hands vertically and scooping the soil underneath. And just doing this with my hands, the feeling in my wrists and lower arms came all the more distinct, like water freezing into its solid form. My arms were laid out as far away from each other as possible, and I thought it best, though why I thought this I do not truly know, to bring my arms into my body. Over many periods of wake I tried just that. Slowly slicing my hands through the density and brushing it past myself. My arms itched closer.

Ultimately my arms found themselves by my side. The first touch of myself felt like victory in itself, I moaned with it. As if in that act I had all but freed myself of the place; though it was just the end of the first step.

Once they were by my side I attempted to slide them up onto my face and chest where I could again try to funnel the soil above me to below. Nevertheless in the end, most of it was abandoned at the side of me as I compressed it into the little space that was there. It is important to claim here that I still existed in an almost slumberous reverie of wake. My body moved through desired action yes, but my mind still could react little to the consequences of anything I did; it seemed my actions starved my mind of what little energy did reside in my frame. I moved the clumps from my face and let it settle down the side as I tried to find myself a new platform to rest my head on. It felt wonderful to have space by my face again as the soil above stuck there, creating a tiny cavern. But as I tried to breathe in the air I hoped would exist, there was only nothingness to inhale. Exhausted, I decided to sleep with the comfort that my face had not the pressure the rest of my body suffered.

This only lasted a while, for the weight of the world collapsed under its hollow cavity of support. Crashing onto my face as agonising as anything. I felt like the bones in my nose and skull had shattered, though I know it was not the case. I violently began coughing and screaming. Exhaling and inhaling, soil dropping its persistent self into my orifice. I could only swallow.
I wanted to die again. It passed.

I slept again and woke with positive intentions. I forced the heavy soil that compressed upon my chest to the side and under myself, arching my back as best as I could to get the small amounts as a new platform for myself. Because it was a very gradual process I never realised it happen, but eventually I found my back was nearing a diagonal angle as my legs remained outstretched; as if sitting on my bed back at the farm whilst leaning casually against the wall. Once I recognised my situation and progress, my energy disappeared, I had to rest again. But in moments like these, when movement could not take my mind away from the strife of my existence, the aforementioned tears and sweat stuck the horrid mud to my face and most angering eyes; my anger was for the man who took her from me, not my predicament. I lost myself in a mind of whirlwinds and rain clouds, despair of all despairs.
I came back to myself as if from a nightmare, though the reality I awoke to is no worse than any dream I could have imagined. In some strange way I expected to wake up again, to

find myself in a quaint inn deep in the heart of Scotland. We would be sitting at a wooden table by a cosy fireplace that flickered and crackled through the evening. I almost could smell the drinks on the table with their fine scents, our ornaments. And across from me, my Rebecca would be telling some endearing story as her complexion buzzed with enthusiasm. Delicate bliss.

All was a lost dream.

But more than that, I could not give up on her, the girl who spoke so gently was not in that state, her life was at his mercy. He had whispered his claiming of her to me, and what that meant I could only guess, but I knew her fate with him was infinitely worse than mine. He had followed a cart trail across a border to take a harmless girl, there could have been no small reason. Was she then his prisoner? I had to move, to be free to save her.

I endured the pain once more in the hope I could make my way to the surface. My plan to escape was to continue my funnelling action with my legs to raise them, but with many painful and hopeless attempts I could scarcely do any good with them, there simply was not enough strength to do so. My legs were decaying I thought, withering; but I would not allow them to, not without seeing her one last time. Lacking the ability to progress with my legs, I continued to raise my torso and head.

I could only imagine they had buried me in a shallow pit in the ground, for trying to dig a six foot deep grave and keep Rebecca waiting obediently by my lifeless body, would only be a hassle for them. It would have been in their best interests to bury me enough only not to be seen by anyone passing by. And with this in mind, at this stage, I had raised my head roughly three feet above the level of my lower body, yet I could feel no sense of salvation. No world above me, the void was endless. Had they then buried me all six feet down into the earth? Possibly. Had they buried her too? A thought that had not crossed my mind until then. In panic I screamed her name, but the only answer that came to me was that of the thick mud that plummeted into my mouth. Hushing me with its simple authority. The void of nothingness remained around my arms in that moment and so I was able to pick with my hands the majority of the mass from my mouth, though it seemed like polishing boots with dry faeces. I tried to relax myself but such could not be done, and I had not released my frustration with that solitary scream, I covered my mouth with my hand, screaming until I could no longer. Every exertion of energy felt futile and empty.

"My Rebecca, my sweet darling Rebecca are you buried too? Are you suffocating in an airless arena?"

The mere thought of her alone and scared forced me to action. I began shovelling rapidly with greater urgency than I knew I could. The sweat that formulated was a pleasant feeling on my itching dry skin and I continued without thought, like a madman on a murderous mission.

I somehow found myself in a position where it seemed I was almost able to stand upright; still with little feeling in my legs. I tried to find solid ground to stand upon but there was nothing, I only remained in place from the compressed soil behind my leaning back.

The Hell seemed as endless as the notion of space itself, and as perfectly inescapable as crawling out of time, yet I decided to worm my hands up high above me, to see if I could find the surface. With both hands directly up, reaching for the skies, there still was no surface within my grasp, destroying all the nothingness that was my faith, oh so miserably. I wanted to end myself again, make a noose of the dry earth, whatever could be done; until the image of my Rebecca in the inn came back to me. Her loughs of azure, and smile of allure. My will to know what story it was that she so spoke, what delights she had in store for my ears filled me. Yes continue. I began with thoughtlessness to shuffle directly upwards, but sleep soon took control of me.

I awoke to a strange sound, like the soft peaceful hum of some sensual Goddess of a dead kingdom; quite agreeable, dare I say. But as I moved to a more conscious conviction, it became apparent to me it was the sound of rainfall. I knew not what to think initially, the idea of moisture on my skin would have been Heaven, but on the other hand my sensory orifices would be filled with the damp mess, and there would be no chance of finding myself in airless space. Would it cause me to sink lower, creating a bog about me that I could not free myself of? I panicked and flailed the best I could, thinking it paramount I move as high as possible before the rainfall would ruin my chance of freedom. I extended my arms frantically, wriggling my form ineffectively. The dampness came through the ground slowly, I could feel it around my fingers first, then slowly trickling its way down my arm and onto my face. But I could not be hindered by thoughts, the rain would drown me if I waited a mere moment I told myself.

Then I felt it, the rain drops themselves patting down on my finger tip. My left index finger was out into the surface of the world. I could feel the cold air of an atmosphere and a gentle breeze blowing over. Such an enormous pleasure pulsed through me. I almost died of happiness. I could go on to save Rebecca. I was out alive I thought, as if already dancing on the surface of the world, glee of glee! Then my eyes opened to the awful place I had still not left. And once again the energy that kept me awake through my struggle was slain by the thought I was already free. I had not the strength for the surface, not before sleep. Thankfully caressing my finger was only mild rainfall, I doubted its intensity could cause any hindrance to my efforts.

My feet and ankles were drenched in a quagmire when I awoke and my finger had retracted into its natural state away from the surface. I thought nothing of those facts however, for I had a struggle up to the Heavens that I call earth at hand; and nothing could have stopped me during that period of wake. I reached for the cool and fresh air that I could dimly feel above me but only the tip of my finger could reach. I tried to jump myself higher. And I kept trying for a time I know not how long, however my unresponsive legs and the bog about me rendered it impossible. With my spare hand I tried to find a clump of strong

127

and dense soil that I could use as leverage, a platform to pull myself from. I fumbled and funnelled, finding a stone that was lodge in place well. I pulled myself up through the sticky damp mess, bursting my other hand out into the bubble of the world above. So cold, so wet, and yet it was everything I wanted. I tried to clutch onto the surface for my next platform of leverage. I could not see a thing above me save for a deep blackness that burnt my eyes, still, I pretended to myself that I saw the light at the end of the tunnel to the surface; to true existence. My heart trembled, I was so desperately close...

Chapter II: The Three, The Fog, The Lough

Nocturnally helpless and weak in the light, depending on a prayer

Pacing deserted roads to find a seed of hope

Mikael Åkerfeldt

I could feel the cool air on my forehead in a vibrant bliss. My arm fought its way out into the openness, pulling with all the might in the world and the smallest of sensations. But despite that fact, the world upon my arm felt so real. And squeezing their way to freedom, my shoulder and neck wedged out into the open. I let my upper body flop to the surface as my legs remained in the pit, stopping my movements to let the treasurable moments become reality. The myth of the world above did exist.

The breeze was a slow drift in itself at most, but still, its icy chill scratched at me with sharp tentacles. I adored its free movements as it floating by me, caressing me before flying up into a gap in the trees; I longed for it all over my aching skin. The world with its space and its moisture, its freedom, was mine completely as I lay motionless. With my face in the damp soil and thin grass that tickled my face, I wrinkled my brow, rotated my jaw, feeling the cold further and comparing the sensations in every muscle on my face. The pain did come back to me somewhat when I strained my complexion, but I cared not, the existing world was a remedy in itself. I was in such a deep debilitating love with the atmosphere of the world that I could not possibly pay heed to any agonies of the form, like the love of God had changed the taste of the world, infecting its smell. I wanted to hear the day, to hear birds chirping in the skies and the sound of running water nearby, but all was silent, all was still save for the sounding of the soft winds.

Only my legs had remained in the ground, and it was a simple task to drag them out; deepening my ecstasy of freedom and of existence. There, as I lay on my back, the winds picked up into a gust, whistling past me, I loved the full sound as it pounded into my ears as a real sound, not the dull murdered muffled sounds of the grave. And the moisture within the winds, dense and cool like drinking from the sea of humid liberation, if such a thing could be. I felt like a new-born child as it comes out the mother's womb to breathe in its first taste of air. My lungs filled with a deep, rich and wet inhale as I drank the air of the gods, I sucked it in as if in any moment I would sink into the airless soil again. I had taken for granted the air so easily in my life previously; I almost could not breathe again for the joy and relief I felt. Another thing that I had taken for granted in life was the ability to walk and the freedom of movement. Using my legs one after the other and looking down at the ground knowing you are an agile being, not a slumberous thing that could not get off the floor. But I had achieved my impossible goal, I had thrust myself back into the world, my own morbid renaissance had begun.

I was still not adjusted to the atmosphere of the world, to how freely I could move my arms without a large bulk resisting me above. Beyond such, it seemed that I had forgotten how to move in any human-like manner; and I had no energy to move myself. But for all this strife against me, I cared not, for my hell was over.

Wet mud stuck to me still, locking my hair in clumps, haunting my mouth and eyes. I held onto my thighs and shook them slightly so they could remember their use and feel the muscles they had forgotten; and though it hurt, I was glad to have some sensation back.

I let my torso fall into a comfortable state, crashing to the ground and feeling the vibrations running through my limbs like a tremor before an earthquake. I analysed the impact as if I had never before engaged in the mundane action.

Trying to maintain my composer, I spoke into the soil. 'My God. My Lord, the Son and the Holy Spirit. I pray you help me overcome, I pray you help me find her. I will search until my last breath and beyond! Please oh God, help me, please hear me on this wretched night.' Muteness, mild peace. I opened my eyes slowly, half expected to see the effect of my prayer instantly, hoping, as if God would light his lantern of good fortune for me, the sun. But the world was no different.

I rolled over slightly to get a better sighting of the world around me. It was a densely foggy night, I remember so vividly, the white moisture floated all about the area of a woodland. It was like a snowstorm that would not fall to the ground; though there was no brilliance, just a scentless smoke.

The soil in my throat remained hard to swallow, it was so dry, and I could not shape my tongue correctly to gulp it down; yet the call to drink something had come, the call to relieve my mouth of the dirt and moisten my oesophagus. Once I realised my thirst, my body screamed in a relentless yearn. I opened my mouth and faced it up into the moistened air, but I felt nothing, only saw the moisture within my breath drift from my mouth. I removed the mud clusters from my eyelids and took a few deep breaths, humanising myself, getting back into the stable routine of what that entails. But water soon left my mind for her.

I searched for the road I had so religiously travelled but could not see any sign of it, wherever I looked there was only trees, thick and unending like being lost in the deepest insomniac's desert. "Can we go back to the capital now?" ran through my head, they were taking her to London! However, with that fog, I could not discover which way South was. The fear also came that she could have meant Edinburgh.

I lay my fatigued hands on the ground, brushing the grass across my palms as the greenness tickled me immensely; I was feeling existence again, as well as preparing myself to rise up onto my feet. It seemed the air, the moisture, the vague sense of light had done wonders to my form. I knew I would still struggle to walk, but I felt at least capable of rising to my feet. And I tried. Pushing myself up with determined strength, the sudden free movement pulsed a faint dizziness to my head as it moved two feet off the ground. I closed my eyes quickly, trying not to see the movement that sent me sick, preventing worse. I got to on my hands. The next step was to get my legs to move, to grip the soil, but they only clumsily scraped along the floor; like a rodent being dragged by the tail from the mouth of an impatient feline. I attempted again. And again. In my mind, I tried to force my feet through the soil, knowing that to my then current capability, such a force would only render my feet stable upon the ground. With the tips of my toes roughly controlling my form from toppling down, I managed to plant the rest of my feet down upon the ground. With eyes closed and a mind trying to suppress the idea that I was moving, I raised myself up, standing tall and upright. My knees creaked awfully as I rose, almost making me want to give up and fall down, but I did not surrender. Slowly, my eyes opened to the world, I could very faintly see the moonlight breaking through the trees and fog, creating a white walkway into the treacherous forest.

A step, an arduous one. As I stamped my foot to the ground, the vibrations ran through my leg as if being stuck a mortal blow. I loathed it, though I knew I needed the pain to bring back my sensitivity; like striking an arm crippled with pins and needles. I closed my eyes once more, trying to rid myself of all thought. But I could not, and maintaining my balance proved too complex as an icy chill brushed into me, disabling me to the floor and the air was knocked out of me. For a few moments I could not breathe, and though I panicked initially, it made no difference, I was fine. More distressingly however, I felt so outright hopeless, for even the gentle cold winds could defeat me, and cripple me to an unmoving, unbreathing thing on the floor. What chance had I of saving her?

I ate at the soil my mouth fell on, gnawing aggressively. I can only guess it was the frustration, perhaps it was the collapse of my sanity.

Remember the inn I told myself, I would not allow myself any other fate than to meet her there one day.

I tried to lighten my own moods with thoughts of her, of delight in a mist that I had never seen so strong before. Yet the mist itself was a bittersweet beauty, for all its mysterious splendour it clouded me with uncertainty and isolated me from any sense of belonging in the world. I did not even know where I was. I shouted in a rage that boiled my blood, and heaved in a deep agony; lying with no conviction to do anything but digest soil and scream in helplessness. Bleak and dark existed the night, it shivered through me. And the trees held their own layer of shade from the stars, there was no hope.

Where on earth was I? I recognised not where I lost her in this place. I began to doubt I even remained in the same Scottish wilderness.

Time passed, all strength within my body, and most crucially, my soul, faded. A lesser being would have cried, but I had no sentiment for my lack of walking ability, I had not the time anymore for emotion. Yet for my strength leaving me, the fact I still remained a consciousness thing, was some miracle in itself I thought, and with that, some strength returned.

Onto my feet I willed, and with a real struggle and pain, I did so. The dizziness returned, but like my idea of planting my feet through the ground for a stable footing, I did the same for a stable mind, locking it motionless; again I had no time for faintness or vertigo, for a wandering mind or incoherent thoughts. I had wasted enough time underground.

My steps were slow at first and unbalanced, I had to learn to walk again. Needless to say I failed many times, stumbled down to the damp ground and questioning if it was worth my trying. The white air all about me seemed to laugh in a pitying way, drowning me in its mockery. The trees with their sharp broken branches pointing at me, shaming the mud covered man who was incapable of himself. And I had to accept it, I had to accept that I could not walk. I let the fog and trees win that battle.

'Continue to mock me! Continue to shame me to the most unhappy corner of my mind!' I said, I would just try to crawl away instead.

Like that dying rodent moving to its final resting place, I crawled, the cat known as life had had its horrid game with me; I cannot put it any simpler my reader.

All the nerves in my body pulsed with searing fire, it felt death would be the only release. I should have remained in the ground I thought. I wished and I prayed for the strength to place myself back into the grave I rejected. But in my despair as I aimlessly crawled, I heard the sound of water to my left, and the scent too came more distinctly. The same relief that stole me when I came from the grave stole me once more, my mind grew weak in it, I hurried my crawl.

I do not know how long I crawled, it could have been a matter of minutes, it could have been hours, but with the sole idea of finally reaching clean water narrowly filling my mind, time seemed not to exist, I simply arrived there.

Behind the density of mist and fallen trees, placed with the idea of relieving any wanderer from the unending suffocation, a small loch existed. Pitch black it was in its very depths, though a silver light shimmered off it progressively. Had I been myself I would not have liked such a dark shade of water, like an inky malice, but I would have drank anything in those moments. Over the water, the air had space to breathe and the fog there was much thinner than in the clustered wood, I could just about see to the other side.

I must have been within ten yards of the water, my body aching with desire for my own opium, when something caught my attention. The fog had remained still throughout most of the night, never moving, only lingering fixed in its place. The same I had witnessed out over the eerie loch. Yet floating near the centre of the darkened waters, the fog seemed to move alone, drifting strangely in and out of itself. It was barely a thing worth mentioning when I first noticed it, just an odd draft I assumed however mysterious. Then progressively turning in and out of itself, it appeared to have some design to it. The size of myself I guessed of it as it swayed most absurdly, moving subtly a foot from side to side; it was then that I knew it was of intelligence.

Despite the ache in my neck from holding up my head, my eyes remained fixed on the phenomenon. I was still on my hands and knees but I moved my lumbering body into a more comfortable pose, kneeling, looking out at the fog. The swaying, almost dancing fog in the centre of the water appeared a different shade of white than the rest of the cloth mist. How could that be? Confused was I, with fumbling hands I rubbed my jaded eyes, but that only clouded my sight with further earth. Was the mist gently expanding? No, its vague shape was swiftly coming closer.

My heart dashed ahead of it capabilities, the throbbing nerves in me contracted with a nameless emotion most closely linked to the fear of the unknown. What was it that moved so fast toward me? I strained my eyes again, looking into the depths of the endless shades of white, but the most fine, the most opaque was that of beings. Women. Three Women. Milky pale, seeming to form from the threads of the twisting fog into gradually distinct forms. Garmented in thin white night-gowns, but little more could I define as they hovered over the water with wide aggressive strides. I thought myself hallucinating when I initially defined the smoke as women, "it is just the trick of my weariness" I tried to oppress myself with; but something in the horror of them made the sights undeniable. In my panicked alarm I stood upright, forgetting my debilitated condition, forgetting everything save for the strong stance I tried to radiate, for two of those oncoming women could have been two of the three thieves of Rebecca.

As the swaying shades moved closer, and their figures became more defined, shocked I was to realise the dreadful truth. The three, were ghosts. Only ghost could exist that pale I held; almost the same white as the tasselled gowns they bore, a perfect shining moonlight white. I was too bewildered to truly be disturbed, nonetheless, I knew too perfectly well that if they could, and tried, to harm or abuse me, I had not the strength to yield. I could barely crawl let alone brawl three beings. They were coming closer. They were going to reaching me.

The swaying, that at first appeared a simple side to side motion, little more than a yard, was not swaying at all, or it was, but in the form of something strangely seductive: then they were not to harm me I inferred. Yet when they were close enough that my eyes could see the blank expressions on their shapeless faces that fixed keenly on me, I could not help feel mortally afraid. Running was no option, this was the end, a scream of terror trembled deep inside my loins. I reclined a yard but fought back all other manifestations of anxiety.

It seemed an age before the white mass of cloud that was them reached the end of the loch, but when they did, they placed their hovering bare feet onto the soil. I could see the materialised muscles move with the work of weight, these things were real and of this world. Something else changed in them when they made contact with the earth but a short distance from me, their faces softened somehow, without altering a thing, they did. And because of such, I noticed how plainly luscious they were with their large soft eyes and narrow cheeks. I could not believe my sight. Increasingly from little more than slow movements, they sensuously dance to a melody I could not hear. Their arms turned in the air hypnotically and their hips moved with charm. Circling and prancing, moving directly towards me.

I remained watchful, patient, unsure of any action. A scent distinctly metallic radiated from them, intriguing me brilliantly, what would their starry skin feel like? My heart rushed its beat, my breath too, as a yard separated me and the striking three. They closed the gap between us with the gentle motion I began to crave. Then they divided themselves, one either side of me whilst the other remained in front, I would have felt flanked had I not been taken a fool by the erotic sway; I was, and am, a weak man. The ghosts on either side of me became mirror images of themselves, raising their arms, signalling for both of mine to be outstretched. I could only obey, yet it was with all my pleasure. They pulled up my sleeves gently to reveal my flesh; the ghostly tassels tickling the hairs on the underside of my arms finely. I looked to them both with an unknown delight, and they at me, with curious wills and serene desires. The one forward from me stood dancing to herself, yet her complexion of lust paced across my form.

With swiftness I have never seen, and of them being the cause, irrefutable, the fog swallowed us up in an instant and naught else could be seen. The two that flanked me held my arms with their icy soft hands, a softness no human could have. A softness where the mass almost gave in to the shape of mine, leaving me with the feeling that I was scarcely touched at all. It was something incredible.

The two lowered their faces to my arms as I watched on in rising anticipation. Sniffing me at first, like thirsting savages, before gently with that same inexpressible softness pressing their lips to my arms; like the deepest frost in a liquidised and misty form, oh perfection. Their passion seemed to seep into me with their faint kisses as they slowly worked their way up my arms. I let my head fall slightly, and my breathing too became slower and deeper, as I could only enjoy the moment with its festering ecstasy and obscenity. I filled myself with their arctic life, perfection still.

The frozen being facing me stepped into me with that calm yet desirous stare. She was white as angelic stone, yet the night and moon let dim shadows create her impeccable shape. I looked back into her enchanting eyes, eyes that appeared to have natural shades despite being all white. Yet I struggled to hold my gaze in them, for with her, I felt unbearably weak.

She no longer danced or swayed, only stood with a soothing brilliance. I looked to her bare chest that glittered fine, wanting to see her contours of life; though not wanting anything at all. She raised her delicate hands up to my face, carefully resting them on my cheeks as her tassels dangled over me. The other two had found their ethereal embraces on my upper arms, pleasing ever so. And with quiet conviction the one that stared into my soul puckered herself. It was then that I felt the hunger in me come to the fore with a hoarse and uncomfortable thirst. And in the centre of that hunger was a sort of anger I did not understand. Though it most certainly was not aimed at them, she must have thought it was, because before I knew it, she was gone. All three were.

I looked all around me, even to the skies, but only could I see the density of fog that they brought into the world. Simply as one would assume of ghosts, they vanished. With a wind blowing peacefully, the fog began to dilute. I fell down to the ground and mourned their departure in some sense, and mourned the loneliness of solemn silence upon foreign lands.

Eventually I made it into the loch for the reason I moved there in the first place, to drink, and to clean myself entirely of the filth that awfully clutched to me.

I lay down by the side of the loch, freezing from the bath and the bitterness. I gazed up through the white vastness at the moon, it shone half-full and glorious; and as I often did in my earlier days, I felt I could hear questions of life sung from its being.

My eyes grew heavy, and so too did my head, tiredness was slowly beginning to take control of me. That is when I heard my own mind's words assertively whisper "what are you doing? Rebecca needs you." It came and went in the night with humility, but it affected me like a life altering revelation, with guilt, I could only heed the words. She was the victim, not me, and I lay by a loch daydreaming. Strength found its way inside my veins with those words. From the clearer air and the moon I could gather the direction South was, from that my route was chosen. I moved onto my feet with not nearly the same struggle as previously. A hunched stagger at first, but soon to a purposeful march did I move. My feet began to remember their stride, my arms, their swing.

And I ran. I galloped like my horses could not. Rebecca, my love, I ran for you and you alone. The agony still remained, burning my acid muscles, tormenting my entire nervous system; but I carried on, so much so that I managed, for the most part, to forget. I found the road me and Rebecca travelled on easily enough, it existed just beyond initial sight of my gravesite. And from there, I knew the way at least to Northumberland. I did consider the thought of them burying her with me again, but it seemed implausible they would chase us so far simply to murder and bury her. They surely wished to take her with them to the capital.

The cold fog throughout the night perpetually strengthened then died away again in the winds; and whenever it was that it reached its pinnacle, I thought The Three would return to me. But they never did.

I ran to the height of my ability until dawn, and surprised I was when I noticed the sky growing lighter, I felt the night would never actually end. And whilst the growing grey light in the sky dawned, the fog began to die away completely in the winds. The dimness shone above me to my joy, signalling the end to such a queer night. However the madness was not over yet.

At first sight of the rising sun piercing through the winding woods, I collapsed in the road with unbearable agony. I knew not what the cause was to begin with, but it soon became clear it was the sun's heat that was scolding my tender flesh. I screamed a bloody cry of encroaching death, my God the pain was enough to kill me. I thought my eyes were on fire as I looked to the dim radiance of the sun; and that sensation followed in my limbs and further. Was I really so weak the heat of the sun was enough to harm me? Surely not, I could run. Baffled I was and chaotic with frenzied fear. I panicked, I trembled a humbling defeat, looking towards the sun for the unknown reason, but it only extended my suffering. My sight became lost to yellow and red patches and my aching mind grew heavy as if it were sinking through my skull. For several moments I cowered on the ground, my body tortured endlessly towards its end.

'God why?' I managed to shriek and roar as I was enveloped in imaginary flames.

I opened my eyes desperately, seeing only enough to functionally move, but that was enough. With the most basic survival instincts I crawled behind a thin tree to avoid the sunlight. Unsuccessful, I was still dying of scorching potency. Confusion thumped at my wearied skull as I screamed with fright for my life.

'Rebecca I love you, oh so eternally.' I willed them to be my last words before I died despicably.

With my consciousness on its very verge, my body ripped at the ground, tearing blindly at the soil, burying itself in a last desperate hope to avoid the burning flames of the sun. I did not think for myself in those moments, if I did, my rational mind would not have decided on such a thing. I would have only lingered there and debated the true cause of my pain as I withered away. But my body acted for me. My face burrowed into the soil and somehow I covered myself into the darkness. I fell unconscious immediately, unbearable strife and a lack of air does that to one; yet I seemed to live through such events.

Chapter III: Goodbye My Dear. Forever

But long or short though life may be

'Tis nothing to eternity.

We part below to meet on high

Where blissful ages never die

Emily Brontë

Much like the previous nights, I awoke in a confused daze unable to breathe or see, unable to move; and my agony seared deep within as I wandered in and out of consciousness. You by now should know the state of affairs I describe for you, so on I move with my tale.

It was around the fourth or fifth time I came to knowing consciousness that the thirst and hunger inside myself kept me from falling back to sleep. My insides were empty completely. Not just my stomach of food, but my lungs of air too, I felt like there was an open abyss inside me. I wondered to myself how much time had passed since I had last eaten anything, yet I could not fully comprehend a time scale for anything; how long since I had seen a real person I knew not. I let my body control itself, the survival instinct always labours its job I told myself, I let it do as it wished.

A sound, near me. In the soil. Another slumbering creature, moving ever so slowly near to where I lay. And the hunger. I thought of the fresh meat in the moving thing, my God, I had to eat it! The certainty came over me and into every inch of my being with such an overwhelming, despairing urge to swallow its life-force. I was half disgusted at myself for having such an uncivilised thought enter me, but the other half of me was incapable of coherent thoughts. I simply reached out my limp arm to clutch the thing from its freedom.

I believe, without certainty, that the little creature was a mole. Whatever it was, as I gripped its stubborn self, I could tell in its primitive animal brain that it was magnificently confused by me. Of course he would have been an odd little thing to have expected such a large creature as myself positioned under the soil there with him. His fluffy movement felt bizarre to my scarcely awake fumbling hands. Pulling the thing through the soil towards my mouth, it writhed desperately for a release, but so too did I. My emotions swelled to disgrace, my body itched away as I moved the thing to my face. An awful filthy scent came from its fur, yet my urge did not yield, it could not in the heights of hunger. Reluctantly, with hardily the strength to pierce its skin, I bit into the creatures form. How wretched had I become? Eating animals whilst they were still living. But once my teeth traced through the hairs and the mud and found a taste for what was inside, the overruling savage impulse only increased. Before I knew it I was tearing at it, gnawing at its sides to obtain the taste of meat. I scarcely chewed the strips that fell to the back of my throat in eagerness, and the warm blood along with other liquids pulsed into my mouth oh so beautifully, warm like the delight of a spring-time dawn over a windswept meadow; washing away all the clusters of soil lingering in my mouth. It squealed a horrid sound that died into a hollow dog-like cry before ceasing all together.

Despite the grotesque manner in which I ate, everything of life seemed so simple, I felt the nutrients of the flesh and the organs of the creature enter my depths with high emotion. In the moment it seemed absurd that I had never done so before. The new world of ghosts and fiery dawns was forgotten to me, anxiety left me for the first time since I lost her.

Pushing the empty body as far away as possible, trying to forget it existed, I lay in pure elation. I could feel the fresh meat revive my mind, my body and my soul. I fancied I was weightless, capable of simply floating out of the ground and flying to Eden for my woman and her three serpents.

Yet time always passes, and as a consequence the severity of my actions sunk into my conscience. Guilt formulated around my revived soul. I told myself I was dying, and humans are on top of the food chain, yet savagery is not easily excused by a human mind and eating a living creature is an awful reality. On the farm father would tell us humans are the only animals with souls, but that meant nothing to me, they still felt pain.

With my regret, loneliness too developed quite suddenly, so suddenly that I found it unbearable. Rebecca, where was she? I began to quiver in my chest, in my hands. And something of anxiety began to rise again in my heart. Vomit and claustrophobia gushed from out of me violently. Any thread of optimism that I still clung to was bitterly lost. Chunks of the flesh from the gruesome meal spewed out of me, and with nowhere to be dispersed, it could only rumble over my face and fall a wicked emperor to my mouth.

So miserable. So dejected. I willed myself to unconsciousness.

Fortunately in my psychosis I buried myself only necessarily deep, unlike the night before, and when I found the will to move, I made my way out with relative ease. As I entered the world's real atmosphere once more, it was not the world I awoke to the night before. No shiny whiteness. No loch nearby and nothing of mystery, just the commanding darkness of a bleak night as the gusting winds pounded a terrible sound.

I wiped my face of the vomit on my shirt and wandered the night with dripping soil falling from me. I felt so aimless, no longer a person, just a body that continued to walk itself down the murky dirt roads of the Highlands. My sorrow for my loss was bottomless, and strenuous. I constantly constructed in my head the moment I lost her, wondering how, if at all, I could have defeated our villains. Things seem so simple with hindsight. But in the end, the more I endlessly pondered, and still do, the more I conclude that it does not matter; for hindsight is the foulest thing to emerge from our conception of time. My task then was to accept the fact she had been taken from me for the time being.

Whether it was the burning I suffered the previous dawn, or a more general reply to what my body had gone through I could not move for too long that night, I could not run as my will wished of me. And for this I took many breaks, before moving on again until I could no more. During one of those breaks, I tried to forget all and clear my mind of thoughts, but that proved impossible. A lingering idea that often circled through the front and back of my mind, sending dreadful shivers through me whenever I acknowledged its possibility, was that I was dead. It began to plague me. What other explanation was there for living through being buried alive and unable to breath, only to find a loch of ghosts on the other side?

Dead. I was dead.

What a devastating realisation. I had so much to live for, the new life we were to live, the wealth of spirit we were to find together; and our own children. Yet I was dead. And she was gone. I dropped to my knees and looked up to the sky. To the stars who ridiculed me unfairly with their scouting flickers through the gloomy clouds.

'My God, why?' I asked in a soft tremble, almost afraid to utter those mildly blasphemous words at first. But with merely an exhale separating those words and its repeat, I screamed them in anger. His answer to me was a silent world and a fear for what would become of me followed. Was I to eternally wander the earth as nothing more than a ghostly spectre? I would not accept. And the fate of my love in his hands, I could not.

Once again, I began my attempts to run towards home, and though my legs did give way several time, I managed a finer pace than previously; quietly proud of my progress. The sour ache in my flesh still ravaged of course, nevertheless, I would not let it win in our battle of persistence; not ever I vowed. Every time I collapsed to the floor with unbalance, stumbling and falling awkwardly in every which way possible, I let the pain swell, have

144

its fun and game with me, before I fought my way back onto my feet and continued to move down the road, to England, with as much steady pace as my stamina would allow. At times I could only manage a limp, but then at other times I could manage what a healthy man would call a light jog as barren dry thirst frothed from my mouth. Yet I willed it all to the back of my mind, trying ever so hard to ignore its call for water and sick depravity. The only desire I would answer was my need to reach Rebecca as quickly as my legs could take me.

Numerous nights passed this way, with me travelling South on weak legs and a pacing heart, continuing until the sun barely kissed the sky with its outreaching light, and every dawn, I was scolded almost to the edge of my durability. Every night I tried to keep moving and embrace the light, naïvely believing that after a few days I would become accustomed to the sun's warmth again. But that never happened. With the same panic as always, I found myself desperately tearing at the soil about my feet, nothing could I do but bury my head in the sandy earth. How miserable a state of affairs, but that was my life in those mystic nights.

Where was I running to you might ask, I was travelling back on the roads that had led me North yes, but I have yet to display my plan to you, my reader. I guessed that he had lived relatively near mine and Rebecca's home, that seems obvious enough when I had seen him on my land and witnessed his influence on her on her own land. They could only have chosen Rebecca by a chance meeting, but for The Man Of The Lonely Tree to have stalked us so cunningly, he must have been living locally. I did wonder if searching for his home would be rewarding; if I could find it, perhaps I would find why they were going to the capital, and maybe even his unknown nationality. That was my hope. He had a continental accent, that I knew without doubt, however I knew little more than my own enforcedly taught, well spoken English, Rebecca's more north-western sound, and my local community speech in the North-East. And of the woman's reference to 'the capital', assuming they lived in Northumberland,

and knowing she was an Englishwoman, 'the capital' had to mean London, our capital, not Edinburgh, the capital of the soil we happened to be stood upon at the time. With only these fragments as clues to where she could be, my plan was as follows: I would go to my own home first and try to take some food and clothes without being seen; then I would try to find their home, if at all possible. I would go to Rebecca's home and see if she was there, because if she had escaped, since they were passing South, she most likely would have fled to her home. If I had no luck in Northumberland, then I would have to travel down to London and search for her there. And if London proved fruitless then my last resort was to find the country in which he was from, and try to find them there. Though that was as hopeless as searching for a needle in a haystack, that was my duty to the girl, I would have searched the world for her.

And so it was, I ran and slept in the ground like a mud demon for many days, suppressing my irregular hunger that never came for normal food. A few times on that journey I saw berries growing solemnly from winter bushes, and even though I felt repulsed by the very notion of eating them, I felt I had to as it was grossly unnatural to have gone as long as I had without real nourishment. I picked them into a small handful and reluctantly ate them, however they came back up within but a few moments of my swallowing. And though the mole creature partly came back up too, I felt significantly nourished with him whereas the berries gave me nothing. It was clearly evident that something gravely disturbing was wrong with my hunger, I knew it from the moment I came out of my grave and I fancied a ghost would not have a need or desire to eat anything. Eventually, the day came when I could no longer deny my hunger, as I shall try to explain.

Having moved past Hadrian's Wall a few nights previously and coming close to my own home, I awoke with my strange hunger worse than I had yet experienced. It was painful with perfect conviction, yet hollow and somehow illusive inside me. I repressed myself and found my feet back on the road quickly. But I was not running, the hunger inside me ravaged my strength entirely and all I could manage was little more than exhausted meek steps. That night was fairly warm with compressed air of low grey clouds though not a droplet of rain had fallen; I guessed it was waiting for the sun's companionship to dance its magnitude upon the surface of the world. As I trudged down the increasingly familiar land, with guile crossing my path ten yards ahead, a slight fox scurried, stopping in its tracks half-way across my road. It looked up at me, and I towards it. Through the dark those inquisitive eyes gleamed into me like little orange moons, yet I perceived a trace of fear. And I did feel a deep sorrow for him, I did. As greatly as he tried to hide the melting of his nature from his expression, the usually cunning creature that hunted with perfect brilliance appeared before me frightened at the sight of me. Unsure of moving we both froze still, glaring at one another in wonder.

A warming sensation seemed to bubble inside of me from my stomach, it did so with narrow width that slowly twisted its way up into my chest and spread its heat through me. It was the hunger swelling inside me. An urge to eat the poor startled creature existed on the edge of my control; I was slowly being toppled off the cliffs of sanity into the deep sea of savagery. I was appalled with myself for the thought of eating yet another creature alive, but I could not withstand the craving. I almost wept with apprehension. I contemplated killing him and cooking him over a make-shift fire, yet all I wanted was to eat him as he was, alive. My weight, without my knowing it, had pressed itself forward in eagerness, because of this, I hesitantly stepped an extra yard ahead of myself to regain my balance. That confirmed to me I was going to lose the battle, I had to take him.

My self-control snapped like a twig in the night and I paced for the creature with the fury of a malnourished predator. It coward a few steps before trying to flee my frenzy, but did not get very far. I wrenched at his form with hands of steel and pulled at his warm red fur, salivating beyond cause as he moaned and squealed for escape. I bit into the thick and dirty hair and found his warm meat. I felt like the despicable deity Saturn from the darkened home of Goya gnawing at that small body, yet I could taste things I had never tasted before. Odd yet perfect salts and sweat, and bile bubbling into my skin as I burrowed deeper into him. It was euphoric, I cannot deny it, and I will never forget it as long as I remain. Just like my devouring of the mole, all the confusion, loneliness and misery I had endured since I had lost Rebecca became forgotten in an instant. With that fact and the opiate joy I felt, I knew I could not suppress the peculiar and barbaric hunger again. It seemed some kind of sin to me, but it was the only pleasure reachable for me in that time. His struggle dimmed quickly, but his life did not, and as he turned his stare my way, almost melancholically, I imagined he realised the pain he had given others before him; yet he knew how unbearably perfect the moment was for me.

Little remained of him by the end, fluids of all shades flooded onto the road from the contorted sack of bones and dishevelled organs; I could not help but stare at the ruin. The blood on my hands and face that turned cold in the wind was real. The creature was unrecognisable to what he had been but minutes before, and that quickly, his life-force was extinguished. I wonder if Saturn too felt guilt afterwards. I found the horror of it all soul-destroying, I even pushed him in attempt to wake him, hoping to reverse my act, but it did not work. We both found ourselves crossing paths for the same reason, our loved ones. I in the name of Rebecca, but with him mother and cubs would be waiting for his return with food. Yet they had already seen him for the last time, and the harshness of winter was only setting in. They did not deserve my actions. In those moments of reflection, an abrupt pain surged in my chest, causing me to retch violently. Vomit heaved out of me and splattered over us and the road. I could not endure any of it. I whimpered a desire to be anywhere else. Not covered in mud and sick next to a cadaver. I had had enough of whatever my new lowly existence was.

Moving to a tree by the road, I dug a hole in the stiff manner that becomes of us when we are in deep despair. The mind turns in on itself and facial expressions turn blank; the body without direction from above simply gets its work done. The night was still young, but the thought of staying awake a moment longer was intolerable, I was sick to my stomach of existing. And so underground I went, without thought of my duty to save Rebecca. And sleep came to me before long.

I awoke in a rut, my eyes opened naturally when consciousness came back to me, thus vexingly soil filled my eyes; and claustrophobia tinged when my reactions were denied.

I climbed to the surface soon enough. Down the road I moved again as the breeze caressed my face. But however much I tried to imagine the winds affection was The Three touching me, loneliness bore me as its defenceless victim; I fell to the floor without the will to get back to my feet. I realised I had not seen a real human since I had risen from my grave, and how long had that been? It felt like half a year. So close to my former home I was, to my family, and yet I felt further away than ever. Reaching my destination was unimaginable, like I would finally arrive on the land of my birth to find no buildings there anymore; I felt lost in all ways but the literal sense. I looked to the darkened sea of clouds above, to the rolling fields of our northern meadows as a few trees were scattered about threatening and tall, creating each their own menacing shadows and sizes; yes I was home. Everything around me was so picturesque, yet a wholesome solace swallowed me. I looked upon my homelands but I felt the desolation of being in an endless desert.

I lay in middle of the road, thinking of her, dreaming of her. I wondered if they had killed her, but I kept telling myself he would not have chased her so far to simply kill her like a common murderer. Still, his real reason for chasing her so far was something I wished not to speculate. Then to the sister that was less than a night's journey away my mind turned; Mary, a being that I missed dearly. Being so focused on myself and Rebecca, I had not given any thought to her; however the thought of seeing her that night gave me the courage to continue when all else of happiness seemed irretrievable and far. I took several moments to gather myself before finding my way back to my feet. I moved with tiresome effort to see her, but one I would not give up on.

Over the gentle hills I went until at last, I looked over my family land once again. It seemed like a surreal dream. When I left I assumed I would never see it again, and yet there it lay with candles and the fireplace in the parlour radiating a warm household. I ran the distance to our closest field instantly, filled with an unnamed feeling. It was a pure desire, there was nothing else in life to speak or think of, I had to be stood upon our land, to have my feet past the threshold of legal property. And once I had done so, my knees buckled from underneath me and I lay down awkwardly, burrowing my hands into the ground; into my father's work that once had been mine. I was home again, and I felt wonderful, I really did.

But when I came back to myself, I looked up slowly, and with perfect clarity I saw on the far side of the field, directly forward from me, The Lonely Tree. It stood slightly hunched on one side and foreboding in the dark, bowing down as if waiting to whisper its own riddle to me. I willed its whispering words, hoping it knew something of my villain who seemed to trust it so. I moved to The Lonely Tree and stood under it, looking up at its claws with wonder and mystery, yet it did not speak.

A strange feeling came over me. I felt as if something was watching me. I looked into the night to see if he was here again, by his ever-trusty tree. But it was not them that watched me, it was Jonathon from the kitchen window; seeing a silhouetted male figure stood by The Lonely Tree. I felt cold quite suddenly. Yet all I could do was jump behind the tree and watch him peering into the night. He stayed for several moments, watching with the certainty I once had of someone being there. When he disappeared from sight, I knew it was only a matter of time before he would be out by the tree searching for me, and probably yielding a weapon like I did. I had to move fast. With my failing body I ran as low and fast as I could back off my father's land, and watched for Jonathon from behind a hedge.

No short time passed before I saw a lantern held high in the air, and a man wielding a cane over his shoulder coming to see if he could see anyone. He stomped with driven feet and looked about in every direction, straining his eyes to the night, but not seeing anything that could confirm what he saw. Thankfully he had not looked for footprints, when I was him I was dealing with beings that seemed to appear and reappear at will, therefore footprints were fruitless, but he was searching for a weak limping thing. And I was not sure what was worse, him finding and striking me with his cane, or him finding his weak brother in the fields and bringing him back to their father. I could only imagine what father would have done to me had events turned that way.

I found watching Jonathon quite fascinating. He was the first real human I had seen since my ill-fated night, and he seemed magnificent. His broad shoulders and arms whilst holding his weapon presented a humble power to the world.

In the end, Jonathon went back to the house without much of a search, shaking his head and mumbling to himself as he went back. I waited a long time before daring to move closer again. I looked into every window for long periods trying to judge if anyone was there, particularly the dark rooms where I fancied Jonathon would be sat patiently on guard. I was not sure if he truly believed what he had seen, or if he had gone to see only because I had spoken to him about a man by the same tree. Either way, when I felt safe no one was watching me, I crawled my way slowly to the house.

Once I came fairly close to the building, I heard faintly yet with distinct clarity, the sound of feminine tears. I remained hiding in the shadows, but crept up alongside the house and worked my way round to where I could hear her, and stopped outside our open window. My experience with Jonathon told me perfectly not to risk being seen with Mary; but there was no choice in the matter that I had to see her myself.

Silently I moved my head to the window, peering in timidly and hoping that she was sat on her bed, which would mean she would be facing the other way; and she was. The sight I saw, to my torment, was of her weeping harsh and bitter tears as she held her hands up to her eyes as if to hide the surrender from herself.

It broke my heart to see her like that. I ached to jump in and comfort her, to hold my baby sister and tell her whatever it was she needed to hear. But I could not promise her conversation of peace. She would surely have questions and I would not have pleasant answers: Rebecca had been claimed by a demon and I believed I had died? What comfort could the ghost of her brother be when she believed me to be alive?

My mind whirled with grief and knotted itself in tangles. And I had travelled so far, my feet were wearied. I sat myself below the window with small release as her laments and sighs distressed me. It began as nothing, only a flicker of candlelight in the depths of a valley, yet that queer, ravenous and savage hunger crept up on me with hardly me knowing. Very quickly my stomach pained in stark and unbearable emptiness, it took all my strength to not groan aloud. Rest was not yet mine and I moved quickly for the kitchen, hoping to relieve my hunger with some bread by climbing through the window quietly.

I did so to perfection, creeping along the side of the house with my head low and out of sight; though no one seemed to be out of their chambers. I pulled the latch of the window and sneaked in, stepping softly on the counter and down to the ground without so much as disturbing the air. After retrieving some bread and cheese I wiped my muddy footprints away and climbed back out, carefully placing the latch back as I found it.

The smell of both items nauseated me worryingly however. Though I knew they were not, they felt rotten to me as if they should have been drowning in mould. But I knew I had to eat something real, and I ate them with the haste of a starving pig. It was a bizarre experience, I felt like I was eating tree bark. I tried to ignore it, and focused my thoughts on the relief of eating moderately civilised food again, even if in an uncivilised manner.

Not long after I devoured the meal of stale bread and mouldy cheese a regurgitation I could not supress came over me. Yet by it I felt more curiosity than pity for myself; curiosity how without fail, every time I had consumed something since I came from my grave I could not keep it down. My mind turned to the ghosts then, the somewhat immaterial entities. Surely they did not eat, and perhaps I was not supposed to either; and my cravings of hunger were just my body remembering its human needs. I knew nothing of the matter, but that seemed a reasonable guess. Indeed nothing seemed to make sense in that chapter of my life. The world had been flipped on its head and broke its neck as a result; and like a common thief, I was outside my own house having to steal food. I felt the need to see Mary again, and without thought for the problems I would cause us both if she saw me, I moved back to our window and stood with my forehead pressed up against the wintry condensation. I longed for her. I longed for one of her long mothering embraces that always washed away my troubles.

At that moment she had for the most part relieved herself of her tears and sat trying to gather her composure. With slow elegance, she raised her handkerchief to her face and dabbed her eyes. I fancied I could hear her lethargic heart beating a beautiful throbbing thunder; and I noticed mine pounding itself faster and faster in unease as my hunger rose again. She only scratched her arm as mundane as ever, but it turned my mind to the flesh underneath her skin. And its heat and its potential. I could feel myself beginning to salivate and it sickened me. But I found myself shaking with desire, and sin. I closed my eyes in hope of losing the unthinkable thoughts I began to think, but it was useless, my mind only knew of famine; and she was defencelessly alone. I challenged myself to consciously lower my pulse to her calmer beat; I trembled and squeezed my knuckles into my palm, but managed to do so. As I gathered myself together I raised my hand to the glass and whispered softly 'goodbye my dear. Forever' then rushed swiftly away, over the hills and as far away from her as possible.

I ran and ran and ran with a thousand emotions swelling my sanity, though predominantly it was loathing that I felt, loathing for what I had become. And I hoped not to come across anyone, for my restraint was wearing thin and I feared I had not the strength to resist another encounter with someone.

I found myself standing in the middle of a field half-way between mine and Rebecca's houses, there I screamed as loud as my body would allow straight from the agonising depths of my soul. The hideous noise that came from me as I pounded at the ground even frightened myself. Why had my life come to deprave hunger for kin? It was incomprehensible, I thought I had to be dreaming. With a prayer for my maker, I pleaded for him to wake me from the desolate wasteland of Hell. I looked into the skies and the clouds with a questioning of him, waiting for him to awaken me.

Nothing. As ever when I prayed in my deepest despairs, there never was any guidance. I cursed his name for the first time in my life. And for all the anger I screamed to him, he showed not himself. He only mocked me with his silence. How could I not question his existence? He had apparently spoken to those with lesser issues yet he cared not for my plight. I could only conclude that throughout life I had delved too deeply, and squandered the obvious and bleak fact, that there is absolutely nothing.

I gathered my thoughts, my will. Lying there had killed my hunger from desperation to a neediness; delicately, I placed myself upright, balancing patiently before wandering on without direction. But I was not aimless, I wandered for a purpose, yet I pushed it to the back of my mind until absolutely necessary, I was searching for an animal. Three or four fields I moved through before eventually two field mice crawled my way, almost as if they did not notice me. I knelt down quickly, grabbing them both and biting into their little frames; disgusted at myself whilst doing so. After the agonising experience with Mary, I scorned the notion of consuming life; yet however much so I despised it, I was in some way relieved I would satisfy my cravings, even if only minutely, and know I could last the night without turning back and ultimately harming Mary.

With my hunger quenched I paced myself at my highest speed to reach Rebecca's house. I had felt such love and joy at travelling there on so many occasions, but that time, only a sense of diabolic circumstance went through my mind.

I reached her home with little of the night to spare. But as the house came within my sight, I knew something was not as it should be. As I looked down at the stately home the front door was wide open, swaying in the subtle winds as its creaking hinges moaned in the night and no light could be seen through any of the windows. It looked as if it had been abandoned altogether. A cold chill ran through my spine, but I had to continue.

I stepped down towards the morbid scene cautiously. Initially fearing terribly the devils were inside, but increasingly hoping they were, for she would be with them. But I also thought of frightened parents, searching for their lost daughter, and in desperation to be out searching for her, their minds lapsed in shutting the door.

I heard nothing as I came to the property and peered inside. Everything appeared in its place as it should have been, but a hideous atmosphere radiated from within. Warily, I drifted beyond the threshold and into the home that I had never been welcome in. I navigated through several delicate and ornate rooms that in any other circumstance would have filled me with marvel, yet I felt a strong murkiness as if the walls were painted with it; and the thick tapestries abjectly guarded the starlight from the gloom. As I opened them for some light, the disturbed air revealed to me a thick scent that enveloped me. And I knew the scent. Dried blood. What ill monstrosity awaited me I could not guess. I wanted not to step another yard, no good would come of it I thought, yet I knew I had to. For the sake of Rebecca, I had not the time for emotions spawning inhibitions. I entered the room I fancied the smell was coming from unnervingly, lit only by the starlight from the room behind me and listened for the breathing of anything hiding in the darkness. On the carpet near the centre of the large room, lay a dried pool of crimson and half a dozen sickly rats scurried by, sniffing at the stain. And from that stain, a trail led to the corner of the room where lay the gruesome cause. A man, drenched in his own putrid and crispy blood that for the most part was dry. Of the man's ghastly face, it was her father's; lifelessly pale as horrid patches of decay corrupted here and there. I gasped at the sight. He was still in the majority of his form, which made it all the more horrific, for a black leathered corpse would at least have spared me the semblance of a man. But his eyes still showed the decisive terror he died with.

The sight of a human being that far in decay is an experience I wanted to die having never felt. I had no care for the man in life, as you know, and though I wished a similar death to her thieves, I could not wish it on anyone else, not even a man I labelled a beast.

I remained still, peering over at him until I eventually gathered the courage to move closer. I knelt down by his side watchfully, as if he would flap back on his feet and kill me at any second. His chest had bled substantially through his torn white shirt that had turned a thick claret; his arms and cranium also had bled fairly. His head wound was clearly caused by the strike of a dull-ended weapon, but his chest and arms were more of a puzzling tale. It seemed he had been mutilated before the rats had come to him; and the sections where he had bled, were the sections where the majority of his matter was unaccounted for. I took in a deep breath and closed my eyes, uttering almost nonsensically to myself, again for a waking from the world.

Then I thought of him, and of saying something for him.

'Rest in peace. May you be beyond the gates of Saint Peter forevermore.' Silence. The night waned on.

An apprehension came to me that I too should have been lying in the lush meadows of Heaven; but for some reason I had remained. I sighed miserably before pacing up and down; my way of preventing tears and keeping my fear at a distance. I itched to close his appalling shallow eyes that seemed to watch me as I moved about the room, yet I could not bring myself to touch him, not even for an act of respect.

I sat myself at the wooden desk on the far side of the room, positioning my back to him and trying to dissolve my horror. But what did this man's death mean? They had come for Rebecca and seeing she was not there to be claimed, they decided to kill the other residents in frustration? Though I knew not how many days had passed since we had left together, the body seemed in too early a stage of decay for that to be the case. Yet why else would he have died in such a violent madness if not murdered by the same heartless demons? It had to be them that had killed him. I was certain, but in that conclusion we were both killed for her, yet I continued on and he did not. Why that was I could not fathom.

In the end my guess for the tale of him, was that on their way down to the capital they had passed through Northumberland and killed the captive's family, meaning the mother would be dead in another room; and this was most likely all committed in front of Rebecca. I trembled and winced at the thought, in that very room she had probably wailed in horror and thought I was still buried in the ground, never to rise. I had to reach her, I had to save her from her torment.

In the corner of my eye I glanced to him once more as he stared at me with that horrendous complexion; he was calculating his ability to pounce and murder me when my back was turned, I could feel it in him. Yet as I kept my eyes on him, I contemplated his death and mine. We both were the same human flesh. I, like him, was too substantial to be a ghost; The Three were of some substance softer than us. I hit my hand on the desk to test my own existence, I was real, too real to be incorporeal.

Life in those moments was as insufferable as I can ever recall. Death is the only certainty in life, and no one truly realises it until its cold decomposing leathery face stares you in the eyes incessantly. I had to leave the place. I had witnessed enough foul tragedy for a lifetime, but more vitally, she was not there. She would not have left him to rot had she been there with her own sovereignty.

'I will avenge you, and your lost daughter. By my hand, your murderers will be brought to their just demise.' I spoke towards his hideous face, before running off into the twilight with a burning desire to exert my will. I did not stop until I could no longer endure the sun's rising.

Chapter IV: The Yorkshire Creature

Fair speech may hide a foul heart

J.R.R. Tolkien

I awoke from an abominable existence threatening the lives of those I loved, only to find myself in the empty pit of purgatory; and I knew from that night on, whatever it was that could possess me to deliberate such a violation of kin, whatever foul madness had become of me, was gravely despicable, and I fancied it would never desert me in peace.

The start of the new night was thick with bereavement, I thought of Mary and her tears, the sister I would never see again. I also thought of the dead father who had lain in his own dried blood and the stare that emancipated from his harsh eyes. Yes I was indeed in purgatory, limbo, some grim realm between life and death, sighting those I had once known distinctly in life yet they were completely transformed into nothing but flesh and bones. Everything around me was in the same shape, planted in the same soil as I had known, yet the very soul of nature had turned black with morbidity.

I knew not the road to London, only a road that continued down into Yorkshire, which I guessed would continue further South. They would have walked themselves, I guessed, a party of at least four would not be able to move with speeds, not when one is captive, and so my hope was to advance on them and catch them before they reached the capital. Yet if they had already reached their destination, I would have to find them there. I ran half a dozen nights, going as cunningly and patiently as I knew my search needed to be.

The woe of her loss still tormented me of course, but a major alteration in my life that drew me somewhat deeper than such grief, was the lack of sunlight. I seemed to awake within a black sky and have it not change until a few moments before I slept in filth, waking only to the same endless darkness. Time no longer existed in those skies, and when time seemingly no longer exists, life only becomes a dream-like blur fading into an unifying madness. Further still, when I did return to the world from the grave, anxiety bubbled in my chest when I found the surface, only to realise that yet again, I had missed the day. I was forever to miss the sunlight it seemed.

One cold night, as I moved down my winding country roads the same as any other, as the endless line of forest around the barriers of my path began to mellow into further open space, I could look over the land in which I was to travel. I enjoyed how the contours of the earth seemed to drift into moderate valleys, before some several miles into the distance those plains of grass reached the same height that I stood upon. I wondered if the earth that lumbered silently below the vast horizon was increasingly becoming the notorious moors. If not, perhaps I was to pass through at some point. That night the sky was a strange shade of blue with a slight fog, hardly noticeable without a keen eye, but the mild mist gave the air a lighter tone as so often frosts can do on wintery nights; forming a new genre of daylight that I cherished.

Those crafty trees that did guide my path swayed in the wild winds upon those high lands, creating frightening silhouettes in the moonlight upon the overgrown fields, stretching out beyond sight in the mist. I had been moving but a short while, in relative quiet, before I heard in the distance behind me, travelling on the road, the plodding and clicking of several horses' steps to a wearied rhythm. All thoughts came and went through me like a flash of lightning in the realm of my mind. I stopped in disbelief, and in curiosity; for on my lonely road I had not seen a sign of mankind, nothing since I was in her home. Now one such being came. What scheming criminal would it be moving my way? Only those men would travel these roads at night with a dull struggle in the steps of its disobedient beasts that wished to go no further. I turned to face the oncoming thing with as much anxiety as anticipation; I held my ground in the middle of the road, awaiting the arrival. A faint scent of horse trickled through the air to me, dancing its memories of my own horses; my own carting adventures.

Crawling out of the smoke, a figure approached, forming more distinct with decreasing distance. A darkened carriage it was, swaying to and fro on the rough road from its four horses. And yielding the reins motionlessly on the dark square mass sat a black shadowed figure by a solitary candle; from a distance I could articulate nothing more of him. He in the gloomy night appeared much like the man that took my lady from me, but somehow, based more in faith than thought, I did not think it was him. As I looked, I calculated against the reluctant stallions that his frame would be somewhat larger than mine, again similar to that wretched being, but perhaps the sense of calm sophistication that inaudibly roared from this man into me rendered him beyond the dark menace that stole her. The wheels chugged on in the dirt road, the horses stepped closer. Closer.

The carriage behind him looked simple at best. It appeared black in the dark but as it drew nearer it became clear to me that it was made of a dark wood; and peculiarly the windows I noticed on one side had been covered up completely. Brooding serenity I felt, but it seemed false somehow, who was this faceless merchant? Nervous I became as to his motives, I stood ready for confrontation but hoping for otherwise. Ten feet away from me he ended the drifting advance; the beasts sighed to themselves a cold breath as the man stood up and called
'Morning' in a deep tall man's Yorkshire voice.
'Morning?' I replied with a questioning.
'It is morning to people like us, or something along those lines.' He had a voice and certain manner that sprang out intelligence as he spoke. He stepped down from the height and approached me. Pulling down his black hood, he revealed his face to me and looked down upon me. I saw a man of around forty years of age. The lines of wisdom were forming under his fairly long unkempt hair which was brown nearing black as a goatee of a similar tone

surrounded his mouth. Yet the eyes were the most striking of his features, they were small but commanding, dark and glaring; and worrisome when he held his gaze upon me for a few moments. I could not be certain of him, though I continued our speech.

'People like us?'

'Let us not bog ourselves with these little formalities my friend, you know what I mean. We are both dead. And we are cannibals.' Such tragic and vile words he uttered simply, inferring barbarism of me with little care. I would not allow such, no one would judge me of cannibalism. I had come close yes, but such an horrific act I had not done, and I would not accept being called such by a stranger who knew me not, what grounds did he have to accuse me of cannibalism?

'I am no cannibal' I called with a sharp tone, staring deep into his blank soul and trying to unnerve his conviction. I failed.

'Give it time my friend, give it time.' He was quite a few inches taller than me anyhow, but his sturdy black boots caused him to tower over me menacingly. I tried to stand up to him as an equal, the slender man who stood in his black trousers, grey shirt with a tie, and long black coat. He offered his hand to me.

'Mr Edgar Horn, 'tis a pleasure' he spoke as a warm smile formed on the right side of his face.

'Mr Robert Fletcher, nice to meet you' I shook his gentle hand politely.

'Well Mr Fletcher, I see you are travelling South, and you were running earlier. Would you like a carriage ride and some company on the way?' The dark eyes remained the silent image of evil, yet he spoke with an etiquette I could not refuse; and his stance was that of a reserved, honest man. I looked to his coat and imagined it closed, considering if he was dressed similar to those wraith-like things that stole Rebecca, and he was. Yet still, something irrational made me trust him. This Yorkshire Creature seemed quite courteous.

'That would be swell and most kind of you Mr Horn.' Replied I, and that minute smile on the side of his face formed once again, before speaking

'You must be tired from all that running. Come…' he turned back to his carriage, casually strolling then sitting on the bench outside, holding the reins. I sat myself beside him on the cushioned surface as he so gestured. We rode off pleasantly.

A few moments of silence passed.

'How long has it been since you died?' He muttered quietly. I looked to him with natural reaction as anyone would, but the stare he reciprocated with pierced right into my soul's depths. He made me feel uneasy. The man was like a caged demon trying to hide his cannibalistic barbarism behind an insignificant black tie. It reminded me of what father used to say to us, "a man can get away with any crime as long as he wears a suit." But of the man's question, I sighed in defeat, the reality I had died was still a dreadful truth I could not comprehend. When I was wandering on my lonesome I could easily push it away to the dustiest corners of my mind, yet at that moment, when the creature asked me such a direct question on the truth, there was no evading. I had to engage and accept the truth.

'I could not tell you sorry. A couple months? Maybe longer. I have been falling in and out of consciousness.'

'Same happened to me my friend, fortunately I knew the date I died and the date I regained my wake in its entirety. It was three weeks for me. If you were anything like me then it would have been about three also.' He spoke gazing from me to the outstretched land. He was at peace.

Three weeks. If I had been in the ground that long before I found true consciousness, plus the time it took me to reach out into the surface, coupled with my time moving South, then they had had Rebecca for surely over two months. My heart sunk, she surely suffered greatly in that time. I thought of asking The Yorkshire Creature of her

'Have you seen a young woman within the last two months? Taken by demons, or ghosts, I think.' I forced as friendly a manner as I could within my desperation.

'No I am sorry. You are the only person I have seen for quite some time.' He became silent in thought; and the hope of her died in me as quickly as it had formulated. That sunken-heart feeling returned.

'Your woman, she was?' He continued rather sincerely.

'Yes. Rebecca was her name.' I could see in his complexion the second he took to sink the name in his memory, a moment of respect for my loss.

'Tell me about her?' A feign smile I showed him, his beam told me to cherish what my words were about to tell. I just wanted her back in my arms.

'Rebecca was the most wilful being I have ever known. So wilful she suffered much from her father for our love, and with hardly a word of complaint. Her will and love had me camping our way to Scotland in the dead of winter. But I would do anything for her. She was my angel that God sent to me, I know that, or at least I did. Before I died. She was simply beautiful; with tranquil bright eyes. She *is* my reason, my one; my life and fate. And oh, the way she danced as her golden tresses swayed about the air. We were about to start a new life together...'

'Before they took her from you?'

'Yes.' He had a look about him through his coarse hair, as though he knew not words to speak. His eyes just flickered here and there about me, trying to understand my emotion, before seemingly dismissively fixing his eyes on the road ahead.

'Are you hungry?' He enquired.

'Oh no, I could not eat' I replied in a careless manner, though my thoughts were disturbed by his previous accusation of cannibalism. What in the name of all things sacred would he have offered me had I whispered positively? Those cold black voids turned to me eerily slow, looking directly into me again

'You know, you have to eat eventually.' I shared the glance for an instant only, I could not peer into those reflective things. I could not accept that path of barbarism for myself, it was grotesque. The word 'cannibal' was only disgraceful. I thought of the pleasure that pulsed through me when I ate the fox alive, how I felt that I could no longer resist my urges for such satisfaction, but not cannibalism. Foxes were one thing, humans were simply beyond any ethical code I would adhere to.

'I was like you' he spoke with artless and hoarse words, 'I would not accept the truth either. And good for you, it is very noble indeed. I assume you had a beautiful moral frame before you died. But you will eventually succumb to the cravings. And it will not be in any way pleasant for you, or your victim. But once it is done, you can move on through life. And let the guilt fade.'

'I am no cannibal' I repeated, this time with a harsher and louder tone.

'Alright Fletcher, I mean not to offend or cause distress.' And I believed him, he had sincerity in him although I could not place why I thought so. And with that, in my anger I had spoken out of turn, and had offended him. I tried to rectify my doing.

'I am sorry. Thank you for your company Mr Horn. I appreciate having a person to talk to, I have been losing all sense of sanity.'

'I know Fletcher, I too felt that, and still do. For me it never seemed to fade, I just learnt how to cope with it. I believe once we die, sanity is no longer accessible. To think and remain in the shell of our bodies beyond death is unfathomable to any being with sanity. What would Descartes have thought? Cogitare Ergo Mortuus Sum?'

We rode for quite some time on our winding road as it came and fell down the hills. But eventually we stopped for an hour or so to let the horses rest and chew on the rough grass. We found ourselves wandering gently uphill about the meadows

'Mr Edgar Horn, have you ever seen a ghost?'

'No. As far as I am aware. Why, have you?'

'Yes. And I am unsure as to how many. I saw three come out of a loch a matter of weeks ago. They were not impious as such, but ghostly temptresses, and the moment they took me from myself, they vanished into nothingness.'

'O' in that deep voice was his instant reply. His small eyes seemed to scamper around the darkness for understanding; a man who had more knowledge of our existence than me seemed surprised to hear an account of the reality of ghosts. He straightened his stance and looked over me, the wind drove through the back of him and into me wildly, I hid behind him to shield myself.

'This world sometimes throws things at you, in which you do not know how to interpret.' He had an aura about him, sort of unpretentious and yet bursting with power and intellect. I sensed a man who was content in himself and yet irreversibly damaged inside. But the most admirable of all that I saw in him was his humility. The type of man I had yearned to meet when I was alive. But that was the past, in this life, whatever I had become, I had met him now, and I was truly glad to have done so in spite of the awful black ice that was his eyes. He spoke again trying to comprehend my revealed truth, 'ghosts you say?'

'I do. Pale in sight, and oddly metallic in scent; soft like a thing I have never felt. Have you borne witness to any queer creatures in the night?'

'A dragon'

'A dragon?!'

'A dragon yes. In the distance over the North Sea.' Ghosts were one thing to discover as truth, but rationally they could have been argued as lost, sour human souls; but a dragon can have no unassuming explanation, they were completely mythical to my equilibrium except for the father I once knew.

'Dragons exist?'

'Yes I believe so, I question myself as you do now. But I cannot reach a conclusion other than it was in fact a dragon. I was not dreaming. It was there my friend.' Dragons flying our skies, how terrific and terrifying at the same time. What could I say? I was more dumbfounded at this knowledge than I was when I saw with my own aching eyes the ghost women.

'I think I would like to see a dragon sometime.'

'Frightening' he muttered. This all came with an implication to me, an implication of other beings, what other beings could wander and fly and float about the night?

Our conversation came to a halt for a short while, he seemed fascinated by the wild land lightly sloping down as we reached its height. And I was thinking of all he had told me in the short time we had spoken, a sort of inner reflection of the conversation if you will.

Always my mind returned to the last moment I saw my Rebecca, the slightest of smiles that traced across her face, she was some long ago dream now. But my companion in offering his carriage had become my dream-catcher. I still had some fortune.

I looked his direction in my melancholy as the wind still harmed my eyes. He stared behind me into the distance as his eyes twitched at something ahead. I could see nothing.
'The sun will dawn before long. I must eat before we sleep Fletcher. Are you sure you do not want to eat? You get hungry my friend, and then it is harder to control yourself.' I knew he was right. That was unquestionable. But I could hardly bear to eat another live animal, doing the same to a human was simply out of the question. I would not. He must have seen in me a scared child as I sat frozen and deliberated an answer to his question, but I knew not how to answer. And all he said to me was 'let us get back to the carriage.'

We walked back calmly. He never once pressed me for the answer, but I thought of every possible excuse why I would not go with him. It seemed like a fair walk when we moved away, but on the journey back it seemed but an anxious minute before we stood next to the carriage in the soil. He faced my direction but his attention was elsewhere. I had to speak.
'I wish I had the mental strength to join you. But I know I do not.' His tiny eyes darted my way as if sprung from his focus, gazing at me with slight empathy, his tall stance seemed to melt with my words and he became an equal to me. He placed his soft hand on my shoulder.
'My friend, do not concern yourself for tonight, I shall go alone. Hopefully you will join me to-morrow night. For now stay with the carriage, I shall return before long.' I almost saw a complexion of kindliness in his dark brow, before he walked away with evil conviction emancipating from his presence towards what looked like a small home.

I sat back on the carriage frightened he would turn around and bring his sinister will upon me. I watched him disappear down the hill and become a mere speck in the shadows, and only when he was out of sight could I rest my head back. It fell hard on the wood, but I cared not, for the solitude and silence was glorious and sweet, and for the first time since that tragic night, I could rest by my own accord.

I was centre piece to two fields on either side of me, some trees lay scattered but in general it was open land. The fatal truth I try to explain is this, that sound could travel far up to me. And the world had ceased its windy breathing. I loved the stillness, the silence, as if the anxious stress of my new life had left me so calmly in that passing breeze. Years passed in these moments, I drifted towards sleep.

A shriek.

A loud female scream of horror pierced my ears, and I awoke abruptly. Immediately following it I heard a deep guttural moan by that same woman as if she was unable to repeat her first frightened noise. Gravity pulled my flittering dreams back down into the reality of life; I knew it was him. My new and only friend, he was doubtlessly eating her flesh alive that second. Such depravity revolted me, sending shivers of disgust to harass my brittle skin.

I tried not to judge or condemn him for such vile behaviour, for that would most likely be me before long; but it is only condemnable. The longer I did not eat he told me, the harder it would be for me to contain such will. The meaning behind such simple words haunted me. I tried to accept my fate, but her shrill screams were resounding in my head, repeating themselves like a chorus of every wretched fear imaginable. I loathed it. I wanted to fade into another realm and escape him entirely. But I could not move. I felt the need to stand, to scratch, to strike something, but for all my wants, my form remained unresponsive. I managed only to put my face in my hands and squeezed it to feel that I was actually awake. Yet as I pressed the fingers and the nails into the flesh above my eyebrows, I felt nothing. My temples swelled under the pressure of my cracking thumbs, but still I felt nothing. At the time I did not know why I did such a thing, frustration I assumed, but now I know it was to relieve the sweltering agony that grew inside of me to something more endurable.

Footsteps. Oh the grim inevitability, footsteps brushing against the straw grass and stamping in the damp mud, growing steadily nearer. I detested him for what he stood for, and I could not bear the sight of him again. I only wanted to sit alone, to beat my face into a pulp and try to weep to release from myself the torture that built inside me. Alas, there was no such release, and my harsh frenzied fingers only carved deeper. Those oncoming steps were sharp and slow, almost cautious of coming back into my presence, though he pounded his heavy steps as if to warn me of his impending arrival. If I would have had sensation in my legs, even in some minute uncontrolled sense, I would have run from him until the end of time, but in the end, what good would that have been? I could have run from the evil man true, but I could not run from the evil of him, the evil that I feared I would soon become. As unbearable as it seemed in my emotion, it would only be in my best interest to stay in his company.

Regretfully, between my fingers that hid my face, I caught sight of the fiend's moonlit silhouette trudging towards me. And I could feel his small eyes glaring on me sickly. Something warm trickled down my palms, down my cheeks; at first I thought it was some unpleasant crawling beast, but it became evident that from under my sharp muddy nails, dripped blood. I needed to scream, to run. To scream myself into an ear destroying panic as I ran free of him. I felt only that would help my soul bare the droning, oppressive agony; and then the scarlet from my brow seeped into my right eye, humbling me. I had no will. Those plodding footsteps closed in on me.

'My friend' his dark voice called, I remained silent; unable to reply. 'Is that blood on your face Mr Fletcher? You plague yourself with anxiety needlessly.' His voice rang with compassion yet sounded hollow in its overtly coarse nature, it was a marvel and a menace simultaneously. His steps remained awfully cautious, I did not understand how footsteps in damp soil could be that wretched, but somehow they were. Big black boots appeared in sight through my reddening fingers, no more than three feet away when they halted. A moment or two passed in anticipation of everything and nothing. It was as if I expected the doom that was him to end the world in but a mere matter of seconds.

He simply moved round to the other side of the carriage and made his way by my side; then he touched me. His cold sticky hand gently rested on mine, hinting that I release my face from the grip; though all I could think about was what gooeyness it was on his hands. With soft hands he forced me to look up at him, and I saw a man who sat with frigid movements, as if he was not controlling himself but being guided by another being; or perhaps he knew the empathetic touches and motions that he should do, but his true self knew not how to be connected with them. Whatever it was, I could not look directly into those hellacious eyes, the eyes of a killer of women, the eyes of a cannibal! Without wishing to, I found myself looking to his hands, he had wiped them somewhat, but I knew what had dried on them had come from that woman. He could not fool me; though I do wonder if he particularly tried to.

'Are you alright?' He spoke honestly with his ugly voice, pulling a white handkerchief from his pocket and wiping the blood from my face.

'I cannot go on, just kill me, eat me if you must, just please end my grief' I called simply, vacantly staring towards the ground in defeat as my arms fell flaccidly. The pain in my wounds festered into reality, and I spoke out to the sky 'I cannot exist in *this* world.' All that I held in for so long was released in one moment of woe. I was done with breathing, existing; done with no sunlight and waking only to the moon's haunting reveries.

But I heard my words in the third person, divorced from myself, and in that I knew how pitiful they sounded. I fancy in those moments my soul had left its form out of shame; watching the body deal with its woes and having no part in its ruin.

He calmly turned his position to face me, both his icy hands reached out and clasped me tightly, stealing me. With both hands on the sides of my face, I was forced to look into his narrow eyes. I blinked reluctantly, squirmed an inner turmoil; he waited a moment until my unsure gaze had settled. I still recall how terribly bleak the night was behind his face as conviction shone from the man.

'Rebecca needs you to continue.' He released me.

Those five words from him seemed to echo in the open fields and float around my clearing mind. He was perfectly right. I had to continue for her, the girl was in desperate need of me to do so. She would not be a compliant prisoner I knew, and they would treat her terribly for it. Yes she needed me to continue. And I needed the hope of her to continue, for without her the thought of dwelling in the wretched world another second was insufferable. The man who was trying to gain my attention had eaten a woman not ten minutes previously. Ghosts had tried to seduce me, devils had taken my love from me. Everything it seemed was testing my will for life; and I was on the brink, looking over the abrasive cliffs of life and spitting down on the rocks of fate. The only thing keeping me from jumping was my belief that I was on their trail. Like she was the last known star in the desolate sky, and I waited for the clouds to pass over, to see if that star was still there once the rain had moved on.

'How do I continue in a world that is completely unrecognisable and yet has not changed at all?' I called to him, more in a childish "I cannot go on" manner than an intelligent man who searched for an unknown answer. I wished I could take back my childish words, but I could only wait for his reply. As I looked to him, he seemed as if he was trying to mass the words together in his mind, then he spoke

'By accepting who you are. And what that is. As dead humans we must eat living human flesh.' His dark complexion was the tranquillity of Lucifer as he looked into me before continuing his words 'the wise man adapts to the changes in his life, the unwise man becomes bitter whilst reliving past glories.' Yet for all the wisdom he spoke, resounding in my head miserably, I could hear his croaking speech "we must eat living human flesh". I sat there in silence, frustrated, conquered by anguish, when all I wanted was to scream until my lungs bled.

'The sun will burn us before long' he added and moved over to open his carriage. 'We must sleep, let your mind settle my friend.' He gestured for me to get inside the carriage and as I walked round to do so, to my surprise, it was completely empty. All I saw was the wooden panes and nailed tightly curtains covering the windows. There were not even seats. It was not meant for quaint comfort, it spoke to me only of necessity; but I still relished the idea of sleeping in there rather than under green and brown. I was assuredly confident that the sun was not going to reach me in there. The cannibal stood motionless, holding open the door with his candle in hand.

'This is better than the soil I would say' he laughed to me, but his meaning reminded me that I was still covered in clumps of mud, and was desperately in need of cleaning myself compared to the civilised standard he set.

'I cannot thank you enough for your hospitality.'

'You just rest my friend, I shall find a hidden spot for the carriage and will join you shortly.' His dark face brightened to see me somewhat relaxed.

I sat up against the side of the carriage, smiling as he closed the door, and darkness filled the womb I rested in.

It felt queer to hear laughter, to smile, my cheeks had forgotten how to mould into such a peculiar position; they became strained by it. Quietude possessed me, and I felt contentedness for knowing how the night would end.

A short bumpy ride took place before he climbed inside the carriage to join me.

'Sleep blessedly' he uttered with his hollow tone as always, but I knew the meaning was meant.

'Same to you.'

He laid himself spread out in the fair-sized carriage as I sat pondering everything of him. His darkness and his kindliness. He spoke of not accepting himself as a cannibal as I was, but no such signs did he show. The shriek I recalled from that woman was appalling, and when he came back into my presence he showed nothing of remorse. I glanced over at his barely visible figure; he had already found sleep. I perceived an evil sleeping giant, but how evil could he have been if he believed he had to eat people to survive? There is no evil in physiological necessity. But a truth came to me I had not fully realised the significance of, I was still alive having only eaten animals since I had died; and that had been time enough to die of starvation. It seemed perfectly true that consuming life meant the dead could continue living, but not necessarily human. Satisfied I was by my meditations. I would tell my companion at night that we do not have to consume human flesh to live. The mind was liberated, I did not have to kill people, and I found blessed sleep shortly afterwards. Unless you have experienced the hideousness of being buried under soil, it would be pointless me explaining how infinitely divine my rest that night was.

By the time I opened my eyes, my companion had disappeared from the carriage and left the door partially open. His candle greeted me upon my return to the night, a generous gesture by the agreeable fiend. Something in the air told me he was nearby, but of what he was engaged in I could not guess any further than eating someone. I wished not to be in the proximity of such acts, nor did I want to hear another terror stricken scream. But was it not inevitable that I go and search for him? Like a child needing his father, I could not face the wide world alone, no matter what horrors finding him would distil in me.

Taking the candle in my hand I wandered out into the forest he had claimed as his daytime abode. The woodland was perfectly dense and bare, the trees were thick and secretive. It almost seemed too cramped for a carriage to fit in; he was right we would never have been found there.

Hoping to find the cannibal Edgar Horn, I strolled in my own time with an uncertain plod. The sun had just set, and though it had moved out of sight, its remnants still floated into the sky. The fallen branches and breakable leaves below my feet crackled delightfully, and I could hear owls hooting into the distance about the trees beautifully, as if they were calling me to go and greet them. I was overtaken by the beauty of the night and the woodland, so much so that I did not notice him standing in front of my path in the dark, hidden in shadows. His arms were folded by his chest and his dark eyes loomed over me.

'Glad you have woken my friend' croaked he deeply 'have you come to join in the feeding? You must be starving.' And I was, I had not realised the extent before his words, but once I heard them I knew I unbearably was.

'We can eat the flesh of animals' I called desperately, remembering my meditations.

'No my friend. Unfortunately we cannot' he walked towards me 'doing so stops the hunger that begins to envelope us true, but it does not replenish us in any way, shape or form. It is illusionary, only. You have become weak because you do not eat my friend. And you would turn frail and wither until you could not pull yourself from the ground if you continued. And you could be no help to her stuck in the ground. No Mr Fletcher, only consuming living human flesh and vomiting it away once the life is absorbed in us, will keep us lingering on for our loved ones.' He smiled at the absurdity of his words, but his eyes fell down on me in that awful way they did, I wanted to retreat and flee. He tried to be firm with me for my own sake, he knew how overwhelming all had become for me, but nothing could help the grave reality; nothing could. It was beyond words what I faced. I tried to justify cannibalism alongside farming, but it could not be done. Forcing them to breed, fattening them, killing them for our own wealth, the real depth of it made me grimace in shame. But food being my own species, creatures with higher emotions and fears; creatures who could judge me for the horrendous actions that I would perform, that was something infinitely worse.

'Fletcher, Rebecca needs you to come with me and feed. Besides, you will need your strength to reclaim her.'

'I am not *claiming* her, she is not a thing to *claim.* She is a respectable woman who deserves no part in all this horror and danger and eating of human flesh'

'I meant nothing by it' his voice became colder. 'Do not snap emotion towards me when it comes from another issue. She needs a strong and healthy rescuer, now, are you going to feed with me or not?' He was right, I felt far too weak to rescue her from three villains. I had to do it. I tried to say "let us go" something of the phrase "I give in to cannibalism, take me to my greatest sin" but all I could muster whilst deep in my internal chaos, was a poor and nervous attempt at a nod. Rendering such a despairing act as an affirming action, The Yorkshire Creature moved forward into the perilous night without any attempt to usher me his way.

I barely followed him. I did not fully choose to, it was his powering command that seeped into the ground and dragged me along with him; like a loyal dog trailing his overly curious master. As we walked into the tunnels created by the trees, the hint of daylight left in the sky fell, along with my hopes. The candle I held was too suppressed by the unfortunate proceedings.

The road we had travelled upon was just about in sight, I could tell by the shadowy clearing of the trees; this was when he turned to me.

'Are you sure you are ready for this? Once you do this deed, you cannot undo it. Each murder will be a tormenting opus of horror for eternity. This is not a light matter, do not take it lightly.' The seriousness in his brooding voice forced my lowliness to the surface. I was terrified, and again came that barren and raw need to flee from the world.

'To release her from harm and torture, I will do anything' I said 'and if anything means committing cannibalism, then this I will do. I have to, for her.' He smiled slightly, the way he did.

'The sooner you do this, the sooner you can bring her back to yourself. A lonesome man is riding a carriage on his way South and will soon come past where we stand. You shall remain here, I shall damage him and bring him to you, to feed. Best to have it simple and manageable for a first experience. I will give you a man more or less free from suffering, it will be on my conscience only.' His expression was cryptic, I guessed I saw a mingling of both empathy for me, and fear for how I would cope. 'Put out the candle Fletcher.'

As he sauntered to the edge of the broken woodland, I felt the last thing I expected to feel in such a moment, hope; a hope that the path before me was becoming clearer, even if it was ever-turning bleaker. I imagine I would have spiralled to lunacy had I been left to deal with the hunger alone, and for that, I was fortunate to have him there with me.

Rebecca, my love, all my actions were in the name of our reunion!

Wheels, ticking over stones, the carriage was moving close. I peered into the overwhelming dark to where I thought my friend stood motionlessly, but no longer did he linger there. Where he had moved to I could not see, however as quickly as I saw my mentor had gone, the realisation of imminent murder shot up my figure as if I was struck by Zeus himself; it was on my conscience. I had to turn my back from the horrid event, I closed my eyes to the harshest extent my eyelids would physically allow and clenched my teeth together; dreading the moment I would be presented with a half dead, half eaten man who had had a whole life ahead of him before we interfered. I lost the strength of sensation in my knees and fell to the ground, closing my ears with defiant hands and screaming a diaphragmatic panic.

The world was still. I could hear nothing but the humming of the northern winds. All sound of the carriage had ceased to be. I hoped the man had fallen into the hole of never having existed, but I knew the only explanation for the carriage stopping was the will of The Yorkshire Creature. My time was fast approaching. A mourning wail sound came from above me atop the trees, I looked to sight the source, but only a darkened sky and scattered stars I saw. Some sort of bird I thought, a bird that knew of my looming fate and lamented the death of my innocence. And then it came, the horrid sound I fiercely feared, a thing that caused me to moan profusely in anxiety. A man cried out in violent agony. I covered myself completely, searching for a new womb to hide from reality. And worse still, I could hear his footsteps coming closer. Each footfall on the carcasses of leaves fell with as much ease as when he casually left me, and yet he should have been carrying or dragging a body. My curiosity could not force a glance, I could only recoil.

His plodding came closer. Plod. Closer, plod. Here, little more than a few yards away. A sudden crash fell to the ground behind me, something similar to my size. And the air carried a scent of something warm, musky and appallingly familiar. 'Rebecca needs you to do this my friend' reluctantly he spoke and paused for a moment. 'I shall be catching my breath in the carriage, take as long as you need but know we continue our journey South when you make it back. I imagine you will want us doing so with fair speed.' He took his leave as soon as he spoke, giving me no time to react or speak myself. I felt an impulse to turn and plead him to stay with me, to help me through my agony, but still I could not move. And behind me, near to my ears I could hear harsh hissing sighs, some man's almost in vain attempts to breathe. A man whom I was yet to look upon. 'Rebecca I love you, oh so very much' I called out. In my mind she heard my words, her presence came to me in some form or another. It calmed my wild emotion.
'I need you to give me the strength for my deed; we were there for one another in our perils and doubt. Be here for me now.' But I felt her no more. I felt nothing, only shame for behaving like a frightened child, cowering in the dirt so feebly. I despise feeling shame. Because of such, and because my will only wanted to save her, I tried wearily to collect myself. I pulled myself onto my feet and stood upright, focusing only on myself and my balance. Then I controlled my breathing, forcing it to that of a peaceful man sat

on a beach by the sea, as the stars shone their white brilliance on the vibrant impressions of each wave; no metaphors of fate here, just aesthetics. But falsities fade, I came back to my own world. The atmosphere swallowed me harshly, I could only see a darkness that shadowed me with grief.

It was then when feigning bravery and composer, I turned around to face him, and to the most unexpected horror, I saw myself in him, for he too, feigned bravery and composure. Yet deep in the white core of our souls, we screamed together in Banshee anxiety within the abyss that surrounds life and death.

He was an average looking man, youngish, brown hair, lying in the poorest of states. All his limbs fell crooked, possibly broken or something similar. His shirt was torn, and a bloody chest through the tear oozed dark scarlet. The bravery in him soon turned to a cold raw confusion, and his expression increasingly gleamed past me.

I cautiously moved the two yards to stand over the dishevelled dying body, whose glance vaguely followed me. I steadied myself for the evil act I had to do, to commit a human sacrifice to Baal; to Rebecca. I thought of his mother, somewhere; she would have been horrified if she had been there to see her son not only brutally murdered, but eaten to a savage nothingness. Was I heartless to stand over him in weary lust? Thought of such acts was despicable enough, but the poor man was already on his deathbed by the hand of another, I was an opportunist only. I tried to lay it back on his conscience.

I peered into the cavernous depths of his dying eyes, they were of a bright green, yet a thin muddy cloudiness spread over them. Those meadows of his steadied their questioningly rapid earthquakes into an insignificant twitch, then with the heavy wind from his nasal passage, he passed into oblivion. And that was it. His life had gone. Gone before my very eyes. The simple ideas of life and death are perfectly bipolar, and because of such concepts witnessing someone become the opposite in less than a second was inconceivable to me, but unpleasantly there it happened.

I tried not to flee, to only stare and take into myself the true depth of what had happened, it seemed the best way of handling the man's death. I knelt down by the side of him, his wearied face was too pale for comfort considering he had just died, and he had already begun to turn cold. Much like the dead father I once knew, I existed fearful he was not dead, that he would jump up to his feet emphatically, and with the dance of Mephistopheles' jester he would murder me with cold hands. That feeling never left me.

It was then that I realised the nature of my hunger. It was still burning, and it was still savage, but the shock of all that had happened stopped me from feeling anything momentarily. Now I could feel it again, swelling me, and there was human flesh just by me. And it did not smell or seem inedible. And he had not been dead that long. He did not need his flesh anymore.

I moved closer to him, feeling the warm density in the air above him; still feeling that it was intrinsically wrong to do what I planned. Slowly I pressed my mouth down into his bloody chest, tasting on the tip of my lips whatever so came out of it. I closed my eyes and thought of anything else. What came to me I cannot recall, though it was not enough to clear my mind of the passion and sourness. My jaw opened, teeth above him for a moment, Rebecca, before cutting into his broken skin. The scent of blood was intoxicating in ways both good and bad, but I had to go through with it, to prepare me for a live man, there was no option I told myself.

I barely chewed before spitting the mess out frantically. The blood and saliva that trickled wildly from my mouth as I tried to free myself was a grim violation. I spat and retched and spat again to rid myself of the gruesome red, but it would not leave my orifice. I ate a handful of soil and then spat that out to soak up the remains of him, but the blood was not just in my mouth, it was on my hands also; and that could not be undone. I clumsily fell down beside him, wishing I was him.

179

Two insensible victims we lay, one fatigued, drowning in despair and wallowing in self-pity. The other, existed only in a forlorn cadaverous serenity.

Chapter V: The Tale Of Mr Edgar Horn

Because I could not stop for death,

He kindly stopped for me.

The carriage held but just ourselves,

And immortality

Emily Dickinson

       I must have lost consciousness as I lay next to the corpse. I can only assume I lost the will to live and that manifested itself in the deepest of sleeps; for when I came back to my senses, it was the next night. Mr Horn, The Yorkshire Creature, sat facing me inside the carriage holding a bowl.
'Good morning' his words, followed by an unobvious smile.
'Good morning' muttered I drowsily, bewildered as to how I had come from my God-forsaken predicament, and found myself inside the unmoving carriage. But I could not think, my tiredness pulled the heavy sheets known as eyelids involuntarily over my sight. With fatigue I opened them again, looking at the starlight through the open door just behind him, then to the candle placed by his side that flickered warm and dark shadows about the lines of his face. Those shades about us were perfect for drifting into sleep once more. My body sunk back into itself, my eyes dwindled.
'With the phrase "good morning" comes the feeling my waking hours are going to be pleasant and joyful' he spoke, and whilst he did, he offered to me the bowl. I took it, and he continued muttering to me aimlessly 'mornings of the past. The sun's light dancing off my skin as I rested in our yard, our dog would bark at the birds that soared so high in the sky, and my mother would yell at him to be quiet. But I knew he just wanted to fly.' He paused

for a moment from his far off gaze, his eyes flickered to me with strange intent, before looking back out of the carriage. 'Last night I thought I could start your journey with the simplest of steps; and you would then be able to progress over the nights.' I nodded in drowsy agreement. 'I thought that "simple" step would be the feast of a severely wounded dying man, who would not bear the strength, and most crucially, the will to fight back. I was wrong my friend, and I apologise for that. The simplest start, is eating human flesh as a man eats his cattle, civilised, relaxed. And with you distracted by words, wearied from sleep and unquestionably starved, I handed you my bowl...' The graveness of his inference did not hit me directly. I yawned and scratched my watering eyes as my mind reluctantly deciphered the riddle. Then as my tongue still lapped at the tastes in my saliva and the meaning in his words slowly came to me, I looked down into the bowl. A raw and badly torn chunk of meat lay in the dusty thing as an unclean, clear but lightly pink liquid collected at the bottom. I had eaten without thought or glance. The cunning fiend had worked on my impaired judgement with perfect conviction and the deed had been done.

His dark brooding eyes gleamed over me with sparkling interest, calculating the thoughts in my head. Yet what they were with particulars is for the most part impossible to say. My initial emotion was something of repulsion and I had to repress a gagging sensation. I also felt a harsh sense of violation on his part to me, for he had disregarded my will on an ill-matter that would degrade my soul in its entirety. However there was something else I felt, it was unmistakable, and born more from my carnal suffering than anything emotional; it was joy. A joy that the deed had been done, and it had not cost the fate of Mary; how, then, could I feel anything but relief?

I could feel a warmness growing inside of me, branching out into my veins and through my body like no animal had done for me. It was a subtle wonder yet it gave me a sense of life that I could scarcely remember.

'Thank you Mr Horn, I do not know what would have become of me without your guidance and patience' I eventually spoke in a weak and timid voice, trying to forget what the act of cannibalism is and instead only being grateful for the long needed nourishment.

'Congratulations my friend, the new life starts here.' He smiled at me before entering into himself, his manner sank and his shoulders fell lethargically. 'I do not know what I would do without your company either Mr Fletcher. This world is so barren and lonely.' He did not seem sad or melancholic in his words, but more fatigued by the fact. I let a breath drift in between us before replying

'Have you ever been married Mr Horn? Or felt love?'

'Neither.' It seemed as if the word poured out of his dark eyes as they flickered back towards me with an expression I struggled to understand, was it regret? Self-pity? Or a yearning wonder for what my term "love" truly meant? He spoke further, 'I cannot be loved my friend, only my mother achieved such a thing' he laughed to himself softly 'my heart is cold and riddled with cobwebs, has been for some time; but I believe I can be warmed to the failures of emotion. I hope to be.' My judgement of him was beginning to change, though I had never truly believed in objective evil, despite The Man By The Lonely Tree's best efforts, I expected to find it in The Yorkshire Creature. In these moments, however, I was beginning to see in him a man whose heart was kind in nature, but his loneliness had turned him distant, and subsequently threatening in appearance. As I was learning more about the nature of this beast, and trying to map his past, I had to ask of him

'How did you become such a creature?'

'It is a long tale my friend, it contains devils much like yours, and the loss of a woman who was deep in my soul, however in my case that woman was my beloved mother.'

'It may be a long tale,' I spoke, 'but I am journeying a long way. I believe with fair certainty they are taking my Rebecca to London, and so I will travel with you, as long as you wish, and as far South as you go; so long as your horses travel faster than my wearied legs could carry me. Where is it you are heading to?'

'London. Aye, I could go there. I move for something fresh, I travel South yes, though no destination has been in mind. Yes, we shall move for London, the great city of the grand Empire, that is a perfect destination.' He spoke more to himself than to me. I could see him imagining himself there, and all he could do and achieve. Eat.

'Such a long journey would give us more than enough time for the most detailed account of your tale as you could possibly tell. My friend, Mr Horn, would you tell me the tale in its entirety?'

'Very well then, let us be on the road before I begin.'

And we were in no time. Riding with steady pace on the dreary roads that I knew had I been running, I would not have kept pace for nearly as long as they could. The silence of the night was haunting and exquisite, it breathed with that peace only English country roads can in the thick of darkness.

'Where do I begin' he spoke, holding his small golden candlestick along with the reins as the wax fell carelessly onto his gloves. He had no tone in his meaningless words, yet I knew from those words alone that I heard the greatest timbre of all the men in Yorkshire for the narration of a strange tale. He lowered his head in a sort of nod that never raised itself back into place, and staring towards the ground with those deep and fierce eyes; he tried to cast his mind back to the emotions that shaped his life.

'My father was born into a wealthy family, one that from his mother had become a branch in the family tree of the Earls of Yorkshire. Our name had changed, but they were still our kin, and because of this, we had all the land and wealth we needed.' He smiled to himself and paused for a moment. They say the youngest years are the most joyous, and by the way he smiled I guessed such was so for him.

'My father died before I was born, and with the house belonging to his mother's extended family, his parents had the power to take the mansion from the pregnant widow and give it to another one of their children. But they did not. It remained in their names yes, but they insisted my mother remain there and raise me as planned whilst also giving her the money she needed to do so.

184

She often praised their generosity and loved them like her own ancestors. In my younger days there were nursemaids, educators too. But they had all gone by my twentieth year.

The mansion itself was an old and magnificent place, it had been within our family since the last stone had been set back in the seventeenth century. And it was built of the same stone as the castles our distant kin lived within. But even with the old castles in our line, our home was a glorious heirloom in its own right. When I read *The Castle Of Otranto* I imagined Manfred running riot through our own gothic corridors of armoured knights and our halls with timeworn relics from distant forefathers; it would have been perfect for a performance of that wild tale. Outside, at the front, we had a small lake, and by it, the most passionate oak tree I ever saw, it seemed to sing the emotive songs of every season that wandered by it.

Once the nursemaids had left for other homes, my mother's health soon deteriorated. During a particularly cold winter she caught a fever. Though by summer she was able to rid herself of the illness, her strength never returned. They say what does not kill one makes one stronger, she is testimony to otherwise. No doctor could determine what it was. It seemed a drop of everything and not a lot of any one in particular. She could barely walk, her sight was poor, and she was short of breath in most moments. She became my child; life in full circle. I was her only carer, and though I suggested calling back the nurses several times, she did not want them. She never did like having others inside the home, and so I continued alone, for her.

By the time of her illness my grandparents had died and the mansion was left in my name. For the two decades that followed, I knew little more than caring for my mother. I thought of my father and his father watching over me, wanting me to create the next forename in the line of Horn's so that our great home could comfort another generation. Had my grandfather still been alive I fancy he would have forced me to marry, but I cared not for continuing the line, besides, I knew other kin would take the home once I died.' He looked up at me, studying my posture and lowering his brow. The candlelight danced about us irregularly from the holes in the jagged road.

'One evening in the darkness of autumn, whilst mother sat in her chair knitting as she often did, I sat across the room from her daydreaming with an open book on my lap, much like every other night I had known. That was the scene when they came, four of them. Wicked, evil, demonic, I do not own the appropriate words to describe them, but you were victim to similar creatures yourself. Pale they were, dressed in black, and reptilian of spirit.

At first I heard faint footsteps out the front of the house upon the walkway. I thought nothing of it, most likely folk who were lost and had come to enquire on how to reach wherever it was that they needed to reach; it had happened a few times over the years in our remote corner by the Yorkshire moors.

I opened the door with little caution, expecting to bear witness to a horse and carriage with some confused man walking towards the property. Of all there was nothing, nothing save the chilling silence that filled my senses. It was as if I opened the door to Death himself; and he not yet showing his face only chose to taint my composure with a disturbing anxiety as I looked out into the darkness. Several seconds passed. I knew I had to venture out, I was certain I heard footsteps on our property. I took a lantern from the porch and explored for the source, moving deeper down the pathway and into the freezing night. I recall how the body of the lake was a horrible, gloomy and liquored black as leathery leaves floating upon the surface distastefully. I stood by and searched out into the obscurity, but still there was no sign of horse or carriage, or lantern or life at all; just a gush of wind that struck me like a battering ram under the retreating stars. Those sudden winds that seemed to move solely into me clouded my hearing, it had been silent as a churchyard only seconds before. But that was the least of my concerns, a chill ran through me and invaded my soul, I knew something about that night was grave and in some way yet unknown, unnatural. I felt hopelessly vulnerable; not the form of hopelessness when you cannot warm yourself on a chilly night, but the being of hopelessness when you feel in your presence an inevitable abyss caressing its stiff hands your way, ready to close you up at any moment. O I grimaced, horror loomed over me, it menaced as if the shadow of some giant god was standing over me, waiting for my next move as his minions pried at the bottom of the splashing black sickly waters.

But it was not the time for inequity, mother was my burden and an explanation of foxes or wild winds would not calm my assailed mind.

Though I feared to move round into the shadows of the house, I knew I had to inspect the back as well. There was no gate or fence so it was quite probable something could have skulked its way there. Still, I thought it was more than skulking things, my intuition was human thieves. I was quite wrong.

I crept with silent steps as if the earth would shatter at the slightest suggestion of footfalls; I breathed soundlessly. Past stone and shadow, past hedge and flowerbed. I caught sight of our sundial before I fully glanced round the corner into the garden, it sat in the middle and at the back with stone chairs set perfectly around. Of the time it would have told in that darkened hour of phantom animosity, none would have been told; and time has ceased ever since for me.

I pulled the shutter on my lantern, not a ray of light was visible, then peering my head around the corner, I caught sight of my intruders. I wish I could say I was startled at the sight of them, but it was a cold terrorising of the soul that tore at the foundation of my being. I moved myself back out of sight immediately and froze still. Had I not a fragile old woman to care for I would have fled into the shadows of the nearby hills and returned on the morrow when they had gone, but such was not so. And for her sake, I slowly poked my head out to see again.

Four upright beings stood in front of our wine cellar door, and I say upright beings because these surely were no men, surely no simple thieves; their movement, and lack of, told me so. They were dressed in black cloaks covering the majority of their figures, their hoods concealed their heads but for the face. Yet in their hands and the side of their faces I saw pale and rough crusting skin. I knew instantly they were loathsome, instantly that they were vicious things; yet despite the threat they opposed, I could not help but stare at them. In the time I did, they stood flawlessly still, not a waver, and neither speaking nor acknowledging one another, they stared at my door as if with their will alone they could smash it into a formless insignificance.

I knew before long they would break through the door, physically or mentally, it would be done, and though inside the cellar the door back into the house was locked, I fancied that too would collapse to their will. I knew I required tactics for dogged warfare, and they were as follows:

Silently I would stride back to the front and into the house, take the sharpest of our antique swords, put mother somewhere out of the way of just aggression, and meet them at the inside door down to the wine cellar. When they finally find their way to it and break it down, I would be waiting with the high ground, in the narrow doorway, and fight them one by one as tenaciously as I could.

Such was my plan, yet my limbs were unmoving, all that existed was my pulse pounding its way up and down my frozen arms, falling through my hollow legs and bubbling in my chest; thought of blood had always nauseated me. I gathered my thoughts together slowly and hobbled several anxious steps away before hearing a hollow croak. One of them hissed something to another in the deceitful calm, and I had to see, there was no other way for me.

I peered foolishly back around the corner. They stood where they had been with their ghostly stillness for several moments, until with the pace of an oily slug with violent intent, the being at the front of the pack moved his head to his right, to one of his followers; O the ghastly terror that ferociously burrowed in my bosom. The pack all stepped backwards, a decisive yard, before the leader effortlessly and with little care kicked the sturdy door completely off its hinges, crashing down the steps into our cellar. He moved as if he meant only to test the strength of the metal bolts, but no, he forced the door down with incredible force. Here it was that I was forced into the action of my design and defend my mother, myself, and honour of the House of Horn.

Mother was easily terrified by the sounds of the wind upon our windows and the creaking of the trees outside, she certainly would have heard the threatening pound of the door tumbling down the stone steps. And from that came a very real possibility that she would begin calling for me, causing them to hear the fragile frightened old woman and follow the sound. I ran for the front door in a panic.' Though the complexion of The Yorkshire Creature never changed, and his voice only broke minutely here and there, I could feel his emotion, his panic, his fear; and his horror.

'As I made it to the porch I threw my lantern back down and closed the door. My heart raced beyond control, I would have had no fear with four ordinary men, my sword would have made them cower and never return, but the sight of those dark entities told me they were not going to cower to anything I could do; and their intensity, their unaltering intensity as they sneered at the breaking of my door, they were undoubtedly determined to their cause. What they wanted in our home all the way out in the empty darkness of Yorkshire I could only guess, it surely was not our wine collection, and they had no carriage to carry a looting of antiques. They had come with abominable purpose, that was undeniable to me.

Onto the first floor hallway I paced, that was where my father's swords were rested above relic full body armours. All my polishing maintained a shining silver, ready for use. Quite a proud sight to see I confess, knowing your ancestors had fought under those plates for the likes of myself, and that is what I was taking the sword for I believed. The honour they had done me. I only saw the armour for a flittering moment and yet I was filled with a warrior's courage, they fought for their children, for their future generations and I would fight for my child, my mother.

The first sword I picked was still extremely sharp, and most importantly it was light and agile, this is significant in how my story ends. I could quickly thrust it where need be, without this fact of that sword, I would not be here my friend.' He paused. His gaze fell from the road ahead to me, my own complexion and the mixture of emotions I concealed. The blackness of his eyes filled more of the white than I had yet seen in a creature. I was wonderfully mesmerised yet gently disturbed, not only at the haunting sight of him, but at the dark chivalric tale he uttered. His story continued

'I flew back down the curved stairs in no time to my mother, hoping the torment of loud noises and my rushing through the home did not take her to a better place. "What is happening my boy?" her trembling words were, as if the world was falling apart all around her. "someone has come mother, he is in the wine cellar" I replied as she half gasped with fear, but I had no time to be concerned or console her, I took her as softly as time could allow over my shoulder and placed her sitting in a small storage room. She was too delicate for all that, I was worried I would accidently snap her bones, yet I was infinitely more afraid of what they could do to her; she was not even in the frame of mind for a conversation with them let alone anything else. "I am sorry mother, please keep quiet, I shall be back as soon as I can" I quivered to her.

Certain was I, that I was to die by their hands. By the way I had run around the building the creatures would have known the residences were aware of them; there was no hiding from the impending confrontation for me. But if she remained quiet throughout as I insisted of her, then I thought they would kill me, do what they came for, then leave, and she would be untouched. She could at least die of her own accord in relative peace.

I took a last look at her face, my eyes grew heavy quite suddenly. Her poor face was so life stricken, her lips had withered thin and pale, her brow wrinkled with apprehension underneath her grey tail. The woman was dying, and I could not bear it, my heart yearned for the youth and glory that once belonged to her,

190

not that crippled outer shell with ill-focusing eyes. I left her there, alone and afraid.' The Yorkshire Creature's face hardened almost scornfully, then he looked away to the darkness to hide his passion. I was captivated. I had forgotten completely that he was a vicious murderer, and in the moments of hearing his compelling story I fell in love with his dark soul.

'Down in the cellar I could hear wine bottles being smashed. An expensive collection we had, of the French from Bordeaux and Paris with a few fine specimens of Valpolicella and Bardolino from Venice. A fine collection, but it could be replaced, my mother could not, and by the continuous noises I gathered they were smashing them to spite us rather than clumsiness; which further obscured the motives of the intruders to me. Then the notion came to me that it would only take one to attack glass bottles, the other three could have been behind me for all I knew. I had to be cautious. I was certain my life would be decided in but a few moments. I ask you my friend, how long does it take one to die?' The Yorkshire Creature looked to me again, holding his gaze.

'Less than a jiffy if you let death have it'

'Ah my friend, but time was ruthlessly killing my mother, and it had been for decades. She was a beautiful woman in her day, and one to admire for her strength of heart I assure you Mr Fletcher. But her illness and old age had devoured all such characteristics from her, from her soul as well as her body. The woman I hid in the closest was only an awful shadow of the woman that raised me so lovingly. Did you not see this in your parents, or theirs?'

'No. I did not know my mother, all I recall is vague images, she died when I was young. My father had aged considerably, but of a young energetic man I never really knew. And I never met any of my grandparents; therefore I cannot truly appreciate how you describe age as taking your mother.'

'You are only young my friend, if you survived to be my living age, you would have seen your father change in such a way as I describe. It violates us. Yes death can be a quick jiffy of confusion my friend, but it can also devour us our entire lives. And with death everything truly ends, leaving only peace and forever silence, ironically what we have been yearning for in our lives. Religion itself was only conceived because people were scared of the way death encroaches. Man in the older ages needed the promise of their youth returned, eternally. You appear to disagree Mr Fletcher'

'Of the different forms of death I could not, you spoke perfectly, but look to the sky my good sir. How magnificent the stars are, like pin pricks in a black sheet that covers the horizon; the Greeks called it Empyrean, a revelation of Heaven. And the moon up there too, glowing a strange shade of white that almost seems silver. I have only recently turned from my Christian deity, but to me, if religion ever did simply "begin", its reason would lie in the grandiose of the stars and their kin. Men knew these great things, the warmth of the sun, the contours of the moon's surface and somehow they calculated the mathematics of their positions. They were empirical witnesses to pure divinity, and what else could simple folk do than create personified deities of the sun and moon?'

'How wonderful and pointless it was, and is. In the end my friend, God either created religion on the eighth day or not at all. It seems it has always been a human invention. I can only see religion as a bizarre creation from a wild and perverse anxiety in the face of mortality. But what of us? We who have died and remain here, what of our religion or ontology? Death is not a Reaper to us, but a vixen as I like to say, The Vixen Of Death, she shapes us beyond belief.'

'Answer me this then Mr Horn, we are both dead yes, but only in terms of our bodies, our bodies are dead and altered by some loathsome mystic happening, The Vixen Of Death's doing as you say; but of our souls or minds, they have to be labelled as somewhat alive surely. Are we really dead? Or are we in essence alive?' He smiled at me softly, uninterested in answering my query immediately, he turned to the grunting of his horses. Then with dark eyes towards me he replied

'In a communal concept of the term 'dead', I am dead my friend. And I travel to London to find what I seek and my heart shall begin to pulse again, I shall live once more; my own resurrection. Then yes, I will be alive in essence.'

I guessed in his riddles that he was a man who had experienced insufferable torment, something that had killed more than just his body. His story presented more altruism than I had seen in him before; what I first perceived to be an air of evil in him now appeared a perverse melancholia, and he was simply trying to relearn the art of company. Though his digestive system demanded him to be a murdering cannibal he forever tried to tame himself from its barbarity. Despite my thoughts however, I could not feel completely safe in the presence of his ominous soul, no matter how much I enjoyed his company. The sound of the horrified scream from his victim still tortured me.

'Back to my story my good friend' he smiled a smile that was hauntingly queer 'my point was this, death is not just the lack of breath and thought, death is more than a soul leaving its body. We may be proof of that. Death is the loss of the essence of life, and life can be lost daily as the will or ability to exist in the world diminishes. This day that I am recalling for you, was not simply my passing into the Ever-Soulless and subsequent cannibalism, but also the end of my mother's dying, who after years of deteriorating finally found that peace and silence she longed for.

I looked all directions fearful they were already at hand, but I could not see any of them; only the chaos of breaking glass on a stone floor in the cellar was revealed. Yet it unnerved me as they intended, and I held my sword extended out in front of me with a tremble.

As I crept towards the door I uttered a prayer to God, more of desperation rather than expecting a miracle; perhaps I got one. As soon as my eyes blinked open from the prayer, the last of the crashing bottles smashed to the ground and rolled solemnly in the echoing hollow room. The silence was desolate, then came the softness of footsteps moving up the stairway from behind the door. They knew I waited on the other side, how I knew, I knew not, dire fear perhaps, but I knew they knew. They expected me like the smashing of our collection was the bait to get me to stand upon the very spot they designed. My own steps repulsed me, I had fallen into the nets of their will.

The steps were graceless and emotionless, and the number I could hear slowly lumbering up morphed into one set; they moved in unison. They wanted me to think the other three were in the house from another entrance, but I would not be fooled. Slowly as possible I pressed my ear to the wooden door, listening for the steps, for the breathing of life; but there was no more steps, no hissing breath, no life. It was an eerie horror to know they were so very close and their menace invaded the room before they even entered it. I delayed for another second before remembering their method through doors ordinary men conceded impassable. I jumped to my side merely a second before the stillness was broken by a thunderous sound.

The shield of the door that protected me burst onto the floor in several dying fragments. With fear and doubt, terrified of the retribution they would retaliate with, I swung my sword into the doorway, hoping to catch them as they came forward. I did strike something hard, uncertain was I if it was man or wall but encouraged nonetheless, I frantically thrust the sword at them again and again. When I saw their footsteps scraping up to me on the landing, I jumped into the doorway, feigning the might of a god underneath the composure of a child.

Still thrusting my sword in all directions in that doorway, I caught the arm of the front man and then severed his leg as he came into sight. He fell to the floor but the three behind him stood silently and unfazed by my aggression; or their comrade toppling down to the floor and bleeding significantly. Yet he uttered no cry of pain. As their partner toppled in a heap down the stone steps, I looked into the faces of the remaining three. They were as pale as the moon with flaking skin, it seemed as if their cheeks would crumble like dust if I brushed it, however I knew their flesh was as hard as anything from when I had struck my first victim. Their eyebrows were a thick black and their eyes were of the same black that my eyes have become. Few words can describe the foulness they were, "wicked inhuman creatures" does no justice at all. All I may say is this, they were positively devils, and I was beyond mortified.

Little time passed from when I first caught sight of their faces until the next movement, and yet every memory I had ever experienced did. I relived the loneliness, the joys, everything. The last flicker of experience that came to me was the face of my mother sitting in that dark closet, weak and scared the way I left her.' He had a solemn look about him, and bowed his head as if in remembrance. 'They flew at me with speed my eyes could not believe, and instinctively I raised my sword. The next moment I fell to the floor several feet from the doorway, realising I had been struck quite fiercely. My sword was still in hand thankfully and I raised it quickly above me in desperation and fear that they were coming for me again with their rapid advance. Luckily such was so, one had dived for me and my action saved me from probable death. I had wounded his upper chest badly and he tumbled back towards the doorway. I had no time for thought, only time for opportunity, and though I fancied the two I could not see had flanked me on either side, I charged at the wounded being in front of me. I slashed at him twice and then stabbed him as deeply in the chest as I could. His cold blood sprayed onto me in thick nauseating clusters, but nothing would hinder me. I do remark his expression decreased in malevolence as I wounded him, each blow seemed to bring that foul monstrous glow out of his hideous self and I took pleasure in witnessing the dark life in his eyes become only a vacant glare.

Up on my feet, I threw myself into the wall by the door and stood with my back up against it; for in that position they could not commit their vicious ambush from behind. My eyes darted wildly for the devils as my heart fell into a panicking frenzy, but they were not to be seen, and I could see no sign of other footprints from the doorway. That was when the dread came, the burning suspicion that they had found where my mother was hidden.

If they had not, and I moved to see upon her safety, it would have revealed to the watchful demons where she was. On the other hand, I felt every second she out of my sight was a second longer she was at risk. There was no time for deliberation, and my instinct was that they knew where to find her; perhaps they had heard her scared quivers.

Cautious as the winds, I searched every possible place they could be. I even reluctantly move back in front of the doorway to the cellar and glanced down the black and bloody abyss where I knew one would have been; hopefully unmoving. Not a sight could I see, not a sound could I locate from the pit below; nor behind the shadowy bannister or behind the parlour table. I moved for the room where the closet was, but my hopes sank when I saw the closet door creaking open by the will of incorporeal ghostly hands. She had not touched the door I knew, it had to be one of them. My throat tensed, violent agony travelled up and through my arms, I shivered and it became a struggle to keep a hold of my weapon. Out from behind the swaying door came one of them. His face was covered by his hood, and he bowed his head downwards into his arms as he cradled mother, and stood unmoving.' Mr Horn stopped. Though he was still, and remained still, I could not help see a trembling in his demeanour. He twirled his black ring a few times round to distract himself from the memory, from the loss I knew he was soon to recall. I wanted to show my empathy for him, a hand on the shoulder or some other simple gesture. Alas I did not, I knew not how to comfort such a man in such a trauma. Yet empathise I could and did; for this moment seemed altogether the same as that when I lay wounded on the floor and sighted my own demon clutching Rebecca by the throat so viciously.

'She cowered in her cradle when she saw me, outreaching her defiant arms towards me with the pathetic little strength she had left; it was like she would fly into the shelter of my being, and that I could save her. As I looked to her, I saw that she knew not the end, only a haunting and incomprehensible fear. And that shattered my heart Mr Fletcher.'

'Sounds all so appalling' my choked words, unsure of what else to say. He only nodded, and his expression became thin with a hint of repressed anger.

'The most "appalling" of it was this, I knew when I saw her in his powerful arms that it would be seconds before she would die, I knew it. Panic became my mind, but my body remained motionless, I hoped my calm composure would cause him to give her more time, and that I could think of some method of rescue. But then, I had possibly killed two of his comrades already, and all without a word being said between us. The only reason she was not already dead was because he wanted me to see her life become lost in his own vicious way. There were no more seconds left for her.'

'What was your mother's name?' I asked; some words to show my empathy.

'Caroline, Caroline Horn.' For several moments neither of us uttered another word, same as when I first spoke Rebecca's name to him. We let the name echo in the air about us and in our minds, our sign of respect for the women we had loved and lost. He then composed himself, slowly speaking once more, 'he let go of her. Did not throw or thrust, he just gently let his arms fall to his side. Aghast was I. She seemed to fall for an age, before landing in a heap; like an aged scarecrow fallen from his stance and incapable of ever moving on his own to break his fall. I heard some of her brittle bones shatter and break. There were many clicks when she hit the floor. But before I was able to see her dire condition… he stamped on her skull with his heavy boots. I winced, I cried in disgust. She groaned a lifeless sound I wish not to describe. I will say though, his viciousness resulted in a coarse retch from her small frame that spewed thick black blood from her unmoving mouth. She fought the hands of death for only a second. And she was gone. It was he, not age, who had the last violation upon her existence. The coughing of blood was her last miserable breath.' I looked towards him, expecting him to speak further, but he made no attempt. The solemn face looked down, deep in thought, and I did not want to disturb his bereavement. It is a delicate thing to do, much like if you woke in Hell, and Satan stood nearby unaware of you, you would not attract his attention, not for anything; I guessed my companion had a similar rage.

'May I ask you, what type of being does it take to murder an old woman like that?' He spoke with little emotion.

'A being not worthy of this world and one who deserves the most wretched of fates. Yet I do not feel I can speak or judge of demons or of evil; this whole cannibal business puts my moral compass into question. Weeks past I would have spoken of God's justice in the afterlife, and evil going to Hell, but I have no reason to believe so now.'

'Perhaps you are right, he was a being unworthy of this world. You raise interesting terms, my friend, 'demon' and 'evil'. I enjoy the term demon, with proper use, it can be artistic and creative in nature. But 'evil' is problematic to me, its essence is to judge others and label their morality inferior, cannibalism has taught me not to do such a thing, for we do not know what madness led them down the path of their lives. And religion is irrelevant when discussing morality, transcendence should not interfere with human law, God would know that. My point in all this, Mr Fletcher, is there was no morality to him, he was not immoral in doing what he did, he was amoral. People often look deep into thoughts and acts as if they were caverns when they are but dents in the rock. He was an animal. A predator. There is no dignity or moral laws to ponder in him. There is only predatory instinct and self-contentment. I fear to say, and I apologise in doing so, but this is what your demon is too. That is the path I could not avoid since that dreadful night. And it is the path you will follow.'

'I will always have dignity in my soul. You shall not think anymore of otherwise. I will always value my morals Mr Horn, without them we are no greater than the savage creatures that eat their own children. My God Mr Horn, did Saturn not teach you the definition of a shameful act? Without morality I would not have the will to rise in the evening. I am not a savage and I will forever hold my deeds in guilt and shame if otherwise. If finding Rebecca requires of me to eat humans then so be it, but I will never

198

murder a soul in such a vile method for it, it is not necessary, and only wicked and disgraceful. When I have courage to do such an act as murder it will be in their sleep and when they cannot feel pain or fear. Do not think me a man who would abandon morality. And never compare me to my own demon, he who threatened and killed me, who claimed and abducted her!' He remained calm. '*Abandon thyself*, this is an amoral existence. Give it time my friend, you are young in death.' His awful black eyes glistened somehow as his words mocked me. A brutal silence roared between us for several moments, the night cried in sour misery. 'I am going for a wander' I called with no intention of returning until sunrise. I intended to hop off a still moving carriage however he brought the horses to a sudden stop before I could. Into the night I stumbled, away from him. I felt his sweltering glare was still on me as I moved, scolding me. For some reason, I feared if he was to rise up onto his feet, he would kill me in his cold-hearted manner. No such moment came.

The night itself was bitterly cold, my own breath danced about me in white mists of life with my despondent step. The sight reminded me of those ghosts I saw; their lust and their brilliance still captivated me. And yes that true emotion came to me, shame; shame that the lust of The Three had caused me to abandon myself for a mere second before they disappeared. 'Morality, you wonderful thing' I uttered in a melancholic and jovial tone, 'serve me forevermore lest I become another agreeable fiend.'

I moved into a small wood not far from the road and sat down on a low branch of a tree facing a wet humble meadow. The trees were thick with fruit, and red summer berries lingered on the shrubbery a perfect scarlet that seemed to sparkle in the night's boggy and wintery gloom.

Oh Rebecca. My love.

I hoped I was gaining yards on her, yet I felt further away than ever. Like when I had awoken to my new existence I had found myself in some other realm that she was not in; and I was beginning to forget how it felt to be in her presence. I wanted either to have her by my side again, or to die in that beautiful small opening. Only one was likely, and it seemed like a fine place to die, I felt a sense of peace there that I knew I would struggle to find again amidst all the horrors of cannibalism. And who would not want to die knowing they were only going to eat human meat for undying times?

That agreeable fiend, The Yorkshire Creature, I had left his company because for the most part he was right. Everything I said to him was truth. I will always value my own morality, just in whatever way I twist it over time to survive. Is that not what every reflecting and conscious being does, shape their own morality to suit their needs and way of living? He was right in his message, I just could not face it; his words of me following my own demon's path not only insulted me, but its potential inescapable truth infuriated me.

The stress of existing had for some time been much too heavy; but always thought of her lessened my strife. For a moment I thought of where she would be that very second, but the idea of her in captivity, violence or worse only brought me more anxiety. There was nothing I could do, no thought would do me good. And so to escape thought and remain ever peaceful, I slept down in the opening, falling in and out. Rebecca lay by my side here and there in the cherry meadow, taking my hand in hers. I smiled, holding her with passion as her head rested on my barely breathing chest. No words were uttered. None were needed.

The sun began to rise and I headed back to the company of The Yorkshire Creature. He had moved the carriage out of sight of the road where we were, but left the candle outside as a beacon for me. He sat inside, waiting for me, I think. I did intend to not say anything, and just go to sleep, but as I crawled into the carriage and on the opposite side to him, the words 'sleep well' rang from his lips. I paused for a moment, before replying 'and you', and we did.

The next night we awoke about the same time. He was keen to get back on the road. We rode on with good speed.

'I apologise for leaving when you sat bereaving. It was selfish of me.'

'You need not worry my friend, it is past now. We lost time, yet with a helping of luck, tonight and one more, then we should arrive in the colossal city of London.'

'Wonderful'

'Grey and silver it is my friend; well, grey and silver for us two northern admirers of all things green.'

'You have seen London before Mr Horn?'

'Once. I was young however, from letters more recent I have been informed it has changed much since that time. We shall see together.' For a while nothing more was spoken. My mind was ever on the beauty of the sight of Rebecca the night before, and the sadness of her disappearances.

'You did not finish your story, of how you became such a being like me. There were two more of the creatures with you...'

'O yes, of course. I shall continue for you' he seemed delighted with the prospect of finishing his dark tale.

'Mother died as I have mentioned' his spirits instantly fell to that low drone of mourning again. 'The villain looked up towards me once his deed had been done, and I almost cried in horror at her degrading death and his awful expression. His eyes somehow screeched his wickedness into me. His skin was wretchedly pale and his teeth were jagged like a feline. Though I was astonished and horrified, I quickly found my aggression overtaking me, and infusing me with power; I could do nothing for my mother, but I could kill her assassin.

I held out my sword in front of me as we both stood still, waiting for one another to make the first move; like a game of chess with the enemy's composure. The thought of the last one still remaining, still mobile, most likely watching me, came to me. I knew I had to strike the one I could see before I got attacked from a blind spot. Sweat fell from my brow and trickling down my nose; I moved.

I must have made it little more than a yard before he struck me, and in that time he must have taken five. It was the back of his hand that clashed with my face like steel. I crashed down to the floor with a pain I had never felt before; and have not since. Now here comes a vital part in my story and my ultimate survival, he thought he had struck me unconscious. I guess his blows had knocked his victims insensible previously, but not I for whatever reason; something kept my light flickering, and the handle still lay in my lifeless palm. His assumption would be his undoing and downfall Mr Fletcher, but I skip ahead of myself.

For a few excruciating seconds I lost control of the nerves in my neck, my body seized and shivered stiffly and my senses flew elsewhere. Then like having a cotton quilt on the coldest evening, warming the body serenely, all my pain warmly numbed. I felt calm, and free somehow. Yet when my sensory perception returned, my sight saw the thing kneeling before me. With animalistic barbarity, he bit my chest, tearing me with serrated teeth, ripping my skin and tender flesh. Such indescribable pain came upon me once more, yet I could not scream my agony into the world, I could barely breathe. In hysterical desperation, I threw the sword at his neck. Scarcely could I feel the sword in my numb grasp but I struck with every ounce of strength still within my power; for I knew if it was a feeble blow, I would not survive the retribution. It was not craft or design, only luck that the tip of the blade pierced through his throat perfectly and caught in his upper spine. It forced his body to move with the motion of the blade and though he tried to move his arm in retaliation, nothing effective could he do. And with mocking instinctive fury, I bit into his flailing arm. My own retribution, my vengeance. I took a mouthful from him before chewing and spitting it out at his face. So feverish and fast did it all happen that I cannot recall the taste, but I do recall the pride of overcoming the demon. That I had defeated the murderer of my only remaining loved one, my mother.

I took the sword and beheaded him. His body twitched and shook violently afterwards, fiercer than I had, which both delighted and mortified me. A few seconds of horror later and he could move no more.

The last of the four came soon after. He must have heard his leaders wounded cries, or anticipated he would kill me alone. Either way, he ran at me with thunderous steps, a vicious complexion and burning hatred, moving as inhuman as the last. I threw out my sword aimlessly hoping to slash him yet I expected nothing. I closed my eyes anticipating one last blow to the skull and it would be the end; the wound on my head was already bleeding badly and knotting my hair into a bloody mess. It was a miracle I could stand after the crushing blow to the head as well as having part of my chest devoured, surely no more luck would fall my way.

The blow came, I flew through the air exhaustedly, crashing to the floor yards away with excruciating agony. I knew for me to stand and defend myself then, after that final blow, was hopeless. Minutely I began to shake again, particularly in the neck. My eyes grew heavy but I refused them to close. I willed to fight 'til the end, however soon that was. Yet the sword was not in my grasp anymore. My fate had to be accepted. Mother had died; I had killed three of those ghastly things, including who I believed was the leader, the one that had killed my mother. Three of four enemies is a fair defence I thought, surely my forefathers would feel no shame as their ghostly figures hid and watched my demise in the corners of the room. I was soon to join them.

I tried to move my legs and stand, but that was useless, I could not move. My arms and neck too would not move. Then something caught my attention in the corner of my closing eyes, it was dark and thin, pointing up into the air. Trying to move a seized up neck Mr Fletcher is something I do not recommend, by God that was painful and its sensation ran down my spine into my pelvis. I screamed out ferociously. Moving my neck was no option. My eyes forced their way as far wide as they could, but still there was no clarity on this gently swaying thing. I judged it to be my sword, and my assailant holding it up high coming to end me once and for all. I quaked, I cursed, here it was, my final end.

However it did not move, not beyond a placid back and forth. My peripheral sight was hopeless, rolling over was the only possibility in sighting this pointed fear that at any moment would swing my way and be forced deep into my bosom. The weight of my shoulders and arms still existed to me as agonising weights on either side of my burning spine, but they existed nonetheless. I could sway myself to roll onto my side. I braced myself for the formless pain, then swayed myself awkwardly until I had the momentum to commit myself to the plunge towards knowing my harrowing fate, I turned. Moaning and cursing once more, but it had been done and what I witnessed shocked me more so than I could have guessed.

It was he, my last foe, lying in an awkward rut. Bloodied was his chest as it poured his hopes so grimly down his sides and onto the cold floor. And of the thing I saw that moved ever so slightly in the air, that dark and sharp thing that I feared could only have been my weapon, was. It stood perfectly through him with the handle pointing in the air; it was the most picturesque, triumphant beauty I will ever know. His eyes were leering at mine with black bird-like feeling; hatred for me, but I laughed at him. We both knew I had won. He would bleed to death soon enough as I would lose consciousness, but in the arrogance of my victory I fancied I would indeed wake from it, despite the wound on my head.

He died slowly. Coughing blood like mother did; yet his stare never altered. The grim thing lost life in his complexion completely and yet his awful glare continued. I turned away several times, hoping it would go away. But it never did. And I could not ignore it, somehow, it taunted my victory. I loathed him, I loathed his ghastly gaze even after he died, for the terror that reigned in my soul because of him was ever unhindered; I cannot put it to words. I will never forget that stare for as long as I linger on, ever sneering its hatred, I could not bear it, I could not sleep without it gone. But in some strange way, that stare which made me cower momentarily, is the stare that gave me the strength to rise up onto my feet, which I thought was beyond possibility, for I needed to end it.

I pulled the sword from the stone heart and beheaded yet another miserable creature. In such delicate composure on the edge of breaking into a dejected weep, I struck the body with as many blows as I could, breaking it in enough ways that it would no longer resemble a human corpse, not one that mocked me the way his did.' Mr Horn paused. Sighed.

'Once the deed was done, I looked at the mess of a carcass I had made. Blood plentiful, in its dark and harsh red, covering my blade, the floor, my face. It was filthy and appalling work. His remains were strewn over the floor, and the white frames of his being were showing here and there. It was a gory sight my friend but worst of everything, I could still feel the stare through the mangled and deformed face.'

'Were the eyes still staring at you?'

'No, they ruptured in my frenzy, however I still saw the image of them upon his crimsoned skull.'

'What about the other bodies in the house? What did you see when you looked upon them?'

'Ah, I shall get to them my friend; the story is not yet over.' His mood as well as the drained atmosphere of grief and psychological terror that his story brought to the night was lifted briefly, before with a stern face his words dived back into the pits of misery. He spoke thus, 'I looked away from the thing to rid myself of his evil stare, to the blank ceiling. No use. I closed my eyes. Then the shock and realisation of the true extent of the enemy I had faced, of all four of those grim things, I had defeated all and had lived. I thought back to when they stood by my cellar door, how inevitable my death appeared. And for all their might and evil, I had survived their wrath, and risen from the skirmish victorious.

I struggled my way to mother's side, limping from both the agony of the soul and of the body. Her face fell to one side, eyes open still. Her eyes screamed at me in such a repulsive manner, I closed them both in respect and in so that I had not to experience them any further. I would have moulded the rest of her face if I could, to something more serene, to the smooth face I recall of her brighter days. Alas, nothing could replace the soul that had left that earthly form. I tried not to weep or whine, and for the most part I succeeded. I sat only in silence as her body rested in my arms. Her bones no longer held their mould; he had defiled her, and she was slowly growing cold. The reality sunk further into me that she was never coming back. The meaningless aggression, the useless hate filled me again. And how pointless it was, it helped not my gut wrenching misery. I lashed out at the corpse that had fatally dropped her to her death. Doing the same damage I had unleashed to his companion, like a ridiculous lunatic. Deformed and disfigured he became as my mind whirled in fury. Nothing good came of it. I felt no better.'

I noticed the body of The Yorkshire Creature seemed slower, his words came at an exhausted pace, drafted with heartache in each breath. I took note of his countenance with patience; and waited for him to answer my eager questions in his own sluggish discourse.

'I lost consciousness then. For as I have already mentioned. Three weeks. When I finally regained consciousness without a true comprehension; I was plagued with weariness. Fancying myself dreaming at times, then realising I was awake, only to conclude it a dream once more.

The first sight I caught in that period was grim and ghastly, and followed only by wild illusions. As my eyes opened, the lids stuck in tiresome fashion. A few seconds passed as I wondered why I lay on my floor staring at the dim ceiling. The wicked horrors of that night came flooding back to me. And I looked to my side, to the body, or the lack of, to the meat that fed gruesome things as dried stains of a foul red spread across the floor. I could not bear witness to such a sight, not for more than a second. I needed to escape from it, from the dread that came in the realisation, it was my mother.

I ran up the stairs spewing from my feeble nausea. The unspeaking knights in armour I moved past judged me, condemned me for the blood on my hands and clothes. "It was not me, I killed her not!" Screamed I as I crawled past. Then behind me I heard the stiff recognisable sounds of metal scraping metal, they had started to move behind me, moving rigidly towards me, coming to life in that narrow corridor. They came to kill me for surviving when mother had died. Emotion fell from my frame like I was shedding skin. I cowered on the floor inconsolably.'

'How many were there?'

'Eight. Four on either side, with footsteps pounding closer in a cold march. It was frightening Mr Fletcher.

When sanity somewhat came back to me, and I saw they had returned to their posts, I willed to be by the side of my mother. I knew I would only see a tormenting sight, but she was all I knew in life. I dreaded moving back past the knights, I thought they were just biding their time and would soon move again to end me. But eventually I managed it, plucking the courage to crawl past those terrifying things and to her side.

She lay, simply, dead. The corpse was severely decayed, the same pale grey colour as her hair had been. The child heart in me yearned for its mother back, not a thing of feasts for little beasts, inanimate and blackening.

There is nothing like a mother's love, your heart can only register them as that caring one who you were entirely dependent on for the first years of your life, even when it had become the complete opposite. She was the only one who had loved me for all my years of life, life after her seemed not possible. And seeing her there recreated in me the dreadful withered face I saw in her that moment she died.' I sat and studied Mr Horn. The hardened soul with broad shoulders who rode the carriage, telling me of such unbelievable grief of kin. A strong soul it must take to live through such violence and loss. I only looked at him with admiration. He continued in a dark voice

'Something was then to be discovered, something wholly evil and chilling. One of the creatures I had killed, his corpse had not decayed like the other three. Those three bodies had decayed much the same as my mother's did. But the irregularity of the last was alarming to the least. His corpse, down in the cellar, was full in flesh. Ivory white still. He lay in a pool of dried blood, having been wounded in the chest and losing a leg; nothing could have lived with such major injuries unattended, not to mention the mass of coagulated blood no longer in his veins. As in that cellar it was dark in too many variants of the term for me to feel at ease, I dragged the body into the light.

I looked upon him with strange fascination, how had this one not decayed? Surely the rats down there would have wanted to consume his corpse. And the other fascination, his face, what was this ghostly thing I stared at? His scaly skin, his frightening teeth. But the worst thing of all was yet to come, I caught sight of something that overwhelmed me with revulsion and did so effortlessly. I jumped to the floor in an awful terror, my veins ceased to distribute blood and I flushed a perfect cold. His eye flickered into me, fixing his late gaze upon me. "You live?" I shrieked trembling. Even now in memory I could scream for how unpleasant seeing his eye move was. He gave me no answer, he could move not. I could not guess what his emotion was, anger or agony? You intuit what you wish, what I did know however, is that he had to die. His greatly shrunken pale skin fell in the shadow of my approaching outline as I stood upright, weapon in hand and moving in murderous manner. I was repulsed, I felt as evil as them. They killed a fragile woman who had no way of defending herself. That is exactly what I would be doing to him.

I made it swift. Another did I behead. And for the entire night I stared more intently than I ever have before at those grim eyes of his, waiting for a flicker of life, a change in direction. But they never did, he was surely dead. Looking back on the ordeal I do wonder if they ever did really move, or if it was the grisly makings of my ruined mind.'

'That creature may well have been capable of it though, who knows what they were capable of, or even us for that matter.'
'Quite right. You yourself say you have survived being buried alive. I received graver wounds than my life should have been allowed, and yet I survived too. One does wonder under what conditions we can survive. But I lose focus.

I did plan on burying mother in the garden by our apple tree. But I never did. I had no real will to move from the floor, I only wished to lie there, in the remains of the night where everyone else had died.

The days came and went without me moving from that spot; though no light entered the room from behind the draperies, I knew that time had flown considerably due to the not quite inaudible clock chiming in the far room. As that endlessly ticked on, a darkness moaned in my gut, a sensation unexplainable. A hunger for human flesh.' He turned to me slowly, with harsh expression and unyielding eyes. I realised when looking back into those black eyes of his, only one human lay dead in that room, his mother.
'You had an urge to eat the corpse of your mother?' An image of infamy ran through him as his eyes flickered away, the solemn face twitched downwards. Of course I knew his shame.
'I ran far away from the home before the deed was done. And have never returned.' I felt relief for him in hearing those words. I knew how unexplainable it started for him, and how painful and disgusting it would have become. However in the end, we had both come through the test without the life-long regret that committing the personal crime would have caused us, gratefully.
'That is the story of how I became what we are my friend.' His shoulders raised, a sigh, finished was the intense emotions of the night he died, yet the darkness was never lifted from him.
'That is not the whole story, how did you became a cannibal? How did you realise you could not live under the sun again?'
'There are more tales of my life my friend, but for now, that is it, they can be spared for another time. What can be said is this, whatever initiation there is of how I became this being, it is within

209

the words of what I have just told you.' He spoke with an assuring tone. And I accepted them.

At the end of his tale I again heard the world around me. The horses trotting on, grunted and making their noises. The carriage wheels constantly turning with muffled sounds on the dreary dirt roads. London was near, I knew it. As I looked away into the distance, I saw the faint light of an alive city miles before me. It was a glory I had never witnessed before. It was like one thousand powerful suns danced together to a silent wonderful tune, I could only admire with glee. The next night we would reach the heart of London I guessed, and my companion later confirmed such as so. He said that we could possibly reach the lights of London that night with a gallop but it would be too close to sunrise. It would not be worth risking the rising sun against finding a place to slumber.

'We should sleep out here beyond the outskirts tonight, and travel into the city in good early darkness on the morrow's night.' 'I agree.' He also made strong the point of finding somewhere to sleep soon after we part so it would not be a frightened, desperate rush at dawn. He expected me to find "somewhere proper", a quaint room to stay in for a small fee, and I let him think so. But I had not the money for such and I would not steal coins from an innocent dying man such as he would, to me that was despicable. I knew I would simply go back to my ways of burying myself at morning light. As if for being dead I somehow belonged to be in a buried state.

My companion slept easy that night, unmoving, dreaming of his mother in happier days I guessed. But I found sleep hard to find with the city and its dim lights in the distance glancing at me. It did not speak to me of everything that could be within the grandest city on earth, not its theatres or people or markets. Not the Thames and its famous bridges, but of finding her, in "the capital"; or at the very least some lead into her whereabouts.

A dark monotonous voice spoke: 'My friend, London awaits our arrival.'

'Eager you seem' replied I in a restless rhetorical murmur, yet my eyes remained closed. He shuffled around and left the carriage. 'All the marvels, all the worldly people. The women. The flesh. The nights here are long and fanciful Mr Fletcher, and soon to be mine. Yours also if you desire it, but I know your quest for Rebecca only. Do you wish to remain in the carriage, I can ride up here alone for now?' It seemed eager was an understatement. I had never seen The Yorkshire Creature, Mr Horn, in such high spirits. I was unsure if it was endearing or downright frightening. 'Tell me, friend, why is it you travel to London?' My words. 'Same two reasons as you Mr Fletcher.' He spoke with a rehearsed accuracy and delivery
'And what are they? To find your own Rebecca?' I answered trying to guess half of his double riddle; having no clear guess to the other answer.
'Correct. As I have said before, the world is a barren and lonely place. I need a woman in my life; that is something that has never been. And I am heartless for it. I shall make her like us and we can live in eternity as one.'
'Correct me if I am wrong, but judging from the story you so impeccably told me, you do not know how to make another like us.'
'No I do not. But I aim to find the knowledge to end my favourite phrase. Perhaps if I make a charming woman go through everything I did that night, to the exact detail, she should wake up one of us. I cannot see why otherwise has to be so.'
'You are a wise man Mr Horn and you are not heartless, the tale of your mother demonstrates that perfectly so.' They were the gay words I spoke, but my thoughts were of the horror of many tragically-fated females enduring such a night as he described. Many women would die by his vile hands trying to create the other half to his soul. How sickening. Let us not dwell.

London was the place we rode for, and London was the place we arrived at. Shortly after the carriage began moving we reached the smaller outer areas of London. The men we rode past walked in casual yet fresh clothes which alarmed me to my own dirty and slightly blood stained haggardness. My friend told me 'Never worry, not a one will notice you for the first night, these folk of high society concern themselves not with unfamiliar faces, the second night however you will need to dress well and conform, as will I. They will start to notice you and your habits then, even the folk of the underbelly will.' I took note of his words, the practicality of existing in this city I had not considered, I would have to be careful.

Under the brilliant moonlight rippling through thin clouds I saw what I believed to be a beautifully constructed city; Mr Horn did not agree. His home had been built of fine stone however, mine was otherwise, mine was self-preserved by my old man poorly. These buildings we passed were shops, which were vastly wild compared to the markets up in Northumberland; despite the fact we were still a long way from the centre, as well as the fact it was evening. But this was the capital and I was only a simple northern farmer.

London was always going to be odd to me. Mr Horn seemed to love the prospects that London would give him, but I was torn in two. The obvious side was how incredible everything appeared, and was. The three-floored houses in such multitudes astounded me. And the further we rode in on the cobbled roads, the finer the men dressed, the finer too were the garmented women by their sides in their immaculate frocks. And yet, I loathed to see so many people together, I had never seen this many people in my whole life crowded around in such a small space. I felt small and insignificant, as one simple, empty soul moving on a road that bulged with countless others of the same insignificance.

We continued to move on into the depths of the city and soon enough we were just one of many carriages on the road. And these other carriages were of much more grandeur than the one I was on, each one appeared fit enough to carry Queen Victoria herself. There with all the carriages delving further into the city, I was simply awestruck. The noise generated from all the people became overwhelming, so many people crowding in public, so many colluding, shouting this and that. The air closed in above the city and became somewhat warmer as the streets narrowed and the people were hunched in together. My reader, my senses were bombarded with more than I could take to heart. And the lighting that illuminated the city through the mist, complimented the moonlight so perfectly. Such bright lights they were, of a type that I had never set eyes upon before; I knew I had to study them when given a moment to myself. And in the very air, trickled the scent of so many flowers that I could not distinguish any specific petal, and it masked the gritty smell of general filth almost completely. Yet I found no flowers were in sight as the source, was it the perfumed people I smelt that fragranced themselves with water and the crushed vibrancy of meadows? I thought so. Oh this all was something else.

We came to a halt in a back alley not far from Trafalgar Square, which he recommended with full confidence that I visit. 'This is it my friend.' He spoke with a smile that was full and honest, yet hideously unnatural. Then again, same could be said of any Englishman.

'Thank you for the companionship, and carriage to aid in my journey, Mr Horn.'

'No thank you for the company, you welcomed me to friendship and for that I thank you. You have given me hope for the future.'

'And you have given me hope in how to exist.' Our eyes sighted each other's for a slight moment, before we both looked away. The image of his small dark eyes trying to portray a sense of happiness and failing to do so under his grim brow, stuck in my head like the flash of flame that remains seen thought it has died. Only a wretchedness could his eyes display, but I had learnt that was simply how he was, and having come this far with him I would have had him no other way. I knew I was going to feel the loss of me and my acquaintance parting ways, yet more critically I was afraid of feeling disillusioned from reality once again in this new, strange and enormous city without the rock that was him to keep me somewhat sane. Nevertheless, we had to go our separate ways, our shared path now found its way splitting in two, he must walk his way, and I must walk mine; besides he was going to kill women in gruesome and distasteful ways. I simply wanted no part in all that madness.

I smiled to him and shook his hand, bidding him farewell, assuming it would be the last time I ever see his awful complexion.

'Farewell my friend, with our eternal lives, may we meet again. And with the company we desire' he spoke. I nodded my head with gratitude, taking one last look at him. Then turning my back, I moved away from his presence.

Chapter VI: The Dark Streets Of London

This melancholy London – I sometimes imagine that the souls of the lost are compelled to walk through its streets perpetually. One feels them passing like a whiff of air

William Butler Yeats

     I wandered through the streets of London blissfully that night. Soaking up the strange atmosphere I thought I would never become accustomed to, witnessing the extraordinary people, and the not so. It was as if I by some divine trick, some holy intervention, when the lights came upon me and blinded me so incessantly, I had come into a vision of the future; and everything of life had been morphed into this new and wholly bizarre world, a world where city-folk wore fancy garments I could not understand. Suits and corsets of an altogether different breed than the ones I had seen on the farm lands up North. And so captivated was I that night that I did little more than wander, seeing the sights, smelling the scents and listening to the sounds of what the city had to offer me. The night by the time we had arrived in the centre was by no means early, but I had the time to stroll and enjoy the magnificence, just enough time to forget my own quest and the reason I had come to London in the first place.

     I slept under the soil like my first nights from the grave, feeling a sense of self-pity that I must return to the earth again. But when night once more fell upon the world and I climbed up to the dreary and wet streets, I was again taken by the chattering high society and their dark gothic city that was London. Climbing from my shallow grave to the surface was quite a strenuous engagement as always, yet before that night I had forgotten the true effort it took from me. The resting place I decided upon that first night was a park not too far from the Thames. I had placed myself under the cover of a shade of a tree, and in doing so, I remained prepared to run as quickly and as far as need be should someone notice me in my demonic rebirth; thankfully no one did. Once I was on my feet I moved to the small lake in the park to wash myself of the dirt that had embedded itself in my attire; then I could act as a drunken man who had simply fallen into the Thames should a soul gaze upon the drenched and poorly dressed man that was me. But when I found myself walking into the open streets where people moved for the inns, and less legal places, I saw upon their faces the horror and obvious danger they perceived in me, the unknown slimy individual. My manner was no issue when wandering the lonely northern roads with only ghosts and foxes to sight me, but in the city I was an obvious sight to even the most unobservant of men. Indeed I had worn my clothes since the night I lost her and they were tattered beyond their initial farming worth; and though I had tried to wash them here and there in several loughs on my way down from Scotland, blood stains were still somewhat traceable. If any crime were to have been committed in the area, officers would soon find themselves searching for the wild stranger without dress etiquette; therefore becoming one unassuming man in the crowd, drawing as little attention as possible, became imperative to me.

My method of survival remained mostly unchanged thereafter, except one thing, which retrospectively I call with some humour. The park in which I had found and slept in, the first night and the second, lay far too close for comfort to the Queen's palace. Less than a mile to be precise and she would have had her guards and her scouts around that park within moments of suspicious activity. I could not stay there one more night when I caught sight of the overtly exquisite stone over the trees and overheard talk of the Queen's palace. In my search for a new sanctuary, I found another garden across the Thames which at first appeared perfect, before realising yet another important building watched over my living grave, I could not stop there.

Eventually, my drunken wet persona wandering along the Thames and innocently gazing upon the decaying piers found a spot where no light from the streets could principally reach. Under the shelter of damp wooden boards that was once a pier, there was enough space for a man to crawl under unnoticed. It was perfect for me. In that lair there was also no need to fully bury myself, all I needed was a mud covered sheet in which to pull over myself and conceal all dregs of light, and with it anyone's sight from me; which I found easily enough in a back alleyway with some other discarded items. My new sanctuary had around three or four feet worth of dried soil before it sunk into the dampness of the river. All anyone would know if they for some bizarre reason decided to venture down where I lay, was a heap of soil in a neglected area.

The river itself became my new wash bucket when I was in need, it was freezing of course, and hardily clean but quite simply, it was convenient for me. I found myself settling into the city with initial ease, but then the time had come when my encroaching hunger needed solving.

It was the fourth day in which I write. I crawled from my hole and slithered my way to a dark and horribly narrow road as the sickly, sweating buildings towered their shadows about me. It was a chilly and altogether solemn night as I stood leaning against a wall, despairing and pondering how I was to achieve my will. It had come to it finally, I would do it in her name... but how could I kill a human being? My vow to kill the demons that took her from me I could face, but not ordinary men whose death I had no right to create. My story and that of my friend The Yorkshire Creature was the same, they were evil, they deserved the fate of non-existence. But his initiation into our new murderous nature was only to defend himself and his mother, I had not that moral convenience. To further my plight, having not eaten for such a time, my stomach began to swell in the agony and I could feel my concentration and reason slipping slowly down a slope of no return. So exhausted, so fatigued. But in those moments a faint flickering thought blew past me in the winds, I had to pick someone the world would not particularly miss. Many men abuse the world's gift of life, I use the word 'gift' with irony, but it was a man of that definition I had to choose.

Slowly I looked up to the sky, holding my gaze for several minutes, searching for the wise words of the deity I had renounced. But the only god I saw there was Luna, whose serene and luminous beauty shone as full as ever, floating alone and high on the clear sky-line. She on that night was something unique, and yet, the same as every other night as she cast a thorny shadow from a solemn tree upon me. Was it the city that changed her for me? I do not know, but what I do know is the sight of her was a gentle reprieve from my dismal complications.

With a calmer mind, I thought of how my deed would be done. Yet in my thoughts, I cast my mind back to The Yorkshire Creature telling me as dead men we must eat the flesh of men still living, and if that was the case, then what I ate from the bowl came from a man who was left alive. I grimaced at the thought, yet hopelessly, remembering the warmth of eating food that was wholly nourishing, caused my mouth to involuntarily salivate, and I whined in the swelling torture. It was vile, sickening, and unavoidable. I simply had to eat, and I had to make it as swift and heartless as I could manage as to not dwell on the trauma of the event. I looked to my left and right, to the darkened windows, listened to the world; it seemed not a soul was nearby. I could hear people, but only from a distance on the parallel streets. My chance of finding a soul who I considered worthy was scarce, yet I began the search nonetheless.

I wandered through the most bleak city streets I could have ever imagined, they were worthy of any crime. Had I still been my former self I certainly would have avoided those places with an overwhelming fear of who may try to interact with me. In such simple strokes, life is shattered a new shell. Down a back alleyway I found myself, one that followed out onto a larger road that had an infrequent few passing by. I lurked in the shadows and remained watchful of those that moved. For a good ten minutes not a person came plodding down the road, until one lone man came by, then another ten minutes would pass before the next

218

brooding solitary figure appeared. Of those that trotted by, some were dark yet perfect gentlemen sauntering home, others moved with wild steps like creatures wielding their canes simply to remain stable. Every man that I witnessed I judged so entirely, asking myself "does he deserve my physiological need?" No, they never did. Like the man The Yorkshire Creature delivered to me, I thought of their mothers who laboured in their upbringing, who would still be worrying of their safety. I only hoped that when I finally did kill someone, their mother was no longer alive to know what unendurable fate they suffered. Yet for all that, every clumsy innocent fool that moved past me so casually off balance, I could have stolen from the light with ease and brought him into the shadows. My mouth dripped its yearn at the thought and I feared it would engulf me and contort me to savagery, I held my hands to my mouth supressing my abhorrent will.

I in the end stayed there all night, watching the walkers, glaring into the windows in sight to see if anyone had noticed me. No one had. But ultimately I could not commit myself to the act, killing a human was still beyond me, yes I was tempted in full by body to kill one or two of the drunken men, but my mind simply could not. And looking at myself in the third person, seeing my lustful will, I was disgusted at myself. I wanted only to sleep, to let the agonies of life pass into unconsciousness forevermore. I spoke a vow to Rebecca as I concealed myself,
'I will find you. I will weep the great flood within my soul until I do.'

The next night I found myself back in that alleyway, drenched again and scouting the night-time men. I suffered still from my quite grave issue of not having clean or proper clothes that would allow me to blend into the crowds, but I was yet to find a suitable shop or home that I could steal clothes from, and I would not do such an act rashly. However, worse still, the thing that created a most morbid anxiety in my loins and limbs was the thing that was most important in my whole existence, I knew all my efforts were far too slow and ultimately ineffective in finding

Rebecca. At that point I still had no knowledge of where the main docks were. And it was only violence and hunger I could think of.

It was bitter that night, and in the world about me I felt a heavy suppression, like I wanted to be liberated into the skies yet I was forced so low and small by the thickness of the pouring rain. Despairing for her I waited for a potential victim to pass unassumingly by. But due in full to the weather the walkers were even more infrequent than the night before. Not a person came near, and trying to limit my anxiety and agitation I focused on my breath floating patiently into the air. Inhale, exhale. Inhale, exhale, drifting a white smoke from my mouth into the sky. Then with a gentle sound yet sudden abruptness of a distant thunderstorm I heard something that was most queer. It was like a soundless beam pitched atop the smoking chimneys that called to me, calling me to find it. I rushed myself towards it like I was following a nightly rainbow, hoping to find my treasure at the end of it.

I moved onto the street I had been watching and then down onto a parallel road, however this one was larger and altogether gloomier. There the sound felt closer, yet it was impossible to call with any real conviction. With slowing steps, caution echoing from my withered shoes that slapped on the cobbles, I looked down an alleyway much like the one I had found for myself. Leaning against the wall almost hidden from view stood a most wretched looking man. He was smaller than me, dressed with a black top hat and a long dark coat half covering his high dress as he broodingly smoked his pipe. The nature of his garments covered not, at least from me, the fiend that lay underneath. Curiously, he paid no attention to me at all as I casually walked past him, and for this, initially, I thought little of him.

I walked to the end of the path as it gently curved and left the man out of my sight. But as I came to my stop I realised that the call I heard, and followed, had completely faded away. And I faced a dead-end of sooty, dirty, and seemingly abandoned buildings. The soundless call felt like the most grand yet humble of things, like it would lead to the most life affirming conclusion; as if Rebecca had created a machine that whistled a sound only my ears could hear. But there no life was affirmed, only meaningless derelict buildings as I stood pondering. It was foolish to believe she was there based on some peculiar intuition, and I was not for searching blindly behind every door for men to kill or garments to steal. I turned my back disappointedly on the sound I thought I heard, and was about to move back to my shadowed watch-post in my own claimed alleyway, when around the corner I spotted that man again, unmoved, obviously scouting himself for some victim to casually stroll by. Oh the reality I had not realised was flawless, the eeriness that led me there confounded me still but I cared not, I obeyed, I had found myself a predator, a marauder, a man of ill-will; and he was to be my victim. I hid behind the wall that concealed me from his view and watched him as intently as he watched for his own prey. I remained there for some time as he smoked his sweet scented pipe and puffing its smoke into the low mists; but there was something in his demeanour that was odd, he had the attentiveness of a man possessed as his eyes flickered back and forth up the main road. He must have assumed I had entered one of the buildings and moved on, for he never gazed for a moment behind him.

As you may imagine, when a lone and young woman moved easily past our little road he could not help himself. He took a simple, casual moment to see if there were any witnesses, and having perceived no threat to his intentions, he seized her. One hand cleverly clasps over her mouth to limit the feminine screams, the other hand dragged her further into the darkness and out of the sight of anyone save myself. She struggled with every ounce of strength she had within her, kicking and clawing at him with desperation, yet such effort was beyond useless, she had no physical presence in comparison, and once deep into the hidden enclosure, she knew she had no hope of escape. He threw her to the cobbled floor ten feet away from me as his pipe so carelessly hung from his mouth. The ordeal was nothing to him, such lethargic precision in every movement, I could see from his methods that he had done this a thousand times before.

It was then that into his inside jacket pocket did he place his pipe with the gay charm of a simple man after a few drinks, before he moved back to the female. Fear pervaded the night from her so miserably as she tried timidly to bring herself to her feet. I could hear the pounding of the fragile heart of hers as the foul scent of trepidation began to overpower his lingering smoke. Before she had chance to regain her stance he wrenched her hair wildly, twisting her neck. The young woman wept some words neither me nor he could tell, groaning and trembling like a rodent in the jaws of a large beast. The man appalled me entirely in being so unnecessarily violent towards her. If he stole her money and let her go I could understand his deed, but no motive had yet become apparent to me, not of theft, or of sexual or murderous intent.

I came out from behind the wall and out of the veiled shade emitting all the power I could. His stern face revealed a bewildered astonishment, you should have seen it, he thought he was cunning, he thought he was the predator there that night, but in a single moment I had crushed all the dominant thoughts he had of himself. He knew he was inferior to me, yet determined to finish his deed, he looked to me for a long hesitant moment, and then moved for the girl. He grabbed her purse frenziedly. She yielded him no restraint, the night woman yearned only for safety. I could see in the way she looked from me to him that she was calculating if I too were a threat to her.

That moment without harm for her lasted only a second however, before the man yet again held a fistful of her dark locks, forcing her to the ground by his feet. She made a quick gasp in her trouble but once on the floor she fell quiet, and made no attempt to get back to her feet, only looked up at him in surrender and patience.

I ran towards the beast. He fumbled for something in his pocket, probably a knife, but I left him no time to react. Broke his jaw I did, with one swing of my arm, and he crashed to the cobbled road with blood spewing from his mouth. He had probably smoked too much of that pipe to provide me with a fair duel, but I cared not, I only stood over his body with a look of disgust. And hunger. So much gut wrenching hunger, bellowing for all of London to hear; alas, I could not devour him until the woman had gone.

I picked her purse from the floor, brushing off the dirt and rain quite nonchalantly; then slowly I walked towards the woman trying to appear as friendly as I could. With my arm held out, she cautiously accepted my gesture and I raised her up to her feet, handing the purse back with the calmest demeanour possible. Her womanly face beamed as her tears started to fade, only for the rain to wet her aching eyes again.

'Get away from here, I urge you' spoke I with delicacy.

'Thank your kind soul, how can I repay you sir?'

'You cannot.' She held onto my left arm in an act of gratitude, I forced a smile and a nod her way despite my hunger, then shrugged her off. She ran hurriedly away.

I watched her disappear, before turning to the man who still lay on the ground in agony. He was unable to get up and was covered in blood that trickled its oil between the indents of the road. I repeated the image of him throwing her to the floor in my head, remembering the sickness inside him and not letting sympathy form with the sight of a defenceless man. My antipathy had to remain. He appeared more confused than angry, and soon his awareness fixed only on the fact that his jaw was failing him. I struck his head once more and he fell instantly unconscious. In some capacity, in a corner of my repressed heart my sympathy did linger, and for what it is worth I did feel sorrow for what I had to do to the man; however I was merely too hungry for it to hinder me. Holding his collar I dragged him to the darkness behind a large container of some sorts, probably a bin. I scouted for people who could have seen me and saw no one. Satisfied that I was alone with him, my deed of no humble return could be done.

I took one last look at him, the despicable man whose face was frozen shut, leaking sincere scarlet. How soft was his complexion, in a state of peace no longer influenced, a state where the blood was no longer felt. With anxious hands I carefully pulled open his shirt, revealing his grey and pale nest. I had to close my eyes with revulsion at the thought, I was not made for it, for such sights and thoughts. But thought was useless, all I could do was act. And I did, I bit him.

He was a sour and sweaty beast, the air that steamed from his wet chest smelt unpleasant to say the least, this resulted in my timidity and because of this, my bite was not strong enough to pierce his skin. I opened my eyes again reluctantly, looking upon the man as purely that, a man, the same as I, or same as I once was. So calm he was, so close to death. Yet, I had tried to eat him, the repulsion was insufferable. I struck him yet again in my own anger and inhibition, lamenting myself and my misfortune. I wanted to be done with this agonising and vexing existence in London suddenly. Its dark streets pervaded my spirit and its surrounding tall, grim and vacant buildings oppressed me; the countryside will always be my arena. But then, as always, my thoughts came back to her, my love. She was the only reason I had the strength within me to attack this man to begin with. I had to bite into him for the sake of her. Yes, for the sake of her.

I pictured her smile in my mind for one moment, then cleared myself of thought entirely. I bit into him again, this time as hard as my jaw would clamp down on him before tearing his flesh and releasing the warmth. My nausea was indeed unbearable, but somehow the sensation as I swallowed him was incredible, such perfect duality. It was almost as if the light of God existed once more, and He wanted me to be free of my woes and my remnant of human morality that clung to its old definition of what savagery was. I bit into him further and swallowed more, chewing amidst the duality and doing so hurriedly as if the man would soon disappear. The flesh was warm, almost sizzling my sensations, and so too was the liquid with it, lubricating my coarse throat. I pretended I was somewhere else, eating a fine rare salty beef stew made by my own Mary. The truth seemed too far into the surreal and grotesque to fully accept; and Mary's meals were quite luscious. As I consumed my beef stew and opened up the seal, the musty air rose up into my lusting face with an intoxicating smell I both loathed and loved. I needed more and I could not deny the gluttony I felt that night, nor can I deny the frenzy in which I ate my fill.

When I finished my awful endeavour I lay down in careless bliss and my eyes fell closed in submission to the pleasure. The taste of it warm and fresh was something else entirely from the watered meal in my friend's bowl, which seemed devoid of flavour and substance in comparison. As vile and wretched as my act was, the sense of feeling I received after was undeniable. Euphoric even. My mind settled itself completely from its overwhelming agonies and woes and I could only hear silence, for the first time, since I had lost her. The circling anxiety that had formed from that night had drowned away.

After a little while lying there with my mind in the heavens, my body sprawled in ease, my stomach from its stillness slowly began to contort itself and swell. Saliva formed quickly in my mouth and slipped down the sides behind my teeth; and my cheeks suddenly went numb with a warm tingling sensation before I retched up his flesh. It came in a deep painful retch that burnt my throat, and my mind. And once I was satisfied I would be sick no more, I could not find myself in that same peace as before. For the sickness itself set my mind onto the reality of my deed, I had killed a man. How awful, how irreversible; the fact would remain with me forevermore no matter how often I offered God my repentance.

How so woeful the night became around me. The man himself, his death and my evil deed; the blood spewed on the cobbles and the vomited flesh to my side. Luna hung above the buildings and looked down at me, shining her light in a ripple through the surrounding clouds, watching and judging me in her tranquillity. Yet her tranquillity, her silence, infuriated me, I felt she was mocking me with her calm as I sank into the cold stones below me in misery; all I could do was shriek a sound unheard before. The despairing cry must have reached all the way into Heaven, and when I too heard it and its echo, I wished it was anyone's voice but my own. "I am a murderer. A cannibal", the only thoughts I could muster. I had killed and eaten a man all in the name of love, what peculiar and mad events had led from her death to this I could not remember, but it was certainly unjustifiable. The disappearance of a girl in the Scottish Highlands could never justify the consummation and death of a man in the back streets of London, no matter how fiendish he was.

I yearned for my deathbed, my hole in the ground under that derelict abandoned wood-walk. After much thought I stole his money. It seemed a tactless and immoral thing to do, but I concluded he himself had stolen the money from many a woman such as the one I saw him choose, therefore I was doing no evil in taking money that in no sense was his. And I cared not for tales of Charon or other ferrymen in the realm of the dead, for I was already in the realm of the dead and there was no ferryman present to help me in the darkness. Besides, I needed the money to finally buy myself some clean clothes. I spoke to The Yorkshire Creature of how despicable stealing the clothes from a dead man would be and vowed never to do so, and I am a man of my word; for the most part.

Towards my hidden and dark hole I moved into the night, with a much wearied mind, walking slowly and thinking ever of my deed, the murder. Anyone who saw me would have thought I had been smoking the pipe my victim had, yet my mind was just clustered with guilt and disgust, Rebecca would have to wait, I needed to lose myself in slumber.

The next night I did find a shop to buy my attire, and it was rather cheap for such splendid clothing. I stood outside the shop for a good long while trying to shake my own inhibition about stepping into the building, to look the man in the eyes and have him reciprocate and think nothing of me. But when I eventually stepped into the place and the owner asked what had become of me, I spoke some fiendish gentlemen had attacked me and

226

thrown me into the dirty river. He looked at the wet, bloodied and withered state of my garments with sympathy and at once found a towel for me, wrapping me warmly within it. He even let me keep the towel; of course I paid him as handsomely as I could. 'What is your name good sir?' He spoke to me sincerely. I hesitated a moment, before answering

'Alan King. And yourself?'

'David Mendelsohn, pleased to meet you.' We shook hands and I noted the shop, he was an useful ally if I ever needed other goods.

I left him with a smile of gratitude, there was something about me he seemed to like, perhaps my victim story had stirred the caring element of his soul, perhaps it was simply his way of getting me to pay him extra in earnest jest. But he was a most gentle man. I could tell instantly by the softness of his handshake that he wished not to impose himself on me, or the world; and that he was of no school of pretence. And for that I held high respect for him.

The clothes I left with are as such: A long black coat, much like the man of the previous night, and sturdy black boots that yet left quiet footfalls. I also acquired some warm black under garments, a silk topper and a fine cane. I looked like the participant of both high society and the lowly scum of London. The sharp collar on my coat and the edges of my hat, when needed, covered my face in shadows and I became simply another man in the night-time crowds. I also bought a large curtain and clean bag for my clothing.

My routine became thus: I would rise at nightfall out of my soil den where I used the curtain to wrap myself in from the light, I would then wash myself of the little soil on me in the Thames as silent as possible, hidden under the broken dock. I could then dry myself with Mr Mendelsohn's towel, change into my clean garments and go about my nights work and duties, returning just before dawn. I would change back into my torn clothing and sleep in the curtain once more when dawn broke. I was comfortable with this. In my earlier life I had a cold heart for routine, but that was then, and of the time in which I write, it was most settling to have something that made me feel like a directional being again. Even something as small as a regular routine was in some dry sense a sign of living, and from the moment she was taken from me to these moments I write of, little had given me such sense of living.

One more idea of mine for a routine was to be put in place at this time, and for all the withering world it shames me deeply to admit, but I must confess. With my first murder, I left him there dead in the darkness of the small street. The following night when I bought my garments I awoke to whispered words of the gruesome death by those people I came within hearing of. The authorities had suspected it was a clash within the circles of thieves within London's underworld. They were careful to elude details of the missing flesh on his chest and stomach, and of half of it within bile to his side; it seemed the masses were not to hear. Most importantly I was free of suspicion for the murder, yet it was clear to me that with a second thoughtless death at my hands, I would not be so fortuitous. The taking of life must be secretive and hidden, invisible; but other than consuming the whole body what could I do? Oh Rebecca, what I did in the name of your return to me deserves a diabolical death; I tossed the cadavers into the river!

Because of the talk of the town I avoided another murder for several more nights and I turned my attention to that which was imperative, finding my girl. It was to the East of the city where the international docks lay, and it was there that I wandered. I continued along the river watching the increasingly large boats drifting on the solemn waters. It rained, but only a little, barely enough to disturb the gentle waters as the moonlight danced a sparkle on the minor ripples. Those to the East of the city were a whole new variety of persons, not just in their origins and tongues, but of overwhelming numbers of rough and vile Londoners who seemed to dwell in every hole that a human could fit in. I thought I had seen fiendish characters on Trafalgar but in the East I saw demon-eyed folk who would stare a loathing to anyone else that merely breathed near them. I felt quite safe however, I still lamented my kill, but it gave me new faith in survival, I guess that is the silver lining of being a murderer, you know you can cross the threshold if need be, and you know the strength of mind it takes to do so. Of course I scouted through the fields of solitary walkers for a sign of something not quite right, for anything that could give me an inclination that they were like me, or the thieves of her, but nothing did. I moved with guile and caution, stopping frequently to keep an eye on the strangest of men before deeming them worthless to my investigation. I realised in those moments how useful a pipe was; no one questions the sight of a smoking man stood against a wall watching people, but if he does not smoke, then the glances he receives are a fearful enquiry into his ill-will.

The rain turned fiercer as I found my way to some of the docks I aimed for. I paused a good distance away from the dockland and sat on a bench to watch one of the docks-men. He wore a thick coat to conceal himself from the abusive weather and bore a stern face from under his winter's hat. He stood a lone figure in front of a boat as stiff men came every now and again to him with questions of price and destination. I did think of asking him about my Rebecca, wishing I possessed a portrait of her to enquire, but in the end, something held me back, something about him. I walked further down along the river and at length I scouted an old and unassuming docks-man whose eyes squinted with an old man's bewilderedness.

'Excuse me my friend' called I, increasingly unsure of myself. I hesitated for a moment, before stumbling further the words, 'my friend may have passed through these docks some weeks ago, Rebecca Evans-Hill. She is a slender being with long fair hair, however there is also the chance she may have used a false name, is it possible you have seen her? Are there any records of who has passed through?'

'No sir I recall no such name, and of faces I forget all too easy in my years. What is it to you anyhow? If your friend told you not, then surely it is not your business to be asking.'

'Any possibility who you work for has records and could tell me of her destination if she has boarded? I will pay you any amount you wish.'

'Any amount aye? If you are a rich man I am sure something could be arranged, though you look not rich enough.'

'I assure you kind fellow, in my land up North, my family have much wealth in the rail-works there. I will pay you a fair amount, it is simply paramount that I find my friend, her life may be in danger.'

'If her life is in danger then officers could find her much quicker than you and I.'

'It must remain private, you must not utter her name to a soul. Your word of silence comes with the price.'

'Alright sir, give me but three days and I can search our records, and I have access to the other voyaging companies of this dock, I can search them too. Of the smaller docks in London I cannot help you.'

'You are a credit to mankind docks-man, and I will not forget it. Hopefully with your help, a life can be saved. I shall return in seventy two hours.'

'What do they call you?'

'In conjunction with hers, my name is safer unsaid.'

'Oh, well... mine too then.' I looked to the wily old man once more as he looked up at me from his dreary eyes, then I moved out of sight. I was grateful for the man's help and especially for his promise of checking the whole records of the dock for her name. But in truth, would they have used her real name alongside theirs? Surely they knew we had fled home and in the Northumberland area, mine and her names would have been reported missing; a minor search would have ensued. It is possible that having not been found, her name, along with mine, slowly but surely would have reached the registers all the way down in the capital. Though this was all pure conjecture, perhaps the state was also looking for her, and with that, perhaps me? This reassured me that I needed still to remain secretive as possible and I was thankful that I did not give the docks-man either my name, or the false name I had given Mr Mendelsohn that then would have been linked to that of Rebecca's name.

The next night I spoke to a few other docks-men enquiring of fair women named Rebecca boarding any of their ships on their docks. No new information could I find, nor many willing participants in my questioning. In desperation and frustration at my lack of progress I began asking questions to different docks-men information regarding the creatures. Questions of which lands settling foreigners who go up to the very North of the country usually come from. But they knew nothing of those details.

'If I mimicked the accent of a man I once met, do you think you could identify the land in which he came from?' I asked of one docks-man, 'surely you have spoken with many men from distant lands?'

'Indeed I have, but that does not mean I will be able to identify where they are from' he laughed, 'but we can try nonetheless, if you must.' And I did. The words of The Man Of The Lonely Tree perfectly preserved in their form within me. I could hear them still, and I mimicked them as best I could.

'"Nothing... yet." "I welcome you" "I do not want, I claim. And it is the girl that I claim." "I admire your bravery young sir, and for that, and my generosity, I shall allow you to live. But step in my way, and I will not. Good-night."' The docks-man gave me the most confused look, as if he had been listening more to the words themselves than how they were spoken. 'Well, where is your guess?' I called to him with slight anger, trying to take his mind off the content in which I had spoken.

'Well, I think it is a Mediterranean accent you are trying to copy. Perhaps Spanish, of Valencia or Barcelona would be my guess.' Though he spoke compliantly, he was unsure of me and I could see in the strange look he gave me that he was imprinting the image of my face into his memory. I gave him a few coins for his trouble, thanked him, and never bothered him again. And that happened several times, when my questions entered a realm they

231

found unusual, and they gave me that same look; I left and never returned to them.

I was delighted initially to have not only a country, but two cities from that man. But upon doing the same performance with others in the hope of reinforcing his answer, one man gave me Rome only, before his suspicion caused me to leave, and another man reluctantly gave me Athens. My hope in finding where he was from was quickly fading.

I wandered further East than I had done previously in a reverie of disappointment for how poor my search had been going. I wanted the lonelier streets, the empty ones where I could find my solitude, but there was none there, the housing and people were too densely situated for that. However in my wandering meditations, thinking of the demons, I remembered a proverb from Hell, "the busy bee has no time for sorrow." Indolence would only lead to lamentation I reminded myself. And so, many men I watched and half-committed to following, a dozen more docks-men I approached with questions, but still nothing new, and it was the next night I was to visit the old man with hope of good news. Yet I would not allow myself to expect he would have any important information for me.

I dreamt of her as I walked alone. I pictured her last smile before I fell unconscious, such tragic fate. I returned to the world only to see foul clouds shadow solitary souls on a lonely street. I held my face in my hands for a moment, trying to fight any tears and squeeze the heartache away. But as my sight opened up back into the world, I saw myself an intriguing man. He was smaller than me, passing calmly from behind me and wandering on in his thick dark cloak. I could not see his face as his topper shadowed his complexion, but even so, beyond that, he wore a black handkerchief around his neck which covered himself further into anonymity, all I could define was the fact he was clean shaven. However I cannot deny there was something odd about him, the way he stepped as if just walking was a mental challenge, creating an air of tension about him. And the hissing breath that came from him itself felt wretched, like from his breathing you could

232

hear the cold echoes of concealed sinister intensions. I had to follow him. I looked innocently up to the church knell tower in the distance to my left, holding my gaze as he gained steps, just enough that I could follow him without being guessed. I followed behind him with seamless calculation. Deep in my mind, though I had not fully realised it, I already questioned if he was a living man.

He liked the same manner streets I did, the dim ones where the only thing seen amidst the murky and oppressive shades were the monochromatic grey cobbles; the paths not fit for most men, and even less women. I kept a great distance behind him, he had been but two feet from me as he walked by me therefore I was aware he could recognise me as the man from a few streets down. He did at times stop in middle of the narrow paths, only God could have guessed why, he seemed not in thought, not to have had something catch his attention, he simply just stopped. However, when this did happen I was quick to scurry over to a door and pretended to be in the action of opening it. My garments left me from behind without any particulars to notice, even the colour of my hair was concealed. Only once did I notice him look upon me as he stopped and turned backwards. I stood by a door fumbling with my inner pockets for the key when I caught glimpse in my peripheral vision that his face fell upon me, yet only for a moment, then his attention turned to the man up the road in front of him. Despite my risk of not turning fully, he seemed to think nothing of me.

Most curiously, he seemed to have nowhere in particular to go, he seemed only to be moving through the dark with aimless precision. Was it my grim intuition again that led me to question if he was something similar to me? Perhaps, but he could have simply been on some peculiar city drug I was yet to witness.

He moved away from the claustrophobic arched alleys and back into the congested main roads, still with that awkward tension in his shoulders. Then with a calm step and aura, brushing past the folk in the doorway completely unnoticed, he stepped into a crowded inn. The way in which no one even glanced for a moment at him was notable, was I witnessing another moonlit apparition? Ghosts were no issue of mine; it was not ghosts that took her. If I knew for sure that he was a ghost, I would have left him to his ways.

I did not and could not go inside the inn myself. I still had the fear of people noticing there was something altogether not living about me. When I met the docks-men, they were stood in the dark on stormy piers, but inside a warm and well lit inn was an altogether different situation. Besides, stepping inside the inn would certainly reveal to the man that I was following him if he already had his suspicions about his curious stranger. I gave him a couple minutes for cautions sake, standing against a wall and out of sight, but once my chosen time had passed I strolled with the pace of the slowest snail, peering casually in through the window. It was a typical scene of drunkards doing what they so gracelessly do. There was a wooden table at the front where half a dozen men sat singing a song together and holding their ales whilst men on other tables held desperately onto their women. But it was in the back corner of the room where my issue sat, sat at a table with a beer of some sort; and despite the oh so rowdy scene he sat with unbroken stillness, staring out the back window as if spellbound by some ghostly figure out there. Because of this he had not seen me, so I moved onto the opposite side of the road and stood against a wall where he was perfectly in my view. I stood facing side on into the road and pretended often to be looking at a watch I did not own, along with other techniques to appear inconspicuous.

I realised, though I had not seen him do it, that having acquired a drink, the innkeeper must have served him, which in turn meant he was no spectre. I watched him eager for my definition. He seemed no ordinary man, but a man nonetheless, until after around a dozen minutes of him being sat there, one of his actions terrified me; and this action continued the whole time he sat at that lonesome table. Calmly turning his head from that back window about the room, perceiving with certainty that no one was watching him, he held his ale to feign a slip, pouring half of it onto the sticky floorboards. I was aghast when I first saw, my deepest fears and initial suspicions were confirmed. I knew his secret, he did not consume the nutrition of living men. He was dead.

When he was finished with only staring out of a dim window and pouring his drink over the floor, the road was even more crowded than it had been and I could face the direction of the inn without fear. But as he moved for the door, I turned and faced the side once more, looking at my watch coolly; however my heart skipped a panicked beat when I saw from the corner of my eye that he made his way through the crowded street towards me. I remained defiant in my act, I was a man waiting patiently for a colleague who was running horribly late.

It then became clear he was moving to me, there was no ambiguity. I assumed he was going to attack me, but to maintain my act, my glance fell his way gently only when he was closing in on my personal space. Here is where I got my first clear glance of his person, he had a strong face with the large black sideburns many of the men had, but it made him look like a harsh scoundrel if anything. As I looked upon the ruffian my weak eyes met the burning intensity that glared from his. And he held his gaze upon me, I could only drop my eyes and portray a confused sense of uncertainty. There was no uncertainty in him, only an appalling stare of detestation.

'Have you ever known the sun not to rise?
And do you know of the dead not in skies?'

Growled he whilst breathing heavily, like a wild foaming thing having just escaped from a hole; his face far too close to mine for comfort. The riddle caught me off guard for a moment, and his complexion searched my soul aggressively for an answer.
'No. I cannot say such. Only on the rapture would such things be possible.' He for a short moment appeared as if going to speak further, but in the end not another word did he utter, he just moved back down towards the small streets he came by hurriedly.

235

Had he known of me? Surely not, there was no reason at all that would lead him to think such a thing of me. And if he had heard the story of my murder and knew the nature of the attack, it could have been Mr Edgar Horn, he could not accuse or imply it was me with certainty. I thought once more of leaving him to his vices, but my confusion and doubt counted for little when the little angry man that scurried away was so far my best chance at finding her. There was no option for me, I was chained to him and had to continue. And I did. Yet with much more caution than previously and from a much further distance away. Did he know I was following him? Did he try and scare me not to continue? Or was he the master of anticipation and we were engaging in a standoff of wills?

He never turned around to scout the shadow that followed him, I was unsure if it was because he was a mad mug or an intelligent imp. I remained thoughtful and as he turned a corner deep into the East of the city, I gave him several moments before peering round to see him. It was a road of gaunt and narrow terrace housing, and he, stood to a stop at a doorway half-way down. My over cautious concern at his intelligence saved me somewhat, as he opened the door. He turned with a grim brow under his silk hat to see if anyone was watching him, and indeed, he held a gaze at the corner I should have come waltzing through, but I hide completely out of sight. With slow powerful steps, he walked into the building and out of sight. I printed the grey building and its greyer door into my memory. I knew my interest in him had just begun.

I started making my way back to my hole carelessly, yet the night had a few hours to spare, and a stroll helps the soul put things into perspective. I travelled down an old dusty alley far away from where that man called home. I was hungry, but not desperate, though as I looked up into the enclosed walkway I had found myself in, it was the perfect unsighted place for a murder, and like the perfect opportunist I thought to seize my chance; besides, I needed all my strength for the next night when I would try to find and follow that horrid, angry and deceased being again.

I waited in the gloom and silence until I could hear the dull sound of footsteps approaching. I then placed myself to sit on the cold floor and held the expression of a weary man in horrendous pain. I was to ask the oncoming man for help off the floor as my foot was broken and I was unable to walk, and once he came within reach and off guard, I would attack and digest him; if judging in that moment he was not worthy of life. But as the person turned the corner only five feet away, I sighted an austere man with an unclean face. He wore the garments of a civilised man of the metropolis like they all seemed to, yet this one was unkempt and torn as if he had come from a mass brawl. I sensed he was a callous man worth ridding the world of instantly, but deep down in the recesses of my heart and soul, I wished he would help me to my feet and show me enough compassion that I would change my judgement, and not kill again. Instead, he gazed upon me with momentary surprise followed by complete rage at the fact I had the audacity to lie in his path. The look emanating from his weary and pale eyes filled me with the same rage he felt, and in this rage my hunger swelled on the edge of control. I rose to my feet immediately and stood facing the man, staring at him with as much loathing as he gave to me.

'What the bloody hell do you want?' His words were spit, his complexion reddening with fuming disease. I had to take him my reader, there was no two ways. He ran for me swiftly, but I was all the more, with only a yard stepped I struck him in the face with my cane, hard. Stumbling a yard backwards, he held his face in agony, but having remained on his feet, I struck him again. It was then that he crashed to the floor as my cane split in two. I struck him further with my fists until he lost consciousness then without pause or hesitation, I ate from him. Blood gushed from his head wounds, particularly from the back of his head where his skull bounced back off the cobbles.

I left an awful sight, one that I wish not to detail, it was horrific and painful to me. Only two facts will I mention: firstly, from this victim I did steal money that I could only consider his, and that was quite a sum. The second fact was that he was the first man I discarded in the river. I tossed him into a bin and then that bin I dragged into the river. Once I was finished with him, I flew back to my hole and slept feeling both shame and disgust.

As you may wonder before I continue onto the next night my reader, the man's lifeless body was found, two or three days later I believe, the bin had rolled at the bottom of the river by the waves of the boats and washed up downstream. There was uproar at his defilation for a few days, the talk of the town blamed it on London's underworld again, lady lucky was on my side, there was no search for me specifically by the authorities.

Now onto the next night; I wanted sight of the queer, unsettling creature I had followed. Of reason to guess anything of him being in league with her thieves, I had none whatsoever, but I had no alternative to wonder, to search, and in the end, hope he was, for this one man, I had at least found. Still, he could have had valuable information either of her takers or some other truth in which I could use to find her. Firstly however, I had errands to run.

I visited Mr Mendelsohn and acquired a pipe as a nice prop when standing still and trying to appear unremarkable. I also acquired several bags for the bodies in the hope they would remain sunken at the bottom, and not roll anywhere. A mirror to glance behind myself if need be too; and then both a new silk hat and two new canes, for from a distance that night, the man I wished to follow would see two unrecognisable and distinct features of me. I even made sure one of the canes was ivory lined, very distinguished and distinctly nothing like my previous cane. Mr Mendelsohn being much too happy to see me gave me a good price on all my items and so I gave him a little extra.

'How are you today Mr King?' He spoke, and I smiled to him.

'Splendid my good sir. How is business?'

'Fine Mr King, as always, just keeping on keep on-ing, that is my motto.'

'Wise words indeed Mr Mendelsohn.' He smiled.

The other errand I had was to see the docks-man. I wandered that way expecting absolutely nothing and hoping for everything; I received only what I expected. There was no record of my Rebecca's name having passed through, and without a portrait to question any of the other docks-men, talk of descriptions would not amount to anything useful. In all probability, if she had passed through, they would not have used her name anyway. I paid him for his trouble and confidence, and enquired of the costs of boarding ships to Valencia, Barcelona, Rome and Athens. Though of course, I was not yet ready to leave London, I had my demon to investigate, and his dim abode is where next I travelled.

I searched all angles for the creature watching me in expectation of my arrival from his unclean windows, but no sign I saw, neither from his windows nor from any shadows behind me. I remained and waited all night for him to either come out of the sanctuary, or return to it from his night missions, but neither happened.

Half a dozen nights passed in the same fashion, waiting by and nothing happening, and no one obscure did I see nearby. I started by spending all night outside that place hoping for a sight but by the fifth or sixth night I only spent half the time there. By the way he spoke to me, I was certain knocking on his door was no option, and too that he most likely was more experienced in brawls of death than myself. Therefore I began questioning older docks-men again and wandering the city streets for sight of other demons; and I killed two more men in routine fashion in those passing days.

One night, when I was making my nightly journey to that building and taking the same route I had done every night. A quaint small square I would pass through. The moon shone vividly overhead and the air filled with that rich but densely dark blue that such nights often do. Always was the place crowded and that night was no different, I had no reason to suspect anything suspicious or even that a soul would notice me, but then something caught my sight with a shudder. Across the way from me in that intimate square, I saw him, or more accurately, he saw me. I was a good walking distance from that home he entered those nights ago, he should have known nothing of the roads I used in travelling there, even if he had seen me outside looking in. But there, the hostile man, the thing I suspected of devilry gawked into my form with the face of a gargoyle as his eyes twinkled an ill-fate. The shock of it all struck a trembling of terror through me. I only managed to peer his way for a moment when in the absolute horror that he cared not to be discrete in ogling me, I averted my eyes, trying hopelessly to contain the anguish that flooded me and called me to flee into the crowds. But what frightened me most of all, is that he had so easily tracked, found and anticipated me. He sat and waited for me to move to his sanctuary in full confidence.

I continued walking the direction I had been, the only thing I could do really, and pretend I knew not the gravity of the situation in the hope that I had not lost yet. That was my thought process anyway, but in the end it was only a few more steps I made before the impulse of looking his way again prevailed. And with that, my look back his way was sluggish and in obvious defeat; I had lost. When turning back his way and anticipating the wrath of the Devil, he did the most bizarre and unexpected thing, his glaring fire eyes no longer invaded into the depths of my fickle being, no, he caught my second gaze for just a second before then walking away; almost oblivious as to anything about me.

I held my stare unwillingly in a dazed confusion, he turned his back to me and strolled away as if gaily through a blissful meadow. What did it mean? Did he even remember me? Or was he following me as I followed him? My mind knew not what to think, but most foolishly, as much as every fibre in my body begged anxiously for me not to on that night, my mind forced me to follow him. For Rebecca, for my love. For her safety I had to risk my own. And he had not been to that house in days, I was not convinced I would find him again if I did not follow then.

Behind the impenetrable passing crowd I remained with a melancholic air of regret, hiding behind wanderers of the night. Quite quickly he moved out of the main well lit roads and back down into the still aired obscurity of our favoured violent routes. The man leisurely turned his back a few times in inspection for a follower, but so slowly did he turn that it was unmistakable to me, and every time with ease I hid myself completely out of sight. He never saw me, nor heard me, for I was silent as the shadow I made of myself. I did so with more caution than ever before, often I risked losing him by letting the distance between us become so great, but it was the chance I had to take. Yet for all this, I could not shake the feeling for the life of me that he knew I was there, following him.

Up ahead I could hear the gentle flow of the river, I could smell its stale scent. He was walking directly towards it, I knew, and with that there was much more space for light to be seen, I had to be vigilant.

He turned the corner that I knew must have left him looking over the river. I waited as long as need be, several long eerie and cold moments, then with immaculate caution I peered round the wall to sight him. There by the river and looking over the stone barrier down at the dark current he was, stood with his back to me, as if dreaming of something far away. I knew I could not just follow him until kingdom come, and his calmness made the idea of speaking to him seem like the best option. I thought of my friend in the carriage, evil-eyed and grim of complexion, but nothing he could not help, why this man should be any different I had no reason. I yearned for his possible wisdom, perhaps he could confess the truths of us beings; of where groups of us dwelt in London and in Europe, and from there, ultimately, I could learn the whereabouts of my lost Rebecca.

I stepped a few timid yards out into the open, when behind me, I heard a soft footstep, catching me so effortlessly and most disturbingly off guard, someone was behind me. I turned to see, and crushing me so utterly in despair, dressed in a similar black coat and topper as the fiend I followed, stood another such being blocking my way back through the street I came. His stance was one of unyielding menace and power. Of his demeanour, he was an ugly thing much like the one I was following, pale and gaunt with a brow only anger could define. A brutal chill went through me, all this time that I had followed one, another followed me.

I feared for the outcome, not merely for the sight of him, not for knowing the first one had known of me all along, but because they had revealed a sharp and keen intellect to me. I knew not their potential and I knew not their will for me. I only turned back to that first one I had followed, and he grinned at me as if the Devil himself. I closed my eyes for a moment, praying for some plan to present itself. In front and behind had these creatures been closing in on me, but as my eyes opened again, two more of them appeared from the shadows left and right, holding lanterns in front of themselves that they opened wide. I was surrounded. Surrounded and they were closing in on me. 'What do you want with me?' I uttered in apprehension. 'Hark, what do you want I say?' I further demanded as their advances were measured and grim. Not a word did the vile gentlemen say, my heart burst in panic.

'Where is she? Where is she?' I screamed and screamed, but their faces yielded no notice. I pained for a way of escaping the horror but there was nothing I could do, I was encircled well and truly and was theirs for whatever they chose of me. But what made my heart sink all the more, was the realisation that of these four, they were all men, and none of them was The Man Of The Lonely Tree; these were not the villains of Rebecca.

I was unsure if they wished violence however, for once they reached three yards in every direction, they still had yet to raise an arm at me. And I did not want to initiate violence myself, for that would have certainly led to my demise. The best action for me was to wait on the edge of defence and see what they planned.

However the peace soon died, when within arm's length they descended upon me in malevolence; in unison, they pinned me to the floor. I raved for freedom, "wretches" I called, but it was useless, I had to accept my fate in their hands. Once I was upon the damp and dirty stone unable to move, one of the fouls who held a lantern darted his eyes about the area like a reptile, and seeing no witness nearby, by breaking the lantern upon my skull, he torched me alight.

A blazing agony I had only felt from the sun's rays engulfed me. I cried the loudest gut wrenching demonic howl my lungs could allow. I writhed frantically but was unable to direct my limbs to safety. It was torturous. They risked their own selves catching fire to keep me within the flames that started to spread by the oil they poured on me. Oh the pain of burning alive was yet again upon me. My whole form soon went up in the flames. I could even smell the horrid stench of cooking flesh; my very skin began to melt off me and sizzle. They at length rendered the flames too much for themselves and let go of me; standing by and kicking me repeatedly instead so that I still could not escape. I was frantic in defending myself at first, but it became apparent they were not going to allow me escape. I could only move to the state of acceptance, of resignation, there was nothing I could do except let death come over me. I stopped moving and just waited to pass into nothingness.

My life with Rebecca was all I wished to think of. The first time I ever saw her, outside her home so sweetly, oh the bright and brilliant beaming face. I felt weak in more ways than I can describe, "Rebecca your exuberant smile has been failed again" I thought as mine lay smeared over the pallid cobbles. Thought of her and our last defeat saddened me terribly, so close to dying a final death I was, but something in me could not let them ghastly things defeat me.

'No, not again' I called with what minute strength I could, which probably amounted to little more than a murmur. Yet with it I gained something inside me, I managed to toss my coat and shirt off. How I know not, I can only guess that the flames were too fierce for them to try and stop me by that point; though I still received blows from them, they were few and did not hinder my attempts. I fought not because of the merits of existence, for I believe in no such thing, I fought only for the duty of love, for my Rebecca, whom I promised to protect. Once my coat and shirt were on the ground, I lashed out at them with all the force I could, and gained a moment on them. Hysterically I ran for the Thames dripping skin like bread crumbs and at last I leapt into the dark waters.

I fell with a tumble and hit the stone awkwardly, my burns stung like the water electrocuted me with the greatest lightning bolt Zeus could throw at me. However after only a few moments of that excruciating, ultimate agony, I was left only with a numb perception of myself which I whole-heartedly welcomed, flirting with consciousness quite suddenly, I had reached my dying Utopia.

I drifted down the river peacefully, falling under the waves here and there until I lost the air within my lungs and fell permanently under the surface. Whether it was only the waves of the ships that kept me stumbling on, or I was caught by chance on one of those ships and dragged there, I know not, but my body found itself moving down the river, to its mouth, to what I now know is Southend-On-Sea.

When I regained the strength to open my eyes, I just accepted the complete blackness I saw and the fact my arms defied gravity whilst a strange smell made me cough and suffocate whenever I inhaled. It took me quite some time to realise I was submerged and what I breathed was actually water. I sluggishly kicked myself back up to the surface though I was not wholly awake. I lay in a somnolent reverie on my back, facing up to the sky and taking in air again; until I finally noticed the creeping sunrise in the distance behind the clouds. My body was still numb I tell you, I raised my hand out of the water to see if I could feel any sensation in it and none was my answer. The only sensation that writhed through myself was a wretchedness of deformity, my hand at least was of a greyish colour and its skin had dried in a way I could not describe. With scarce consciousness I knew my form had greatly changed but I had not the strength to comprehend what that really meant; nor the time to ponder.

Now, I could see land in the distance, that is, the vague line in the distance that represented land, but I intuited with the perception of a barely conscious thing that the sun would reach me long before I could make it there and dig myself a grave. They had not killed me in the flames as they tried, but I was convinced that they had in the end killed me, for due to their actions, I could not bury myself from the encroaching blaze. However, I knew what had to be done. I forced the air out of my lungs once more and sunk deep under the water. But in my hope that the water and its depth would be enough to stop the sun's light from destroying me, I was wrong, or at least not satisfied.

I would have been content to simply lie on the seabed until I could sleep no more, for I had proven oxygen neither vital nor necessary to my survival, but I was not satisfied it was dark enough. I hit the seabed with most likely the gentlest of touches, but with my nerve damage it seemed a mighty and thunderous crash.

Oh I pitied myself, I had failed in saving her again. My heart swelled up in its own misery and bitter tears. And the sun was coming. Both anguish and joy came to me at the thought of finally dying.

Slowly did the sun rise and as expected, the light only sent vibrations through me, reminding me I had a body at first. Yet the higher the sun came, the more I felt the awful heat. I dug into the seabed, with weary shapeless hands that eventually led me to safety. If I had been on land in that state, that weakness, I know the sun would have been the death of me; but for the sea dimming the light, limiting its power, my will to save her, and my vow to kill the thieves of her, was not extinguished.

End of Book II

Made in the USA
San Bernardino, CA
15 December 2014